The Case
of the
Greedy Lawyers

The Case
of the
Greedy Lawyers

◆

Carl Brookins

NODIN PRESS

ISBN 978-1-932472-71-4

Library of Congress Control Number: 2008925657

Design and layout: John Toren

Nodin Press, LLC
530 N. Third Street, Suite 120
Minneapolis, MN 55401

For Shell Scott, who never saw a pretty woman he didn't try to bed, or a bad guy he didn't want to take down.

Chapter 1

MY NAME IS SEAN. It's my first name and my last. That causes a certain amount of confusion in bureaucratic circles. My full, official, name, the one on my birth certificate, is Sean NMI Sean. I guess my mother had a sense of humor. I never knew my dad. He was away at war while I was growing up. I think he came back, but not to my life. That's not important to this story.

About my names. Note that the pronunciation doesn't fit the spelling. My names are pronounced 'Shawn' and that's got nothing to do with my heritage. My middle name is NMI. It means No Middle Initial. You don't pronounce it at all. So why am I telling you all this about my name? I think you have to have some idea who you're dealing with in order to make more sense of the story. Besides my name, this isn't one of the usual yarns you get nowadays.

You see, I'm a throwback. I'm passé, out of date, a lost cause. The world is no longer interested in me and my kind. I'm no longer needed. Or so they say.

I'm a P.I., a private dick, a peeper, a shamus. I heard somebody with perhaps too much time on his hands even invented a writer's award named after me and my kind. Imagine that.

They're wrong, though, the people who say nobody needs me any more. People with problems come through my door every day looking for help. Well, almost every day. Most of the people who come through my door are middle class or the so-called blue-collar types. The more upscale don't usually come through the door. They call and ask me to come to their office, their home, their turf. Sometimes it's just a power ploy. Sometimes they just feel more comfortable in their own surroundings. Sometimes they don't want to be seen with me, so we meet in my office or some other out of the way place.

I guess you could say I'm an ecumenical kind of P.I. I don't care about a client's class or where they live; it doesn't matter what scale they are. Upscale. Downscale. Sometimes they're timid. Sometimes they're scared. I don't care how scared they are, or if they're timid or blustery. They all have something in common. They have a problem. When they call me, or come to see me, it's not because I need them. It's because they need me.

I'm the guy they turn to when their polite lawyers in their thousand-dollar suits and seventy-five-dollar haircuts can't find the right writ, can't get the judge to listen to their objection, can't get that protection order enforced. I'm the guy who'll deliver the goods when everything seems lost; the guy who'll find out if the dude is really crippled up like he claims; who'll locate that crucial witness or that one fragile link to truth. I'm the go-to guy, the one who goes down those mean streets, as they call 'em. The one who gets his hands dirty, the one who gets results, and never (if he's any good) gets his name in the paper.

I'm very good.

I've seen it all in my short time, relatively speaking. When I shave, cut my hair and dress up in my good suit— I'm smooth. I fit right in. I can pass for just about any kind of body. Indistinguishable from the hoi and the polloi; that's me, except in the height department. I speak in complete sentences mostly, have been to more than a few symphony concerts, and I generally know which fork to use first at a formal dinner.

I'd just as soon have a good beer and a medium-rare hamburger.

* * * * *

I WAS IN MY OFFICE the other morning. It's not much, and it's not in some upscale location, like Edina or Minnetonka. But it gives me a place to hang out when the weather's too cold or, like this particular day, too hot. So I was in my office. I was waiting for a possible appointment. A tentative appointment, because when the call came in the day before, I'd asked for a name. Didn't get one. The person on the other end just hung up. Unusual but not so surprising. I was waiting to see if anybody showed up. While I waited, I was studying. A detective novel. By Richard Prather. One of my training manuals. His character is a P.I. named Shell Scott. He's an ex-marine out of WWII. That was the last declared war. Happened in the last century.

It was getting along toward eleven and there's a timid sort of rap on the door and this dark-haired...woman pushes it open just enough to peek in. She's feeling tentative, a little hesitant. I can tell that right away.

"Yes? Can I do something for you?" I say. Not every opening line has to be an original, you know, sometimes just words strung together to get the job done.

"Are you Mr....Sean?"

"That I am, ma'am. As it says on my door, Sean Sean, Ltd., at your service." Not entirely true. I don't take every job that sidles through my door. I'm picky. That's why I'm not rich. Being picky also helps me to stay alive and out of the hospital. Mostly.

My high school geometry teacher would have loved the Ltd. on my office door. She sometimes claimed NMI in my name meant No Measurable Intelligence. I don't know why I added the Ltd. Gives the line better proportion on the glass, I guess.

My hesitant visitor hesitated some more but finally she came all the way in. Almost far enough to shut the door behind her. Then she stopped again and looked around at my classically sparse yet utilitarian furnishings.

She was pretty good looking. The hard-boiled P.I.s in the books I read in my spare time would call her a classy babe, a piece, a frail, a doll, a looker. Don't read the line and try to sound like Humphrey Bogart would. I tried it and it doesn't work.

She still looked a little nervous, but she took another two steps in my direction and closed the door. I waved her to a seat beside my desk. Then I sat down in the old chair I use. You know the kind. It's wooden with shaped arms, curved wooden slats for a back, a creaky set of wheels, and a grooved steel spindle in the center that winds the seat up and down, depending how high off the floor you want to be. Since I'm only five-foot-three, I have the seat up pretty high so I don't bang my chin on the desk top whenever I sit down. But that means I have to keep a small box under the desk to put my feet on. Otherwise, sitting with my feet off the floor, I'd be swinging my legs back and forth like a little kid. Wouldn't make a good impression.

"Mr. Sean," she said in her dark, husky voice. "Mr. Sean, I'm in some trouble. I need help and you were recommended to me."

"Really? By whom?" Now right away, see, I've blown my cover. No private dick, certainly not your classic hard-boiled, would ever say *by whom.*

Chapter 2

"YOU WERE RECOMMENDED by my attorney."

I looked at her and waited. She looked back as if she expected me to respond. This woman carried herself in a certain way. Dressed in a certain way. Quiet elegance, I think it's called. A way that suggested money and a good private education. She probably lived in Deephaven.

I'm not uncomfortable with silence. In my line of work I encounter it a lot. But time, as they say, was running on. Grains of sand falling through the hour glass. So I raised one eyebrow in a practiced sort of way. I do that. I practiced it. I think it's what happens when the detective in the book cocks an eye at somebody. So I cocked one eye. My other eye pretty much stayed where it was.

My classy-looking but hesitant guest looked down at her lap and then back up at me. "Yes, my attorney, Ephraim Harcourt Saint Martin. Of Harcourt, Saint Martin, Saint Martin, Bryce—" I held up my hand to stop the stream of names. That firm had over 100 partners and associates. I didn't want to sit through a recital of the whole list.

"I see. I know the firm, I believe." I did indeed know the firm. I've done a number of jobs for them. In fact... well, that's another story. So, her attorney was the current senior partner. That meant she was Somebody in Minneapolis circles. Or she was married to Somebody.

I gave her a meaningful nod, something else I'd practiced in front of the mirror. The woman shifted a little in the chair and looked at me from her wide-spaced, big gray eyes. We waited some more. The pace we were setting here, I began to calculate I'd be skipping lunch again or grabbing a mid-afternoon sandwich at one of the greasy spoons along Central Avenue.

"Look, Mrs...." I stretched out the pause. I still didn't know her name or what this was about and we'd already been sitting in my office for the better part of twenty minutes.

She started as if I'd interrupted her reverie. "How did you know I'm married?"

"Elementary. Third finger, left hand. Now, is there anything you care to tell me about, such as why you're here?"

My visitor moved her right hand over her left to conceal the wide gold band and dropped her small purse on the floor. It made a loud thunk for such a small purse. "I'm sorry. I've never talked to a—a private investigator before. You see, I'm in some serious trouble and Ephraim, Mr. Harcourt, recommended that I hire an investigator. I don't—didn't—want to, but I finally agreed, if I could meet you first." She stopped and bit her lip, then bent swiftly and retrieved her purse.

Ah. Now I got it. A first interview, and if I passed, we'd get into the details. "So, what do you think? Do I pass?" Did I care? Shell Scott, Prather's six-foot-plus ex-jarhead would look at a woman during the first few moments and his keen eye would tell him, "This broad is trouble." I couldn't do that. Maybe I didn't have enough experience. Or maybe it's because I have trouble with the label. Why were women referred to as broads in those old books? Maybe my linguist friend from the U of M would know. I filed that thought away for another time.

"I don't know yet. You aren't at all what I expected. I'll have to think about it some more." She stood up and extended her small hand across the bare top of my old oak desk. I stood too and took her hand in mine. Her fingers were warm and damp. Good manicure, though. I gave them a gentle squeeze and she turned away, clutching her small purse under one arm. I stood watching as she went through the door. She had a nice, high rounded bottom and she didn't switch her hips when she went out. She knew I was watching and I had no doubt she knew exactly what she looked like from the rear. I'd bet she'd checked herself out in the full-length mirror of her dressing room more than once.

Nice buns, I thought, watching her go down the hall toward the elevator at the middle of the building. Those mysterious buns were considerably less enticing the next time I saw them.

In the Hennepin County morgue.

Chapter 3

I HATE THE MORGUE. It makes me queasy. Fortunately, I don't go there much. In spite of what you may have read about private eyes, not a lot of my work involves dead people.

Or shooting.

If I fired a gun as much as Mike Hammer does in some of Spillane's novels, I'd be deaf and I'd have needed joint replacement on my right elbow long ago from the recoil. I remember when I was a kid in the Navy—they marched us to the range one hot Florida day and we got to fire a fifty-caliber machine gun. It bucked so much I had blurred vision for an hour afterward. And the noise was deafening. Literally.

The handgun I carry, when I carry it, for which I'm duly licensed by the City of Minneapolis, is a .45 caliber Colt semiautomatic. Yes, it's a cliché. It is a very large weapon designed originally for military use. The slug it expels is not much smaller than that machine gun bullet I mentioned. Of course the load is smaller, but you get the idea. This weapon has the stopping power of that great boxer, Ali. Colt manufactured a .45 caliber pistol in the late nineteenth century. It was very popular, even if it had a terrific kick, because of its stopping power. One version, the Buntline Special, had such a long barrel it was almost a small rifle and nearly as accurate. But it wasn't designed for quick-draw situations.

Anyway, the Colt .45 semi-auto was the preferred sidearm of issue to the military for a long time, right up through that little action in Korea, because you could hit a man in the hand with a shot from one of those things and frequently knock him down. I always laugh at the movies when some dude draws his .45 semi auto and shoots the opponent in the arm, and the guy yells and keeps on firing back. Never happens. You shoot somebody in the arm with one of these things and if it doesn't take the arm right off, it knocks the guy flat, into shock, and he's done for the day—*if* he lives. Remember the scene in the movie *Shane* where Jack Palance blows away the farmer and the impact of the slug knocks him half way across the street? That's more like reality.

So when I carry, I carry my .45 caliber Colt semiautomatic. It's heavy and awkward, but when I have to bring it out, it gets respect. I don't carry it in a shoulder holster. First, wearing a two-pound lump of steel in my armpit would quickly give me shoulder strain and second, no tailor I can afford could make me a jacket that would conceal the thing. I wear a hip holster on my belt that only gives me a slight list to the left when I'm heeled. Another thing about my gun, my gat, my iron, is that it's safe. If I drop it on the sidewalk, it won't go off. It might break, but it won't fire because it has two safeties; one of which is in the back of the butt where you squeeze it. I haven't had to carry it for over a year. Buying bullets is a major expense. I buy my bullets in bulk, but it costs me almost half-a-buck every time I pull the trigger. Even so, I try to practice regularly.

And I'm very good. With either hand.

About the morgue.

That gray-eyed, anonymous, married woman came to see me on Thursday, and the next Monday I get a call from the police. They want me to come over to the morgue and look at a body. So I go there, not to the first floor viewing room where grieving relatives look at a television screen in quiet comfort, but to the basement. To the stainless steel and ceramic room where the bodies are kept in refrigerated cubicles; where the steel tables with edges and drains are;

where the smell of disinfectant and other things is strong enough to make your eyes water; where the autopsies are performed.

I didn't know the detective who was waiting for me beside the elevators. A big, burly fellow, he towered over me; probably weighed twice my 130 pounds. He told me his name, but I forgot what it was. "Why me?" I said as we took the elevator to the basement. "Who am I going to see?"

"Just wait," he said.

In the morgue, some white-coated dude took us to a table with a body in a heavy, plastic body bag lying there. He unzipped the bag partway and there she was. My Thursday visitor. I'd only seen her the one time, but I have a good memory and recognized her right away.

"Know this person?" asked the cop.

"No, but I've seen her. Who is she?"

"You don't know her?

"I only saw her once. Last Thursday. Around noon. She came to my office and said she might hire me. I didn't even get her name."

"You make a habit of working for anonymous clients?"

"Not really. It was kind of tentative. Exploratory, you might say. I got the impression she wasn't sure she wanted to hire me. What's with the marks on her face?"

"We don't know yet. She didn't tell you why she wanted to hire you?"

"Nope. She didn't have those marks on her face when I saw her. How'd she die?"

The attendant zipped the bag farther open. The corpse had nice breasts, slightly flattened with tiny nipples. No saline implants there. Between them was a small hole, entrance wound from a bullet, it looked like to me. Something occurred to me. "You call in a forensic entomologist?"

"A what?" asked the detective.

"Forensic entomologist. These look like insect bites. I think we have a certified one here in town."

"What for, she didn't die of bug bites. She was shot at close range, one time. See the powder burns? Small caliber weapon," said the man from homicide.

"The entomologist could probably tell you how long the body was out there. What was she wearing?" We detectives always ask that.

"Nothing. No clothes were found with the corpse. So, you're not gonna be any help?"

"I would if I could but I didn't know the lady in this life."

The detective sighed and gestured at the attendant. "One other thing."

The attendant zipped the bag all the way down, and with his gloved hands laid hold of the woman's hips. He pulled the body up on its side so we could see her bottom. Her cheeks were striped and raw looking, with a series of welts running cross-wise on the gray flesh. I felt my stomach start to roll.

"Jesus. Somebody whipped her."

"The whipping took place just before she was killed." My detective was watching me carefully.

"Bondage? S & M?"

"What do you think, Mr. Sean?"

"That'd be my first guess, but that's all it is. A guess. I think you're right. These are recent whip marks. Thursday, the day she came to see me, she didn't move as though she had any pain, or even tenderness in that region. The chair she sat in is an ordinary wooden side chair with no cushion."

"Could she have been wearing padding?"

I recalled my vision of her leaving my office in the snug skirt. "No. I would have noticed. Who is she?"

"Her name is Magda. Magda Bryce." He paused in what I took to be an expectant manner. Maybe he was looking for a guilty reaction.

"Never heard of her. But I assume she's related to someone at the law firm. Sorry I can't be more help, but I've told you everything I know. I don't even know why you called me."

"Mrs. Bryce had your card in her purse. We found the purse beside her naked body. Somebody dumped her near Cedar Lake. She was concealed in the bushes at the edge of the water. A dog located the body."

I wondered if it was the same purse she'd had two days earlier, the day she came to see me. I also wondered where she got my card. Maybe from her attorney. Maybe not.

"Can I see her personal effects?"

"No, Mr. Sean, you cannot."

I shrugged. I didn't really care. I wasn't involved and I'm not one of those people who is haunted by *if onlys*. You know, *if only* I'd been more probing, more persuasive, perhaps I could have averted this tragedy. Nuts. If only she hadn't been carrying my business card, which I hadn't given her, I wouldn't even be here in this chilly room looking down at her dead face.

"The other thing is, you're the last person to see Mrs. Bryce alive." We were walking out of the autopsy room toward the elevator that would bring us back to sunshine and reality.

"Respectfully, that isn't true," I said.

"No?"

"At least one other person did. Whoever shot her saw her alive. Unless this was a suicide."

"Not suicide," grunted my companion. "No gun at the scene, no residue on her hands. Mrs. Bryce was definitely murdered."

We parted ways. And that was the end of it. Maybe I'd call on senior partner Ephraim Harcourt Saint Martin to see if there was anything there, just to satisfy my curiosity. I didn't expect to learn anything, and I didn't think I'd need legal protection either.

Boy, was I wrong.

Chapter 4

MY VISIT TO THE morgue was depressing, and the hot Minnesota summer sun didn't chase away my blue mood. I closed the office and went home. I don't live in Minneapolis where my office is located. I don't live in some sleazy, seedy, hotel or apartment building, either. I live in the suburb of Roseville. It's about equidistant from downtown St. Paul and downtown Minneapolis.

I cruised north on Interstate 35W, took County Dog exit, whipped down the street and into my driveway. My lot is crowded with mature pines and hostas and ferns so I have almost no lawn to mow. Only a little in back. I like living in a small forest. I'm not sure all my neighbors like it though.

Sometimes when I have the windows open, I hear people walking by in the street. We don't have sidewalks in my neighborhood. Hell, it's only been a few years since we got paved streets and concrete curbs. Anyway, with the windows open, I usually notice people walking by. Even with the windows closed, I notice people sauntering by. I try to stay alert. With the windows open I'll hear someone say, "Oh, look at that yard."

I know they're talking about my yard, because all the other lawns on the block are nearly identical—smooth, flawless green, with a few flowers here and there. One or two nicely trimmed trees. A couple in the street will stop and one will say, "Yeah. Boy, that's sure...different." Sometimes the speaker will substitute '*interesting*' for '*different*.' They don't know I can hear them, of course. It's usually the man who makes the 'interesting' comment. I know why. He's figuring how he can persuade his wife to let him do something like my yard so he doesn't have to spend an hour every week mowing the grass. Even on a riding lawn mower.

I mow my grass in ten minutes. Less time if I trot.

My next-door neighbor likes my trees. We share a couple of big cottonwoods that mess up the neighborhood every spring. He just grins and nods when people make cracks about his next-door forest. He's a little round fellow with a constant twinkle, a cute rolling gait, and a nice big lawn edged with flower beds. Some of his flowers migrated from my yard. Or maybe he stole them. He works on his yard a lot. He's retired.

On the back of the house I built a big odd-shaped deck, right off the sliding door to the dining room. It's shady and cool, so I grabbed a Corona and a slice of lime from the 'fridge and went and sat on my deck. It was quiet and relaxing and I considered how I would make my approach to Ephraim Saint Martin.

I took a big slug of beer, and when I lowered the bottle, Thumper was there at the back edge of my little patch of lawn. Thumper is a rabbit. Old, by the look of him. There are always several rabbits in the neighborhood, also crows, 'coons, and other critters.

Rabbits come and go and quite a few get killed by local dogs and cats, but not this old guy. He turned his head and looked at me. Wiggled his nose. Then he flipped his long, gray ears so the silver stud in his left one winked in the sunlight.

Chapter 5

I SWALLOWED ANOTHER slug of beer and when I looked up again old Thumper had disappeared. I tossed the dead soldier in the recycle box and went inside where I pawed around in the 'fridge and located that nice New York cut strip steak I'd had the Byerlys butcher pick out special. Yeah, I'm mostly a beer and hamburger kind of guy, but I also like good food, properly prepared a lot of the time. This particular steak was about an inch-and-a-half thick, and the butcher'd trimmed only a little of the fat off the edges. Then I fired up the charcoal in the grill.

In a cool corner of the bottom of a kitchen cabinet I located my stash of big firm Idaho potatoes. I selected one of the two left and shoved the sack back in its corner. I got out a plastic bowl and poured a couple of tablespoons of water into the bottom. Then I set a small plastic strainer in the bowl. The strainer would hold the potato out of the water.

After I washed most of the dirt off the spud, I jabbed it a couple of times with a fork and stuck the bowl with the potato into the microwave. A lady friend turned me on to that trick. The little bit of water helped give the potato just the right amount of moisture. This way the texture came out just as if the potato'd been baked in a regular oven.

I nuked the spud about the time I flipped the steak. Red juices ran down the sides. That chunk of beef would be just perfect, cool and rare inside. I don't do elaborate pastas or veggie dishes. Haven't time for wimpy stuff like that, but I do like a nice salad. So I whacked off about a third of a head of iceberg and got out my special blue cheese dressing. Most places make the blue cheese dressing too sweet or too strong. I like a nice subtle creamy sauce that lets the essence of the cheese come through clearly. To get it exactly right, I talked a chef, a former client, out of his recipe and then I made a couple of slight changes.

When everything was ready I sat down at my dining room table for a real treat. When I'm on a job, this kind of meal is a rarity. I'm either eating fried stuff or cold stuff, sometimes sitting in my car watching some bozo defraud his employer's insurance company. And peeing in a can.

I hate that.

So, I glance out at my deck, and papa cardinal shows up for supper. I feed birds. They're kind of messy but I like to watch them when I can. My cat rolls around on the floor showing off her belly and purring at me. I take a big mouthful of steak. While I'm chewing, I slather butter on the potato and sniff the cheese dressing.

There's a heavy pounding at the door.

Now, I'm like my neighbors in this suburb. I have a well-lighted, easy-to-spot doorbell. So pounding is really unnecessary. I get up and go to the front door, ready to give this politician, or salesman, or whomever a mild tongue-lashing about interrupting my dinner. It's dim in my tiny front hall because the individual at my door is blocking most of the light from the window.

I pulled the door open and I think I opened my mouth to say something. But I never got the words out. There was a ripping sound as the beefy guy opposite me jammed a gun right through the screen and into my left eye. I blinked and backed up a step. The pressure lessened, but this guy reached around the door and grabbed the back of my head. Not gently. Then he shifted the gun so he could come all the way in.

"What?" I managed.

"Stay the hell away from Bryce and Saint Martin. Otherwise you're fly meat." Then he cuffed me hard on the left side of my head. When I didn't go down, he slammed his other hand, the hand with the gun, against the other side of my head. I saw stars. No lie.

My knees turned jellylike and I sagged back against the wall. My large assailant turned, pawed the screen door out of his way, and lumbered out. I heard a car rev up in the driveway. The guy must have had a driver. There's a closet for outerwear beside the front door. When my head cleared, a nanosecond later, I yanked the door open and reached overhead.

Cleverly concealed in a spring mount above the door is my 20-gauge pump shotgun. The one I shortened slightly. I like a wider spread, so I took a couple of inches off the barrel. It's always loaded. I only use steel, double-ought buckshot. At thirty feet the tiny balls will make the side of a car look like a sieve. Cops frequently carry the same shotgun. It's a very intimidating weapon.

I jolted down the steps onto the driveway. The vehicle in question was maybe thirty feet away in the street, accelerating toward the intersection of D and my street, where he has to go right or left or else take out the house directly across the road. I could have stepped into the street and blown off the rear wheels, but I don't like to bring my work home. This is a quiet neighborhood and people on my block have no idea what I do. When someone asks, I just say independent consultant, which covers my odd hours. So I didn't blow away the car or its two occupants, much as I wanted to.

Instead, I jumped in my own car and tore after them as discreetly as possible. The gray Buick roared left onto D. I briefly lost sight of him until I got to D. There he was, just a couple of blocks ahead. The county road was fairly busy and I stayed even until they turned off and went north up 35W. I closed it up, but there was still too much traffic for me to risk a shot, so I leeched onto their wake and hung on. Then they made a mistake. I don't know if they realized I was behind them, but they slowed and took the off-ramp to Highway 96. The ramp was empty and there was nothing ahead of the Buick except pale blue sky.

I closed the distance between us and stuck the shotgun out the driver's side window. The sound of the shot was mostly lost in the wind and engine noise. In my excitement, I'd forgotten the kick of the shotgun. It slammed my arm painfully back against the window frame and I dropped the gun. I tromped on the brakes and slewed to a stop, teetering on the edge of the ramp. I went out the door and started looking for the shotgun in the fast-gathering twilight.

That weapon had set me back over three hundred dollars to start with. Then there were the hours invested in the modifications. I couldn't easily afford to replace it. I hoped it hadn't landed on the pavement. Eventually I found it, smeared with dirt and grass, lying in a clump of goldenrod. I'd been lucky. The gun had missed the concrete when I dropped it. I held it alongside my leg to conceal it while I waved off the one kind soul who stopped to ask if I needed any help. As he left, I heard his tires crunching on tiny pieces of safety glass that littered the ramp.

Oh, yeah. I'd hit that sucker all right. The car I'd been following. Took out his rear window and no doubt destroyed his trunk. If I'd been able to aim a little lower, he might be sitting up there on the ramp with me. As it was, alone at last, I looked up at the stars for a moment of silent contemplation and then went back to my ruined dinner. The stars were silent.

Damn! What in Hell was going on?

Chapter 6

THE NEXT MORNING I took the shotgun to my basement workshop and gave it a thorough cleaning. I polished up the barrel and treated the scratches with bluing. I used a nice wood polish on the stock, and I made sure everything worked all right. Treat your tools right, and they'll do right by you, I always say. While I was at it, I broke down and cleaned the other shotgun I keep hidden in the house—never mind exactly where. I reloaded both with fresh ammo. My need for the shotgun is almost always a pressing one and I can't afford misfires.

Then I headed downtown. As I drove out, my next-door neighbor, Bob, smiled and waved. Another peaceful, normal, suburban morning. Things at the office seemed normal too. No sign of a break-in or anything like that. I looked in and then turned back to examine the yellow post-it stuck to the glass.

"See Me," it said with a big *B* scrawled below the message. So I went down the hall to the end where first cousins Betsey and Belinda Revulon had their offices. They do computer graphic program design and desktop publishing of some kind. Their two-room office is crowded with computers, printers, cables, wires, a couple of big televisions, and racks of supplies.

Betsey was there, sitting at a console, fingers flying over the keyboard. "That's far enough. Confidential stuff here." She smirked up at me, never missing a beat in her rapid rhythm.

"Belinda here? She left this note."

"Yep," came a voice from the back room. Belinda Revulon appeared in the doorway. She is a big, healthy Swede; I'd estimate she weighs around one-fifty. Fine blond hair formed a wispy halo around her head and showed no sign of gray. The tiny wrinkles that gave texture and character to her face betrayed her age at somewhere over fifty-five. Her cousin, Betsey, was only a little younger, just as blond, and except for her bosom, extremely slender. They treated me like an errant younger brother.

I let 'em.

"See me?" I said, waving the yellow post-it.

"Man came to see you last night after you left," said Belinda.

"Hours after," chimed in Betsey.

"Big, tall man. Like that writer? Harlan Coben?"

"Looked very stern."

"Brusque." From Belinda again. They both knew what questions I'd have, so I just let them finish their routine.

"Asked where you were."

"And what were your hours."

"And when we thought you'd be back."

"I asked him his name," said Belinda. She shook her head and the multiple rings in her ears twinkled at me. "He wouldn't tell."

"Asked twice. I'm pretty sure he's a detective."

"A nameless detective," I said, nodding, and looked at them. Betsey and Belinda looked back expressionless. They didn't get it. Well, not everybody reads Pronzini, I guess.

Betsey's look sharpened. "What's going down, Sean?"

"Yeah, whussup, Dude?" said Belinda. "You're in some kind of trouble again. I can tell."

"Maybe, maybe not. Don't worry about it. I don't want you guys hit by any stray shrapnel."

"All right, Dude," said Belinda. She went by me and held her hand a little above her head. I reached up and we slapped palms in that high-five routine. Then I went back to my office.

So, somebody checked out my office building, and some truant tried to intimidate me into staying away from Magda Bryce. Since she was dead and I'd only seen her once, either these people were not communicating or they thought Magda Bryce had already given me an earful, an important earful. It wasn't likely she'd come to my office to hire me because she had a bad case of athlete's foot. But she could have had a bad case of husbanditis. Except people in town who know me at all, know I don't take routine divorce cases. Harcourt, Saint Martin, Bryce, et cetera, certainly knows that. So where did that leave things?

It left me in the dark with so many questions that I decided to do exactly what I'd been warned away from. First, though, I'd go brace Ephraim Harcourt Saint Martin. On his own turf, so to say. And maybe I'd pop in on Magda's grieving husband as well. That could mean a trip out to Deephaven, but I could afford it. I had a little time and nothing pressing in my caseload. I went out and down to the street. My car was safely parked in my spot back of the building, but I could screw around a good while finding parking near or under the IDS tower where Harcourt, Saint Martin, et cetera, had their offices. So, instead of driving, I sauntered along Central until a cab showed up. There wasn't one right outside my door, like in the movies. What's more, the driver of my cab wasn't one of those chatty second- or third-world immigrants who'd be witty and charming and gives the detective all sorts of significant information while they whisked through traffic.

Tidbits like: "Say, did you hear the scuttlebutt about Bryce? Seems he was about to throw his wife outta the house for malfeasance, misfeasance, or not emptying the cat box." Stuff like that.

This cabby just asked, "Where to?" stuck a black, well chewed, cigar stub back in his face, and never said another word during the ten-minute ride to the entrance to the Crystal Court. I paid him and went inside. I even gave him a tip. A small tip.

The Crystal Court is on the main floor of the IDS tower. It's a big, three-story open space surrounded and topped by glass curtain walls that let in a lot of light and keep out the real city. By that I mean the noise, bus exhausts, car horns, vagrants trying to wheedle money from better-heeled passersby, and the occasional itinerant saxophone player or bongo drummer.

Elevators and escalators connect to the elaborate skyway system that lets people wander around most of the center of the city without setting foot on the street or feeling rain or snow or wind. Or the stultifying heat or biting cold we sometimes get in Minneapolis.

On one side of the court is a set of glass doors that separates the business tower from the public area. Guards are always posted there. Beyond the guard station are the elevators. I went for the second group. The first group only reaches to the thirty-fifth floor. The other set of elevators starts at one, jumps to thirty-seven, and goes to the top. The fifty-first floor. I have no idea what's on thirty-six.

Hell of a view from the top floor. If you have the big bucks you can throw parties up there. On the fiftieth floor. I've been up a couple of times. Once to a restaurant that later closed when expense accounts and the economy tightened up. Great view. So-so food.

I could feel a guard's eyes on me, in my jacket and summer slacks. No tie. No gun. And my high-top Keds. Why was he looking at me? Those guards see all kinds of elegantly dressed people, women especially, wearing walking or tennis shoes at noon and after work. Of course, I admit not many people wear red high-tops with white soles.

The elevator shot up to the forty-ninth floor. Left my stomach somewhere around my butt and plugged my ears. Out of the elevator to my right was a set of tall wooden doors that looked as if they'd require two strong men to open. Not so. I knew from experience they needed only the touch of a hand. So I touched one and it swung open, nice as you please.

I hadn't been up here in quite some time. Most of the jobs I did for Harcourt, Saint Martin, Saint Martin, et cetera, came to me by courier. Somebody shows up with a fat, sealed envelope like a warrant from King Arthur. I sign, the courier gives me the envelope, and goes. Inside I'll find several pages of information and a letter of instructions. If I need more information I could call, but I've been given to understand they don't want me to call them. Or come to the offices.

Frankly, I didn't much care for the idea either. But this was different.

Inside, the atmosphere was hushed, almost soundless. It was quieter than the elevator lobby and that was real quiet. In front of me, beside the halls that lead left and right to partners' and associates' offices, was a big polished walnut desk. Behind the desk, typing at a noiseless keyboard, sat a youngish, big-shouldered, slender man with longish dark-brown hair.

The metal nameplate on the front edge of the desk read *P. HALL*. He looked at me, silent, alert. Not interested, just watchful.

"Hi," I said. "I'm not new here. Don't get up, I'll find my own way," and I breezed right on by.

P. Hall hadn't been here the last time I'd braved these hushed halls of legal wizardry. That time it'd been some broad, a looker, a frail, a—never mind. This guy looked like he could be in the movies, some beefcake costume piece, like *Hercules*, maybe. His brown hair swept back from a high forehead. He had very wide shoulders inside his dark suit. I started down the hall to my left. I moved with alacrity, my shoes sinking into the deep-pile dark mahogany carpet. I left P. Hall in my dust.

Chapter 7

THE CORNER OFFICE that was my target was right where it had been the last time I was here in these hushed halls. The door carried no nameplate. I pushed it open with one finger and entered the outer room of a three-room suite. It was a large room, as befitted the entrance to the Great Man's digs. In front of me across a half-acre of bronze carpet rested another large, polished-wood desk. From behind it, a female person in a severe, tailored suit looked at me with a disapproving frown.

"Is there something I can do for you, Mr.—?" she asked in a frosty tone.

"Yep. You can tell Sir Ephraim Harcourt Saint Martin, or Eppy, or Har, or whatever it is you call him, that Sean Sean is here to see him. Stat!" I had no idea whether she was diddling the old man, and I didn't much care, but I could see from the expression on her face I'd struck gold, or silver, or maybe just a nerve.

She raised her chin, stared down her long, elegant nose at me, and breathed in deeply, which caused her nostrils to flare and noticeably lifted her bosom. "I'm very sorry, Mr.— Sean, is it? Mr. Saint Martin is—"

"Doesn't matter, sweetheart." I'd made a half-turn right and slouched with one hand in my trouser pocket. The other hand held my lucky Susan B. Anthony dollar. I started twisting it back and forth through the knuckles of my hand—remember Bogart as Captain Queeg with his steel ball bearings? *Click, click, click.* I dropped my chin and looked at her across my left shoulder with a flat expression. It was something I practiced.

"Doesn't matter if he's in conference, on the phone, practicing his golf swing, or boffing some secretary in there. I'm gonna see him now. So, sweetheart, do you tell 'im or do I announce myself?"

Now, I don't ever sound like Bogart, and I certainly don't look like him. I seriously doubt that the woman had any idea what part I was playing right then, but it felt pretty good to me, and it had the desired effect. She produced an expression of mild alarm, jumped up, and headed to the door on her left. That'd be on my right, just to keep the orientation clear. She went through and closed it quietly behind her. I counted silently in my head: *one elephant, two elephant, three—*. When I got to five pachyderms, I went across the room and followed the woman through the door.

In the next, impossibly large office, the woman was nowhere to be seen. She'd disappeared, probably out another door, probably to fetch security.

"Excuse me?" Ephraim Harcourt Saint Martin had a good courtroom voice. It was cultured, loud enough, and at the low end of the baritone range. He definitely lived in Deephaven. I'm good, you see. I can tell a lot about a person from their voice. Even just two words.

Of course, I'd heard him speak on several other occasions, and I already knew where he lived.

Chapter 8

EPHRAIM HARCOURT SAINT MARTIN didn't rise from his large, throne-like padded leather chair. He just stared at me, giving me a taste of his famous courtroom stare. That stare had shriveled the scrotum of many an opposing attorney. It didn't faze me in the least. I didn't have anything he wanted. I knew where he lived.

And he knew that I knew.

A long time ago, when I was starting out as a small-time, independent shamus, this firm of Harcourt, Saint Martin, Saint Martin, Bryce et cetera had hired me for a small-time piece of business. After I finished, I'd made some smart-mouth remark about certain small-time illegalities I'd happened across inside the firm. They mostly dealt with sloppy bookkeeping, and although they weren't particularly well-concealed, members of the firm recognized they were dealing with a detective with above-average powers of observation and cogitation. Eppy had responded to my smart-mouth cracks with a threat to my physical being, my corporeal self. So, of course, to maintain some semblance of my manhood, I threatened him back.

Not cool.

Since at that time I had few clients, he looked for ways to get to me. The way that hurt the most was when he began to dry up my contacts. We private investigators rely heavily on our contacts. I was having to skulk around at weird hours to meet subterraneanly with cops and other people who had helped me out in previous times almost as a matter of course. Word had gotten out that a lot of players in and around law enforcement in the Twin Cities suddenly couldn't afford to be seen in my company, or they'd risk the ire of the law firm.

I'd stormed in to Eppy's office and told him I'd get him where he lived. He retorted that I didn't know where he lived. At that time he was correct, but I soon found out.

One fine Sunday afternoon in July when he was having a big garden party for the firm—attorneys, wives, children and so on—I invaded his grounds, his estate, his home. I subdued the two security people working the party. That part was easy. For a little while, I just wandered around his mansion. I didn't break anything, just pawed through some drawers, sampled his private stock from a bar, and left evidence about that I'd found my way to his very private wine cellar.

Most of the people I encountered assumed I was one of the nattily attired servants. But then I decided to make an appearance at the pool. That's where Eppy was holding court, surrounded by several of his firm's attorneys and their wives or girlfriends.

For this appearance, I carried a tray of champagne flutes to poolside. I thought I did it with flair, with a certain nonchalance, and the reaction was all I could hope for. You see, from the bar where I'd obtained the tray of champagne flutes, I'd made a small detour into the bushes along a path, and left my clothes there. All my clothes.

Except for the mask I was wearing and my red high-top Keds, I was stark buck naked. Now, with all modesty, I will tell you that while I am short of stature, I am *not* short all over. I waltzed out onto the fake grass that surrounded the pool carrying my tray of flutes in a jaunty fashion, swaying gently. The air was cool on my naked body. I stopped with my toes just over the ceramic edge of the pool.

I posed in the gentle sunlight, first this way, then that. Never dropped a single flute. Silence rippled around the pool as if someone had farted in the boardroom. When it was dead quiet, I said in my most menacing voice: "You see, I *do* know where you live."

That broke the stasis. The silence was instantly transformed into pandemonium—screams, laughter and imprecations. The only one I saw who had no reaction at all was Mrs. Saint Martin. I recognized her from frequent pictures in the local newspapers. She just looked at me with no expression whatsoever. I set down the tray, leaned forward, and dropped two small plastic globes into the pool. Then I tripped casually back into the bushes where I made like a rabbit, grabbed clothes, and bolted for my escape route.

The water-soluble plastic globes I'd dropped contained a concentrated solution of indigo dye. Harmless really, but sometimes it's tough to get the blue out. The spreading dye caused an even greater outcry, which brought the horde of small folk running to the pool from elsewhere on the grounds. Dressed now, I had only to step among them, allow them to flow past, and continue on my way. I avoided the long fairway-like open greensward that ran down to the lakeshore. The irate adults, in attempting to find me, were impeded by the mass of children. I raced to a gap in the fence line at the edge of the property that I had discovered days earlier and made off.

Was I accused? Arrested for disturbing the peace? Threatened with grievous bodily harm? Of course I was. But I'd had a mask over my entire head, no one had been within twenty feet, and when first discovered, observers had been...er...distracted.

Positive eyewitness proof that I was the naked man with the tray of champagne flutes and the blue dye was non-existent. The cops weren't going to have a full-frontal nude lineup, were they? Plus I'd arranged to conjure up a couple of reputable witnesses who would swear to my whereabouts elsewhere in town at the crucial time.

Let's face it, I hadn't watched four-plus hours of *The Godfather* for nothing.

No-o-o contest.

Chapter 9

ALTHOUGH THEY COULDN'T prove I'd been the naked perpetrator of the pool incident, the message had been received and Sir Ephraim called off his campaign against me. One of his minions showed up at my office a few days later and suggested a truce. They offered to throw a little business my way from time to time, if I would never suggest to anyone that Harcourt, Saint Martin, Saint Martin, Bryce, et cetera, was a client and if I'd stay away from their offices and their homes, and most particularly, out of the sight of senior partner Ephraim Harcourt Saint Martin.

That suited me just fine. I knew they could drive me out of business if they really tried.

No-o-o problem.

So for the past several years we've had a mutually profitable arm's-length arrangement. Now here I was for the first time in several years, despoiling the carpet in the great man's sanctum. The great man was not pleased.

In a word, the man was pissed.

But so was I.

E. Harcourt Saint Martin looked me over as I stood framed in the doorway, sort of like a target. I couldn't exactly feel the intense dislike in his gaze, but he made it very clear I was an unwelcome intruder.

The silence went on for a few seconds. Then he growled, "Well? You have perhaps four minutes before security arrives to summarily remove you from my presence."

I controlled my anger, admirably, I thought, and said, "We've done a bit of business together without much direct contact, but now something strange is going on and I need some answers."

"I cannot possibly imagine that this firm has any dealings whatsoever with you." He shook his carefully coifed mane of silver hair slowly back and forth. "As I recall, I gave absolute orders that this firm was never to employ you again. So far as I am aware, that order—"

Well, of course I should have remembered that my work for the firm was outside the ken of the senior partner. Either that or he was just blustering to keep up appearances around the office. I held up one hand. "Let me get a few short sentences in here and we'll conclude this interview quickly. I'm not too pleased to be here either. I'll mention a few things, such as the city morgue, death by gunshot, a woman you know with a bullet hole between her breasts." Normally I wasn't that blunt. Besides maintaining my image in Saint Martin's eyes, I was digging for a reaction. I advanced slowly across his carpet toward Saint Martin while I spoke and I watched him closely, but saw nary a flicker.

"I have not the slightest interest in your word game, Mr....Sean."

Notice that little hesitation? That's the problem with my name. People don't want to be familiar, call me by my first name. It sounds as if they are, no matter which name they use. And I can take it either way. But it throws them off, just a little. Ruins their timing. Gives me an edge. Sometimes.

I have a choice of several reactions I've developed. One of them is to pretend offense at over-intimacy. Today I chose to ignore the name game.

"Last Thursday a woman came to see me. She said you recommended me."

"Ridiculous." He snorted. One of the few people I've met who can do a proper snort.

"She told me she was considering hiring me. She didn't. Then she left. She didn't tell me what the problem was or why you had recommended me. Interspersed with the long silences, I think we shared no more than a couple of hundred words."

"Are you trying to make a point?"

"Two days later, Magda Bryce turned up dead. Shot."

Now I got a reaction. It wasn't much, just a flicker of the eyes and a slight twist of the lips. "That's part of it. The other part is—"

There was the sound of a door opening off to my right and a male voice said, "Mr. Saint Martin?"

Saint Martin lifted one hand off the desk, just a casual movement; he didn't even get his wrist up. But it had all the weight of an imperial gesture. "It's all right. Wait outside, if you please."

I didn't look around. Whoever it was gently closed the unseen door again. I continued. "Since she came to my office I've made a visit to the morgue, had my dinner ruined, been assaulted by some thug who destroyed my screen door, and learned some other guy has been skulking around my office asking questions of my neighbors. I'm irritated. I wouldn't be here otherwise. I want you to call off the hounds or I'm going to get mad."

"I have no idea what you are talking about. I certainly didn't recommend you to Mrs. Bryce. The death of the wife of one of my partners has upset us all. She was like a daughter to me. The police are investigating. This firm is not. Please depart immediately."

I considered, still staring at him. Sir Ephraim was noted for his insistence on being kept apprised of all the business of the law firm. But in any large law firm like this, no one could know everything, especially if a partner or associate wanted to be secretive and the business was not one of the firm's cases. Or if it was extra-legal.

"Did you send Magda Bryce to me?"

"I did suggest she contact a private investigator. My secretary was instructed to give her names of several competent investigators. I'm quite confident yours was not on that list."

"What did she want to consult me about?"

"I'm not at liberty to say. Moreover, I have only your word that it was Mrs. Bryce who came to your office."

I chewed the inside of my lower lip, not one of my more attractive habits. "All right. I'll fix the screen door myself."

I figured Sir Ephraim would circulate a memo about this conversation to the entire firm. He'd also issue a directive reminding everyone that the firm preferred not to do business with one Sean NMI Sean. He'd want some distance between us, whoever was responsible, until they figured out what was going on. Assuming something was going on.

I made no mention of the whip marks on the body. Saint Martin might suspect I knew about them, if he knew about them, but he couldn't be certain of that. He might not even know I'd actually seen Magda Bryce's corpse. Uncertainties can lead to mistakes. Knowledge is power. Of course, power corrupts.

Chapter 10

I WENT OUT THE WAY I had entered. P. Hall was at his desk, not a hair out of place. I looked at his well-shaped long-fingered hands, wondered if he ever thought about taking up the guitar. His bland look revealed nothing. I couldn't tell if he'd been the one in the concealed doorway. I glanced back at the carpet as I went through the big door to the elevator lobby. I couldn't swear to it, but I thought my foot impressions in the deep carpet were a little fainter than when I'd walked in.

The elevator dropped me to the ground floor, restoring my inner organs to their original locations and unstopping my ear. The guard again eyed me and my Keds as I sauntered to a nearby public telephone. I didn't routinely carry a cell phone. I was considering it, but so far I couldn't justify the expense. I'd rather spend the money on certain surveillance equipment. I dialed the cop shop and asked for my friend Simon, a long-time homicide dick who'd never make it above second grade because he was too wise.

"Hey, Simon, how's tricks?"

"Simple," he growled, robbing me of my next line. "Whaddya want?"

"A little chat. How's about I pick up some buns at Crider's Bakery and we meet in the plaza at government center?"

"Okay. Thirty minutes, give or take."

I cradled the receiver and went out onto the warm summer street. Two blocks down Nicollet Mall toward police headquarters was a little grassy indentation in the wall of commercial and retail buildings. The tiny park held a few tables and chairs. The tiny lawn fronted one of the smallest and best bakeries in the city. Not many people knew about it, and those of us who did, didn't talk much about it. Dan Crider, the baker, made a comfortable living and that's all he cared to do, that and strive to produce the best pastries in town.

His buns were the best—round, firm, perfectly shaped; they attracted admiration wherever they were seen. I picked up six and sauntered through the heating day toward Third Avenue and Sixth Street and the big plaza between Hennepin County Government building and City Hall.

Simon was late and I'd already succumbed to the aroma drifting up from Crider's buns and eaten one. Detective Ricardo Simon, whose name didn't go with his heritage, was a short, overweight Norwegian with wispy brown hair, a prominent belly, and a perpetual frown. At some time in his past, someone had smashed his nose into an approximation of a small potato. Not an Idaho, one of those misshapen round Red River Reds from North Dakota. He was absolutely incorruptible. He grew up in Wisconsin and had been on the Minneapolis Police Force for about ten years.

He and I had been friends for almost as long. We weren't close pals, but we were mutually respectful, and every so often we'd been able to help each other out. I watched him lumber across Fifth against the light. He waved a hand negligently at a driver who screeched to a halt and leaned on the horn.

Puffing, he collapsed onto the stone edge of the central fountain beside me and stuck out a hand. I filled it with another succulent bun.

After a couple of quick bites, Simon looked around and then back at me. "So, what's your pleasure?"

"Monday a homicide dick summoned me to the morgue. A big guy, maybe six-one, heavy, way over two hundred pounds, longish dark hair."

Simon grunted and swallowed. Stuck his hand in the sack between us and extracted another bun. "Sounds like Hank—Henry Holt. Tell me about him."

"Good, solid, honest guy. Establishment type. Not brilliant but good with details. He usually gets the job done. Why?"

"He's investigating the murder of Magda Bryce."

Simon nodded. "You involved in that?"

"I don't know. I only met her once, very inconclusive." I told him about the attack on me and the nameless detective asking around my office.

"So they know where you live," he smiled mirthlessly.

"I don't have a clue what's going on here. I just came from seeing Sir Ephraim and—

"You went to his office?"

"Yes. I told him to call off his mongrels. But I don't know for sure who sent either one."

Simon shook his head and then glanced sideways at me. "You know about the whip marks on the body?"

I nodded. "Something nasty is happening in our fair city and I seem to be an unwilling player. I don't need this right now; I haven't got a client here. But I suspect that the attention I'm getting won't stop."

"And of course, if I now give you the standard speech about letting the police handle it, you'll ignore me, right?"

"Simon, ol' buddy, I can't step out, unless whoever sent that beetle-browed mutant to my home quits now. I won't go around looking over my shoulder all the time."

"Well, Holt won't be a problem, unless he learns you're holding out on him or you interfere with his investigation."

Simon's cell phone gave a muffled trill and he fished it out with a grimace. After a few grunts into the microphone, he left, taking the last of Crider's buns. I sat in the sun for a while longer.

Chapter 11

I WALKED UP FIFTH toward the mall after I left the plaza. I was enjoying the weather and the bustle of downtown city workers hurrying about their business. I liked the downtown atmosphere, the traffic, the energy. I'd have moved my office downtown if I could have afforded it.

The light turned green and I started across Nicollet. There was a whirring beside me and a slender, dark-haired female brushed by and bumped me off-stride. When I located her again in the crowd, she was traveling at high speed on inline skates, weaving in and out among the pedestrians.

"Hey, watch it!" I yelled after her.

As she turned the corner out of sight, she glanced back through heavy, wrap-around, dark glasses. I legged it after her, late morning heat or no. By the time I turned the corner, she was halfway down the block. One of the disadvantages of being short like me is that my horizon is sometimes limited. Since nearly everyone on the block was taller, I had a hard time keeping track of her progress.

"Hey!" I shouted again. The biggest reaction was from the people nearest. They jumped and shied away. The dark-haired skater merely turned her head toward me again and then leaned a hard right into an alley. I knew that alley. I know most of the alleys in downtown Minneapolis. One of the perks of the job. This alley had a couple of branches and backdoors to several hallways. Give it up, I counseled myself. I took my own advice.

I went back to my office. When I got there, I shrugged out of my jacket and hung it on the bentwood coat-and-hat-rack in one corner. That was when I noticed an envelope sticking out of the side pocket. I don't carry things in the side pockets of my jackets. It ruins the lines, especially when I'm heeled. Somebody must have put the subject envelope in my pocket. I knew it didn't happen at the law firm or Crider's Bakery. Simon would have no business slipping me an envelope *sub rosa,* so to speak. That left only the dark-haired female skater. More odd behavior. I gingerly fished the envelope out of the coat pocket by one corner.

It was an ordinary, cheap, white business envelope, the kind you can buy in every Wal-Mart or Target store and probably in a million other places. Unsealed. There was nothing written on either side. So I dropped the envelope in the center of my desk and stared at it. I could see there was a piece of paper inside. The piece was folded in thirds, like you would do to put the sheet in a number ten business envelope. I took two pencils out of the desk drawer and, using the eraser ends, fished the paper out of the envelope and unfolded it.

If the envelope was ordinary and common, the sheet of paper was not. It was white, heavy and obviously of good quality bond. On one side was some printing. Aha, I thought. A clue. But to what? The clue was printed with a sharp-pointed, dark-blue felt pen. It said: *PLEASE HELP ME.* That was all, no signature, nothing else. Not much of a clue. I sat and stared at the paper. No revelations or in-sights came to me. Sherlock Holmes would deduce all kinds of significance from the cryptic note. Not me. I figured it might just be a prank. Finally, I took a large, flat, glassine envelope out of my desk and slid the paper into it. I stashed the envelope in my desk drawer and began to look through my file of receivables.

One of the things the old fictional P.I.s never seem to deal with, except maybe in passing, are the bills and the business of collecting what's due. It is axiomatic that we try to collect a good part of the fee up front, even if we have a contract with the client. Otherwise, considering the kinds of people we deal with, once their problem is solved, unless an insurance company, or maybe a big law firm is the client, it's often tough to collect.

Like any solo businessman, I spend almost as much time sending out invoices and trying to collect on them as I do in the business itself. I can't afford an accountant or a bookkeeper, so I use a simple packaged system I found at an office supply store. My simple system told me a couple of ex-clients still hadn't paid overdue bills, so I decided to do some collecting in person.

There were three really late clients. I chose the one with the largest bill. The exotic dancer.

Chapter 12

"Wut zat?" My sometimes mush-mouthed friend, Detective Simon, pointed one meaty finger at an object on the floor. He hadn't quite finished swallowing his doughnut when he'd posed the question.

"Dunno," I responded, leaning over. The light in the dingy apartment was poor to begin with and the detective was standing in front of the single window. Still, the pale-pink object, half-hidden under the sofa, seemed to gather the little light there was so it almost glowed.

"Don't know much, do you?"

"I know the man over there by the kitchen door is dead. I know who I am, and I know you, Detective Simon."

"Smart mouth on you, like always. Tell me again whaddyuh doin' here."

"Simple. As I explained to the officer in the hall, I'm here on business. He stopped me when I was on my way out after seeing a client who lives upstairs on the next floor." I pointed at the ceiling. That much was true. What I didn't add was that my client, the stripper who worked in the topless club down the block, had first tried to seduce me with wine and her doll collection that appeared to fill every available nook and horizontal surface in her apartment. After an excessively detailed and boring dissertation on the lucrative collectible doll business, it had become clear that she wasn't prepared to pay me my fee in regular old dollars. She offered me a couple of boxed dolls she said were worth considerably more than my fee.

I wasn't having any.

I saw at least two disassembled Barbies in a shoebox on her coffee table. My client then switched to discussing the anatomical proportions of Barbie dolls, and we had a little more wine. When that subject failed to ignite a spark, she started making comparative allusions between Barb's dimensions and her own. That quickly led to our tipsy agreement that the only way to tell for sure which anatomical dimensions were more in proportion, was by a comparison of Barbie's and her dimensions without artifice or accouterments.

While the disrobing proceeded, I generously agreed to a similar comparison with a Ken doll, only to learn that, sadly, Barbie's companion was not anatomically complete.

That all led to closer contact. After we exchanged bodily fluids for a while, I dressed and left, soberer, but no better off in coin of the realm. Her athleticism, honed by her dancing, had been amply demonstrated, but the episode had its drawbacks. In her bedroom, along with hundreds more dolls of every possible description, resided her pet parrot. A big one. The damn bird kept up a distracting, raucous gabble the entire time we were coupling. It was screeching words at us, or at me, in some language I didn't recognize. On my way out, the lady told me it was a dialect spoken by some obscure tribe in Micronesia. When I asked her what Polly was squawking, she just smiled and closed the door.

Now I was peering at a pale pink piece of plastic half-jammed under a ratty brown sofa. The sofa stank of old tobacco smoke, sweat, and of the ancient stuffing in its flattened cushions. I was willing to bet the piece of plastic was a body part from one of the dolls in the shoebox upstairs.

Should I mention my suspicion to Detective Simon? The doll's owner still owed me and if I ever hoped to collect, she had to continue working, a definite factor in my consideration. I delayed my decision. "What else you got?" I asked.

He shrugged. "Look at the bookcase. All those tapes and empty boxes."

The bookcase had an entire shelf filled with paperboard boxes flashing lurid primary colors and even more lurid titles. Titles like *REVENGE OF THE LUST LOVERS*, and *DOLORES DOES IT ALL IN DALLAS, HOUSTON, FORT WORTH AND SAN ANGELO*, and another labeled *SEX, SEX, AND MORE SEX*.

A quick perusal of the bookcase led to two inescapable facts: the library had been exclusively pornographic, and nearly all the tapes were missing or destroyed. Someone had systematically cracked the shells and pulled fistfuls of videotape out of the containers. The tape lay in tangled, twisted loops and sworls, like oily brown snakes massively entwined in each others' coils and spirals. I saw lots of jagged ends, indicating someone had snapped the loops, breaking the tapes in many places. Lying on top of the big black-bodied television squatting in one corner were two more ruptured tape cases with one difference. Each of these broken black shells had a hand-printed label, *GINA I* and *GINA 2*.

Gina Moskowitz, from Watertown, South Dakota, was the name of the doll collector upstairs who owned the parrot.

"How long has the stiff been dead?"

"Not long enough to be."

"Be what?"

"Stiff, Sean." Simon smiled at his lame humor. "He must have died just before we arrived. This dead guy is Simon S. Walker—"

"Yeah? Same first name."

He kept right on as if I hadn't spoken.

"—owned a small publishing and printing firm down on Chicago Avenue. Did pamphlets, a couple of religious fringe things, wedding announcements, sometimes one or other of the free tabloids you see all over town. Stuff like that. Nothing major, but he made a pretty good living at it. He liked to gamble, hang around with the wise guys in town."

"So, how long has he been dead?"

"Oh, 'bout an hour."

I suppressed a shudder. That meant he'd died about the same time I was playing grab-ass with the lady upstairs. The only loud thumps I'd heard in the last several hours had been the headboard of Gina's bed banging against the wall.

"What's his middle name?" I always wanted to know that because I don't have one.

"Schuester."

"Funny name for a publisher," I said. "How come you were here so promptly and know so much about him already? The ME isn't even here yet."

"We was about to arrest the guy for conspiracy to receive stolen property."

"Walker's a fence?"

"Not really active, but he's been known to hold things for important people in town. We think he was holding a special package and we wanted to put the arm on him".

"So, it was just a wee bit of a shock to find him newly deceased."

"You could say that."

"You are of the opinion his death was triggered by your arrival here to arrest him?" My friend Detective Simon merely grunted. It occurred to me he was also upset because the dead guy had a first name identical to his own moniker.

"How'd Walker die?" I asked.

"It 'pears he was electrocuted when he touched his faulty coffeemaker."

"What is that, an espresso machine?"

"Uh-huh."

"How do you know it's faulty?" I leaned over and peered at the back side of the machine where the power cord entered its white plastic body. The cord was in good shape and everything appeared normal.

"There, see where it's plugged into the wall? That smudge looks like residue from a heavy spark. We found burns on his palm. Looks like he wuz standin' here on the damp floor with one hand on the coffeemaker. He didn' have no shoes on so the power shot right through him."

More and more uniforms and police technicians were arriving. I leaned closer and looked at the wall socket where the coffeemaker was plugged in. The powdery black smudge looked exactly like what you'd get from a dead short.

A fingerprint guy nudged me aside and began to do his thing with the coffeemaker and the immediate area around it.

A few minutes later a police electrician came into the kitchen. "I checked the basement junction box for this place. Everything checks out down there." He pulled out one of those light gizmos used to see if the circuit continuity was still okay. The light glowed when he stuck the yellow prongs into the socket above the plug. "Huh," he said.

Simon raised his head and looked at the technician.

The electrician shrugged. "It's unusual for a socket to be live after the other half of a duplex has fused in a short. Okay to disconnect the coffeemaker?"

Simon nodded.

The other man took a well-insulated pair of pliers from the leather kit hanging by a wide belt over his shoulder. He carefully pried out the plug. The brass prongs were pitted and dirty. He laid the plug down on the counter and carefully and gently inserted the wire probes hanging from the continuity gizmo. The light remained dark.

"Simon, what's the deal here? You don't usually invest this much manpower in a lowlife like this Walker guy. Especially when it looks like accidental death." I stood up and stretched my five-foot-three-inch frame and rubbed the small of my back. I was beginning to think Gina had bruised a muscle group back there.

He shook his head. By now most of the other cops had left, as had the technicians, and Walker's body had been removed. No one had found anything, or if they had, they hadn't mentioned it to Simon. I'd been there the whole time.

"I just can't shake the feelin' that his kickin' the bucket just as we arrived to bust him is a little coincidental."

Truth to tell, neither could I.

There was a clatter of hard plastic platform shoes in the hallway outside the open door. I turned away so Gina Moskowitz wouldn't see me, motioning Simon to silence. The woman's steps hesitated, and I heard the murmurs of her voice and of the uniform stationed in the hall. Then she went on down the stairs to the ground floor.

After she left, I asked, "Anybody talk to her?"

"Of course. We canvassed all the neighbors. Nobody remembers anyone coming in or going out just before we got here. Except for you. You were here when he was killed."

"Yeah, I figured as much. But I was upstairs with Gina the whole time."

"Gina."

"The stripper who lives right above Walker."

Simon frowned and pulled out his notebook. "The woman who lives upstairs is named Alice Moskowitz."

"Right. But her stage name is Gina the Gorgeous."

"Zat so? She didn't happen to mention that. Why does that name mean something?"

"Maybe it's these two ruined tapes on the TV set. *GINA 1* and *GINA 2*," I said, pointing at the boxes.

We stared at each other.

Simon blinked first. I shook my head and walked into the kitchen where the body had been found. There were smudged chalk marks on the floor. I pulled a tall chair across the room and sat down, looking aimlessly around the small kitchen. There was nothing much to see, except the room felt odd to me.

For a while I couldn't figure it out. As a rule I don't spend a lot of time in other people's kitchens. But I recognize a bad layout when I see one. This kitchen had been shoehorned into this space without any regard that I could see for convenience or efficiency. All the counter space was on one wall, opposite the stove and the refrigerator. The appliances were two steps across the room, side-by-side. The sink was stuck in one corner opposite the back door to the place. The way the room was set up, you had to stand with your back to the only window to work at the counter. If you looked straight ahead all you saw was a piece of black plastic stuck to the blank wall over the counter.

I reached up and picked at one corner. The plastic didn't budge. I pulled out my key-ring penlight and shined it at an angle to the surface. Right. There was some kind of curved glass set back behind the plastic. I could see a faint reflection. It reminded me of a big lens.

I stood up and my hand fell naturally on the metal base plate of the coffee machine. It was cold but I jerked my hand away. I looked at the countertop. There was a faint rectangle on the tile, as if the coffeemaker had recently been moved a few inches to the side. I wondered if the crime scene guys had done it. I went into the other room where Simon was reviewing his notes.

"I guess we're done here," he said. "No crime, no harm."

"Why would somebody have a television set concealed in the wall of the kitchen?" I asked.

"Say what?" Simon looked up.

"I think there's a TV in the wall over the kitchen counter," I said. "It's hidden behind that piece of plastic on the wall above the coffeemaker."

"Show me," he said. So I did.

Behind the wall was a tiny storage room. It was so tiny the door had been cut down to fit. We looked in and it was obvious someone had built a false wall several inches away from the square of plastic, reaching from floor to ceiling. It was a pretty good job. Being handy myself, I know about such things. But it was clear the wall was built after the floor was put in. The false wall made a shaft about a foot wide from floor to ceiling. It had no door or any other way of getting into the space. I rapped on the wall. It sounded hollow. Made no sense.

"Odd," I said.

"Odd," echoed Simon. We shrugged at each other and went back to the kitchen.

"I'm gonna rip that plastic off," I said, pawing through drawers looking for a strong knife or screwdriver.

"No you ain't," said Simon.

"I ain't?"

"Can't destroy the evidence."

I waved my hands. "Evidence? Of what, pray tell?"

"Dunno," he countered. "Why is there a concealed TV right there?"

"Maybe we'll find out if I tear the panel off." Then I had another idea. I happened across a flashlight in one drawer that actually worked, unlike the flash in my kitchen drawer. Holding the light at an angle and peering from the lowest side of the plastic screen, I squinted up past the TV.

"Hah!" I said.

Chapter 13

"WHAT WE HAVE is a small nine-inch Sony color TV on a plywood shelf. It appears the wiring goes up. Let's go in from the back side. From that storeroom."

I took a big carving knife from a rack in one of the drawers and went into the storeroom. Simon was right with me. He frowned at the blade in my hand but he didn't say anything.

With all my strength, I slashed and sawed through the Sheetrock until I had a cut about three-feet long. By pressing on one side, I worked my fingers into the slit. I yanked. Nothing happened. I yanked again as hard as I could.

Nothing happened.

"Here," said Simon and stuck one hand between mine into the knife slot. We both pulled. With a ripping sound of small nails tearing loose, we pulled a jagged piece of plasterboard free. A cloud of dust and dirt fell on us. I sneezed. Simon coughed.

"See, there's the power cord and a cable that must feed the signal to the TV set." I pointed. "It all goes right up into the sub floor."

"Now I think I'd better get a search warrant," said Simon. "For that apartment upstairs."

"Good idea. What do you plan to do about all the videotapes?"

"Untangling and splicing the broken ones is gonna be a hell of a job. Since Walker's death appears to be an accident, I don't think that work'll get much support in the department. I may not even get a search warrant for Moskowitz's apartment. There's no evidence anybody tossed this place. Who's to say Walker's death wasn't an accident, except for the ruined tapes? For all I know he did that himself."

"But it sure isn't likely," I said. "And this is a very fishy setup." I was already getting some ideas about this setup. Unfortunately, all my ideas led right to Gorgeous Gina-baby's door. Settlement of her bill was fast disappearing down a long dark hall. "What about the timing of his death?" Another element that bothered me.

"Simon shrugged and said, "I don't think there's anything to that. But with the TV in the kitchen, I might have enough for a warrant, so I'll give it a try." We left Walker's apartment building and Simon locked the door. We parted on the street. Simon's car was right at the entrance, mine was down the block. By the time I got to it, he'd driven off. So I turned around and went back into the building.

On the second floor it took me only a minute to work a thin strip of spring steel between the lock and the jamb on Gorgeous Gina's, AKA Alice Moskowitz's, apartment door. It's a tool I almost always carry. Except when I'm on a date. Inside, I went straight to the bedroom.

The bed linen was still rumpled, just as it had been when I was there earlier. I knew Gorgeous Gina wouldn't be back for hours, so I had plenty of time. I stood in the doorway and surveyed the room. A quick glance out the window confirmed that her bedroom was right above Walker's kitchen and her small closet was conveniently positioned directly above the tiny storeroom on the floor below.

There wasn't much to see in the closet, apart from Gina's clothes. Not her working clothes, they probably didn't take up more than a couple of inches in one drawer. I'd caught her act a few times and she usually didn't start out in anything more than a flimsy top and a G-string. The closet held her street clothes. Dresses, blouses, slacks, and a small three-drawer bureau. I shined the purloined flashlight around the perimeter of the room at the floor. Nothing out of the ordinary. But when I pulled the bureau away from the wall, I could see that the plaster had been crudely repaired.

I backed out of the closet and looked up at the ceiling. On one wall, right at the junction of ceiling and wall, was a grille. Not all that unusual in old buildings where heating or air-conditioning had been added or modified after construction. Still, it was ideal if the faint idea tickling my brain cells was going to prove out.

I shined the flashlight at it. Sure enough, I got an answering flash. Standing on a chair, I saw what I had half expected to find, a piece of expensive glass attached to a black box with a thin wire sticking up a couple of inches. Somebody had installed a miniature video camera in the vent, pointing at the bed, a camera with a transmitter attached. I was willing to bet there had once been a small receiver attached to a video recorder somewhere in the apartment below. The distances were short, and this was an old building without much steel or other metal in it to interfere with the low-power signal. The picture wouldn't be of broadcast quality, but the images could certainly identify the people on the bed. Was this a blackmail setup? It certainly seemed like it. Maybe Gorgeous Gina had more money salted away somewhere than I gave her credit for. Maybe, after all, she could pay me what she owed.

But why was Walker dead? Did a blackmailee decide to terminate a blackmailer? Did the blackmailers have a small disagreement over the split? Did one of them want to terminate the arrangement? Even more fundamental, who was blackmailing whom? Too many questions. Eventually I'd need answers, but now I had more searching to do.

I turned my attention to the bed. It was queen-size with

dark red satin sheets and a light quilt. A profusion of large and small pillows lay helter-skelter on its surface. Nothing out of the ordinary there. The shelf on the headboard held a clutter of objects—tissues, several plastic squeeze-bottles of oils and lotions, a black sleep mask, a feather duster, and a pair of handcuffs. There were a couple of hefty ring bolts sticking out of the plaster above the headboard.

On my hands and knees, I peered under the bed. Apart from the usual dust bunnies, nothing. With the flashlight in one hand, I squeezed under the bed and examined the bottom of the box spring. Nothing unusual such as wires or pressure switches there, either. After I dust-mopped the floor under the bed with my jacket, there was only one more place to look.

Using all my strength, I dragged the bed a few inches out from the wall. Again with the help of the flash from downstairs, I peered at the wall. Affixed to the plaster wall was a large brown plastic cone. Obviously a bumper that had been attached to the wall to reduce noise and wall damage from action on the bed. I stared at the cone some more. It looked familiar, but I couldn't connect it to anything else. I reached in and touched it. The cone was stiff but flexible. I poked it a couple of more times, but nothing came to me.

I puzzled over that while I withdrew my head and then shoved the bed back in place. I poked around Gina's apartment for a while longer, but found nothing to excite my interest except an album of Polaroids. They were pictures of Gina and some of her friends, or acquaintances, or clients, or whomever. I didn't recognize anyone in the collection. They all seemed to be having an exciting time, though. I left and thought about the brown plastic cone on the way home. I could have wrenched it off the wall, but later I might have had to explain to Detective Simon. Not worth the hassle.

Chapter 14

I LEFT MY CAR in the driveway and sauntered inside. Scratched the cat's belly, copped a beer from the kitchen 'fridge, and went out on the deck to puzzle over the dead woman, Magda Bryce. What did I have? Not a whole hell of a lot, I decided.

Woman comes to see me, obviously upset, but doesn't tell me much. Gunman threatens yours truly, who reacts by blowing out the rear window of gunman's vehicle. Vehicle disappears. Woman is found dead. Evidence of S & M. Questions from the constabulary. Wait a moment. There is evidence of sadism, all right, from the whip marks, but not of masochism. Okay. Then, High Priest Ephraim Harcourt Saint Martin, from Harcourt Saint Martin, Saint Martin, et cetera, denies knowledge of beetle-browed assault. End of story. Right, except why am I being threatened and warned off, I ask myself? Unfortunately, self has no answer. But let us not forget the nameless detective poking around my office. If Saint Martin is not directing these probes, perhaps someone at his firm is doing some independent work. Or, perhaps there's no connection except me.

I pondered some more to no avail. So I went back inside, threw a Brubeck tape on the player in the big bathroom. This bathroom had more than just the usual appliances. In an extension I built off the east side a few years ago is a large round wooden tub. A hot tub. That is, a tub always filled with hot water. It was a California thing, many years ago.

My hot tub serves as my meditation and conversation pit. It soothes me, it relaxes me from the slings and lumps of the daily grind. I favor the atmosphere around the tub with scents and nice music. Even Yanni, sometimes. Sometimes I invite friends or acquaintances to join me—it is a large tub, and contains many gallons of hundred-degree water. Frequently the friends who join me are of the female persuasion. If you are thinking what I suspect you are now thinking, you have little or no experience of being immersed in a tub of hot water.

What I don't allow is TV or telephones. Once, not too long ago, a guest carried in a cell phone wrapped in her towel. When it rang midway through the evening, there was a startled splashing by three of us and the offending woman was forced to give up the device which we ceremoniously drowned.

I stripped off my clothes, showered quickly, uncovered the tub and slid on in, to the soothing strains of Dave Brubeck, Joe Dodge, Paul Desmond, and Mr. Morello with his tasteful brushes. After several minutes of slowly turning limp, letting my nerves and muscles loosen and stretch, feeling the frustrations and tensions ooze out of me, I decided to switch on the jets. I reached a hand over the edge of the tub and found the Jacuzzi switch. I pushed it and on came the underwater jets. They're powered by a large electric pump in the basement. Now, you might think handling even a well-grounded electrical switch is a bit dicey whilst sitting neck-deep in a tub of hot water. Not to worry. Some clever engineer has created a pressure switch that isolates switcher, me, from the power source.

My fingers traced the outline of the switch plate. It was made of plastic, stiff, and ribbed to give it just enough flexibility. Holy Shit! I snapped my head around and looked closely at the thing my fingers were touching. It was round and cone-shaped, a smaller version of the very object I'd just seen stuck to Gina's bedroom wall. The air switch.

Under the cone was the plastic tube connected to the actual electric switch in the basement. When I pressed the cone with enough force, air pressure in the tube moved the switch contacts into the closed position and the jet motor came on. Push it again, and shut-off occurs.

Uh-huh, I thought. Shove the headboard of Gina's bed against the wall and the recorder is switched on. The switch had to be one way, not push-pull like mine so repeated hits wouldn't stop and start the recorder. Now I knew how Walker had been killed and who had done it, however unwittingly. But why? I settled a little deeper into the hot water and let my thoughts drift.

* * * *

EIGHT O'CLOCK ARRIVED and I was clean, relaxed, almost somnolent. I called the cop shop and left a message for Detective Simon. I'd just about run out of useful things to do around the old rambler. So I headed out, back to the office. Not unusual. I wanted another look at that clue I'd stashed earlier. The piece of paper that said PLEASE HELP ME.

My office is in a four-story brick and concrete building that is nothing special. There were no lights on in any of the offices that I could see, including mine. Of course, it being summer in the northern latitudes, and this being the period of Daylight Saving Time, the sun was still pretty high in the sky. Not as high as an elephant's eye, but right up there.

The hallway was another matter. Only a couple of narrow windows so little sunlight seeps in. The nightlights in the hall were on. At six, building management decreed that the level of illumination be reduced to save money, so only every third overhead tube was still powered up. That's how, our landlord said, he kept our rents so low. Right, said I, and his profits so high, more likely. The building was almost silent when I exited the elevator. All I heard were the soft squeaks of the white soles of my red Keds on the tiled floor.

When I opened my desk, I located the glassine envelope containing the clue right away. That's because it was right where I left it. I carefully slid the paper out of the glassine onto my desk. The words hadn't changed. *PLEASE HELP ME.* I stared at them. There was no indication that the words had been hurriedly printed, or that the printer of the words was interrupted before he or she had finished writing the message. So there had to be more, something else the sender of the message knew would at least point me in the right direction. I stared at the white rectangle in the middle of my desk for several minutes. Nothing by way of a revelation came to me. In fact, I may have dozed off for a minute or so there.

Eventually I registered in my mind that night was intruding. When I walked in I'd only switched on the overhead light, but now I turned on the bright desk lamp that sits on one corner of my desk. And that's when I realized I might have more information than I had first realized. The sheet of paper suddenly became textured from the light flowing across it at an oblique angle. In my desk was a pair of evidence tweezers I'd acquired somewhere. I picked up the sheet of paper and held it to the light. Sure enough, the paper was watermarked.

Watermarks are pressed into paper during the manufacturing process and can identify the mill, the kind of paper, and almost anything else one cares to impress into the paper. There are private watermarks. If you have the wherewithal, you can purchase stationery with your own private watermark. When I examined this particular watermark, I didn't see the obvious, the name of the paper manufacturer. So, it was possible this was a private watermark. Another clue.

I could see the watermark clearly. It was a round seal with some words that looked like Latin around the top of the seal. Around the bottom were some other letters. They appeared to be capitals, possibly initials. I fished out a pencil and a piece of my own cheap non-watermarked stationery and started to draw the seal.

There was a loud crash out in the hall and the sound of breaking glass. I dropped everything in my desk drawer, slammed it shut, and hopped up to run to the door all in one motion. I bent over and stuck my head out. Looked right.

Nothing.

Looked left. At the end of the hallway, a dark figure was reaching through the broken glass of the office door to the Revulon cousins' suite. It looked like somebody was after their computers.

"Hey, you," I shouted and lunged down the hall. I hadn't gone two steps when the realization hit me I was making a mistake. The guy jerked upright and took off toward the stairs. Then something else hit me.

Because my synapses were firing on high alert, I'd instinctively started to go down in a sprawling slide to the floor, but the shadow on my right that came out of the next-door office was also striking down. He hit me with a billy club or a sap. It was a glancing blow that numbed my shoulder. I rolled left and kicked back at my assailant. I had the momentary satisfaction of feeling one red Ked hit yielding flesh and hearing a harsh grunt. But then the bastard hit me again, expertly, over my right ear, and the lights, as they say, went out. For quite a while.

When I returned to the real world, I discovered I was huddled against the hallway wall, a dozen feet from my still-open office door. I had a blinding headache and blood oozed from the split skin over my right ear. My left side felt tender, like maybe my hitter had kicked me. Dizzy, nauseous, unable to focus, I dragged myself back to my office and dialed 911 for some medical assistance. They weren't happy since I didn't appear to be in a life threatening situation, but they sent an ambulance and a couple of paramedics anyway.

While I waited, I stared at my desk. The lap drawer hung open. My clue was nowhere to be found, nor was the partial sketch of the watermark I'd been making. Shit!

Chapter 15

THE NEXT MORNING, late, I was on my way out when the phone rang. I still had a residual headache from the whack behind my ear, and my surly attitude about being suckered like that also hung on. I almost didn't pick up.

"What?" I growled.

Ricardo Simon was on the line. I'd told him about the thug I'd chased onto the freeway, even though I'd made no formal report, and he had some news.

"We have a car at the city impound lot you might wanna take a look at," he said. I could hear him chewing.

"Why?" I still had to feed and water the cat, and I had decided to try to interview Preston Bryce, grieving widower of the deceased Magda Bryce. Even if I had to drive to Minnetonka or Deephaven to do it.

"A dark gray Buick carrying a load of buckshot, that's why."

I nodded at the phone. "Okay. I'll meet you there in forty-five minutes." Magda Bryce's husband could wait. I fed and watered the animal to her satisfaction and went out. My retired next-door neighbor, Bob, twinkled at me as I drove away.

The Minneapolis police impound lot is on the northwest side of downtown. It's a big open lot surrounded by a twelve-foot chain-link fence. The fence is topped with a few strands of barbed wire. I guess they figure some of the cars they drag in there will try to escape when the cops' backs are turned. Part of the lot is covered by a concrete canopy that holds up Interstate 394.

Last winter there was a big controversy when the state highway plows dumped several tons of snow off the highway onto cars in the lot below. The resulting snow bank covered the cars of several citizens and caused a lot of damage. No big deal, ordinarily, but one of the cars belonged to the president of the city council and she raised quite a stink.

Simon was waiting in the small grubby office where ordinary citizens go to pay towing fees and retrieve their property. "Jeezus, what happened to you?" he asked.

I explained I'd been bopped by an unknown assailant in the corridor outside my office. I didn't mention what had been stolen. The office smelled of unwashed floors, old steel furniture, sweat and fear. While I explained the circumstances, I began to get nauseous all over again. The gray counter with its sliding gray metal drawers into which you placed money and documents was topped by a large window filled with a sheet of what looked like bullet-proof glass. The walls were painted a faded institutional green. The short, weasel-featured man waiting with Simon led us through a heavy, steel, triple-locked door and outside into the compound and the sun.

"Where'd they find it?" I asked. I had to raise my voice over the constant roar of freeway traffic passing overhead.

"The vehicle was towed from Burlington Northern property on the north side," replied the attendant. He pronounced vehicle with the accent on the second syllable. "A coupla clicks nort' a Sain' Ant'ony."

We walked slowly across the dirt compound down the aisle between vehicles of every description. I refused to hurry and aggravate my head. I try to avoid acting like some of the macho P.I.s one sometimes reads about who just keep truckin', even after being beat up. My head hurt and I didn't care who knew it. The vehicles were parked so close together I doubted even I could open a door and slide inside. Many of them had sustained serious damage and looked as if they'd been there for months. The place smelled faintly of rust and old engine oil, mixed with exhaust fumes filtering down from overhead. Interspersed with the wrecks were later-model cars, trucks and a couple of SUVs. Virgil, the weasel, hawked and spat on the ground. As we walked he explained that the privately licensed firms hauled in abandoned "ve-HI-cles" that were undriveable after accidents, and, especially in the winter, units that weren't moved during snow emergencies before the plows went through.

The City of Minneapolis passed laws that decreed that during declared snow emergencies, plowing operations would be more efficiently handled if they could plow curb-to-curb without encountering snowbirds. Being creatures with short memories, we seem to forget those rules from year-to-year, which keeps the towing companies in business. I, myself, have been a victim.

A hundred yards from the office we came to a four-year-old dull silver Buick. Virgil stopped and pointed. The Buick was sitting at the end of a file of cars in a cleared space so I could see all of it. I had described the car carrying Beetle-brow as gray, but when I stood back from the rear and contemplated the ragged holes in the trunk and the blown-out rear window, it felt like the right one. I nodded.

"Whatchou think?" asked Simon.

"Looks like the one," I said. "Has the car been checked?"

"Yep."

"And?" Simon sometimes needed prompting. His natural cop reticence, I guess.

"Nothin'. No prints, no stuff, not even the owner's. Whoever had it was real careful."

"So it was stolen?"

"Reported the same day you got assaulted. The first time. We figure the perps dumped the car right after you ventilated it. The way they cleaned it out suggests professional mechanics, which proly means out of town talent."

"Which raises some interesting questions, like who can afford to import a thug, what's so important they need one, and why me?" We were walking back to the office. Since the police had already been over the car, there was no point in my searching it again. Unlike some P.I.s I don't think I'm smarter than the cops. Equally intelligent, yeah, but not smarter. Besides, they'd put trained forensic experts on it. I can pick most any lock in under a minute-and-a-half, and I'm very good at surveillance and undercover work. But I don't do fingerprints or vacuum for fibers, hairs, and such.

"Any blood?" I asked.

"Nope. Do you think you hit one of 'em?"

"Through the rear end and the seats, no, but the back window might have let some shot through with enough force to break the skin."

Simon nodded. "As you saw, there's safety glass all over the back seat, which is tore up some. We found steel shot on the rear floor, but no holes in the back of the front seats."

"If the guy who came to my door was out-of-town talent, he probably had a local doing the driving. I imagine the big guy is long gone by now," I said. We reached the office, went through, and Simon and I went into the small parking lot outside the wire. Virgil the weasel went somewhere else.

"When will you go back to Walker's?"

Simon pulled at his lower lip, an annoying habit of his. "Not sure, I'm not getting any support for a full-scale investigation. Where you off to now?" he asked as he slid his bulk behind the wheel of his unmarked, almost instantly recognizable sedan.

"Deephaven," I smiled. "Imported talent has to mean big bucks. And that means out west, pardner." I hopped in my jalopy and rolled west, onto 394, past Highway 100, past the former Lincoln Del, once home of those sinfully rich cream pies, past Ridgedale and on through Excelsior. I was on my way to see Preston Bryce, prominent financial attorney and bereaved widower of the late Magda Bryce.

Chapter 16

I RUMINATED ABOUT the case, except I had no case. No client, except myself, which meant no income. I made a mental note to check my bank balance when I got back to my office and get some more invoices into the mail. I hate cases with unsatisfactory endings, and the murder of Magda Bryce was shaping up into just that, a case with no resolution. I've never thought about it in great depth, but one of the reasons I got into this investigating business, after I learned I was too short to be a cop, was to help people, to set things straight. Okay, I admit it, even to be a hero sometimes. Only it didn't work out that way. The hero part. Sure, I go to the movies. I read the books; know about Eddie G and Bogart and Hammett and Sam Spade. But I live in Minnesota. No big-time gangsters, no high-profile crimes or political corruption, at least none that I'd seen. I was too late for the time when Dillinger and Karpis, Kid Cann and Ma Barker held sway in these parts.

I found the Bryce address with little difficulty. Their big stone mansion sat on a hill facing south, surrounded by mature oaks and maples, on one of the many winding roads in Deephaven. I suspected you could see Lake Minnetonka from the upper stories. Although it sat on a large lot, this house appeared modest by Deephaven standards. There was no fence, no gate and no external security. I parked at the edge of the wide gravel driveway and walked up to the front door. The doorbell was large and lighted, just like mine, although it looked to be in better shape. I pushed the lighted panel. I didn't hear anything, so after a minute I pushed it again.

Now I detected the sound of a deadbolt being released and the door opened a crack on a chain. I could see it was not an ordinary security chain, the kind you can buy at most any hardware store. The kind that can be torn loose with one good kick to the door. This was a serious security chain attached to a serious door set into what appeared to be a heavy-duty frame.

The face that looked out at me was interesting, and for just one moment I thought I saw something on the face. Not in the eyes, like they always write. Anybody who studies the human face the way I do knows that just eyes all by themselves don't reveal any particular expression. It's the rest of the face, the eyelids, the nose, the brow, the squint, or the way the eyes move that give clues to what's going on in the brain pan. But there was something there. A clue?

"Yes?" Her voice was low, with husky vibrations. It was matter-of-fact with a mildly inquiring tone.

"I'd like to speak with Preston Bryce, if you please."

"Do you have an appointment?"

"No, but I think he'll see me. It's about his wife. My name is Sean Sean. I'm a private investigator." I fished out a business card and offered it through the opening.

The woman took it and for a moment I saw that something, whatever it was, flash again across her face. "Just a moment," she said and stepped away from the door, leaving it ajar. I heard low, almost whispering voices. Apparently there was someone else standing out of sight, just behind the door. I couldn't make out the words.

After a moment, the door eased shut and the chain was unhooked. The woman opened the door more widely and stood there in the frame, searching my face with her intense gaze. I looked back at a short, very slender woman with straight dark hair cut in bangs just above her dark eyebrows. Her hair was longer in back, ending just below her jaw line.

She had high, prominent cheekbones and large dark eyes. She was wearing some kind of dark leather jumper on top. It had a wide scooped neckline that framed her strong jaw and neck. Her tight, hip-hugging, black leather skirt couldn't have been more than ten or twelve inches from waist to hem. It revealed a couple of inches of nicely shaped thigh, which immediately disappeared into tall, dark brown, leather boots. The boots ended in wide three-or four-inch heels. A long, heavy, gold chain that reached almost to the wide leather belt at her waist hung around her neck. She looked like she might have some Native American genes.

"Take Mr. Sean to the parlor, Pol," said a scratchy male voice from someone still concealed behind the door. "Mr. Bryce will be there directly."

Pol—was that short for Polly?—stepped back, her eyes still on my face, then pivoted to her right and led me at a sedate walk across the hall toward the first door in the wall ahead of us. She walked like a model, one foot directly in front of the other, but her hips didn't sway at all. She had nice hips. Yeah, I noticed. I bet she practiced that walk with a couple of full-length mirrors, just like Mrs. Bryce. Maybe they'd practiced together. Did Pol have a riding crop somewhere close at hand?

I looked around as we crossed the hallway, but there was no one else in evidence. I wondered briefly what had happened to the owner of the voice I'd just heard. Pol opened the door and ushered me in. I cocked one interrogatory eyebrow at her, just for practice, but she ignored me.

"Sit anywhere, Mr. Sean. Mr. Bryce will just be a few minutes." I went in and she closed the door after me, leaving me alone in an altogether unremarkable room. There was a small sofa, a couple of leather side chairs, a breakfront that probably contained a dry bar, a tall window on one side, and a few forgettable prints on the walls.

I chose one of the leather chairs and settled down. I didn't poke around. This was not one of those bad TV movies where the detective is left alone just long enough to rummage through personal papers and find some significant clue before the suspect or the distraught sister/wife/widow rushes in. I just sat in the silence and studied my fingernails. They were clean.

After a few minutes, the door opened silently and a thin man in tan slacks and a dark blue coat-sweater over an open-necked, white, dress shirt came in. I stood and looked up into the myopic eyes of Preston Bryce. His heavy, dark-plastic-framed glasses distorted his eyes and made them seem larger than normal. There was very little color to the man. His hair was a washed-out brown, his eyes had no discernible color, and his skin was sallow, almost pasty. If you met him on the street, you wouldn't see him. An altogether unremarkable man in an altogether unremarkable room. About the only color to him was the whites of his eyes. They were red. That, and I noticed a faint pink band of the skin across his forehead, as if he'd been pressing his head against something. He stepped forward, shuffled, rather.

I stuck out my hand. "Mr. Preston Bryce?"

He ignored my hand and fell into the other leather chair with a sort of sigh. The cushion sighed back. I sat down again and looked at him with my detective's stare, probing, analyzing, a look designed to make the mark, the suspect, nervous so he'd blurt out a confession. Unfortunately, he wasn't looking at me so the effect was lost. Besides, I had no idea whether he had anything to confess at the moment.

"Well," he finally sighed. "What do you want?"

"I came to offer my condolences, Mr. Bryce. On the death of your wife."

No reaction.

"It's a terrible thing, to lose a loved one in such a swift and brutal manner."

No reaction.

"She came to see me, you know."

A twitch.

"It was just a day or so before she was killed."

A bigger twitch. Bryce straightened a little and looked up at me. "What about? Are you a friend of my wife?" His voice, like the rest of him, was unremarkable. I wondered how such an unremarkable man could carve such a large reputation in local legal circles.

"No, sir, she said she was in need of some help. I'm a private investigator." I fished out another card. I didn't offer it to him. I suspected he wouldn't take it. I just laid it on the table beside my chair.

"What?" Larger reaction, but not much. "Why would M-Magda do that? What was it she wanted?"

"Sorry, Mr. Bryce, I can't tell you that, client privilege." Bull— If he was any kind of lawyer, he'd know there was no such thing. He knew.

"There's . . . there's no such thing, unless you're an... an...attorney or a doctor."

"All right. Let's just say, professional ethics, shall we?"

The small spark of life in the man that had flickered for a moment wavered and died. He looked down somewhere in the region of his knees and sagged again, settling even deeper into the chair.

"Mr. Bryce, I'd like to help discover who killed your wife. I thought you might be able to fill me in, tell me more about her current problem." I was shooting in the dark here. I'd come mostly to try to assess the people around the dead Mrs. Bryce, but this wasn't going well. I wanted to reach over and shake the man, get him to flail out at me, something. But I was afraid if I touched him he'd break into pieces in my hands.

We suffered another long silence into which an old-fashioned mantel clock intruded its regular ticking. Finally Bryce stirred and shook his head slowly back and forth. "I can't help you, Mr....Mr.—"

"Sean Sean, Mr. Bryce, private investigator."

"I...don't...know...anything. I can't imagine why she... she would need a private investigator." Bryce seemed to be hunching up more and more, bending over as if he was getting sick to his stomach or just curling into a ball to shut everything out.

I sighed. "Well, sir, it was a long shot. I'll leave my card here, in case you think of something." I stood up and touched my card on the table with one finger. Then I turned toward the door. It opened as if on cue. The woman known as Pol stood there. Her calm, level gaze took in the scene and she pushed the door wider. It wasn't often I encountered women with whom I could have a level look. She stood there, in the frame, as if posing. I walked toward her and she backed away, then turned to lead me out the way we had come, just a few minutes earlier.

As we crossed the entryway, I caught a flicker of movement off to my left. When I turned my head, a woman was just disappearing up the wide stairs to the second floor. I caught only a quick glance and then my escort, Pol, threw open the front door and ushered me into the already hot and sunny day. Did I mention that the Bryce domicile was air conditioned?

I turned to make my good-byes, but Pol was already closing the door. "Thank you for coming, Mr. Sean. I hope you have a pleasant day."

And that was that.

I drove slowly back to town, to my office with all the windows open to catch the summer air. It was a pleasant enough drive, but all the while I had a feeling that I had missed something at the Bryce plantation. Was *Pol* Polly? Nobody is named *Pol*. Maybe it was just the way she looked at me, as if she knew something I should also know. Then I thought about the woman disappearing up the stairs. She might be the source of my disquiet. But why? I had arrived at no answers by the time I reached my office.

I could see the Revulon cousins' door standing open and a workman squatting in front of it. He was lettering the new glass panel. I slipped through and found Betsey and Belinda sitting together murmuring in low voices.

"Was there anything missing in here?"

Belinda looked up at me. Her eyes were moist and she clutched a small white hanky. "No, it looks like you frightened him off before he could steal anything."

Betsey stood up and glowered at me. "Damn! I'm going to have a talk with the manager. We need better security."

"I don't think you have to worry. I left out a few details when I called you. I doubt the slug was really burgling your place. He was too noisy. I think he was just a diversion to sucker me into the hall." I went on to describe the assault of the previous evening.

The cousins' concern over the integrity of their office quickly turned to mothering-type noises and gestures when they understood I'd been bopped on the head. I let their expressions of concern go on for a few minutes. Then, having sufficiently allayed their personal fears, and buttressed their maternal feelings a bit, I returned to my office. I looked at my telephone answering machine. It sits on my desk right next to the POT. That's what telephone people call it. POT for Plain Old Telephone.

I didn't mention it to the cousins Revulon, but I was starting to get seriously pissed off. Two assaults in this non-case of mine, plus the removal of that sheet of paper from my office. This was more action than I get in my surveillance cases about insurance fraud.

While I'd been traveling out west, the mail had been delivered. It was the usual stuff. Two bills, several unsolicited advertising pieces that immediately ended in the wastebasket, and a serious-looking envelope of heavy expensive bond paper. The return address informed me it was from that lofty and expensive law firm, Harcourt, Saint Martin, Saint Martin, Bryce, Bryce, et cetera. More evidence that in spite of Eppy's continual protestations that I was never to be a contract player for his outfit, I was indeed. Well, what can I say? When you're one of the best, as Harcourt, Saint Martin, Saint Martin, et cetera was, you expected them to hire among the best. That would be me.

Inside was a routine statement of charges, mine, and dates of payment, theirs. One of their usual communiqués. I fingered the statement, appreciating the feel of the high-quality rag paper in my fingers. And since I'd lately become interested in such things, I switched on my desk lamp and peered through the paper.

Sure enough, there it was. A watermark. This one was a round seal with something in Latin over the top curve and a series of what looked like initials around the bottom.

Wait a minute! It looked familiar. Well sure, I mused. I must have a couple score such sheets of paper in my files after my years of sporadic work for the firm. But then I got a funny feeling and the hair on my forearms rose a little. By damn, this watermark looked like the one on the paper that had been stolen last night. I pulled another sheet of my cheap stationery from the desk. Then I got up and locked the outer door to my office, after checking the empty hall.

It was the work of but a moment to sketch the watermark. It was a Harcourt, Saint Martin, Saint Martin, monogram, the original, from back in the days when the firm had first been established by the three partners. The letters around the bottom had apparently been added at a later time to reflect the firm's expansion. They were the initials of most of the immediate past and present senior partners. While I copied the watermark, I realized with absolute certainty that I was looking at an identical watermark from the note the skater had slipped to me. It'd never hold up in court, but I knew.

After I finished, I thought about the significance of my discovery. That's something else we detectives do. Every case has clues lying around in bunches. Most are insignificant. They send you off in byways and into dead ends. This clue could be important. The paper with that watermark was available to a large number of people in and out of the law firm. I might very well have missed its significance except for the fact that someone had gone to pretty elaborate lengths to keep it from me. So the logical conclusion was that it was important. Significant.

But what did it mean?

Chapter 17

A HUGE CRASH of cymbals and up-tempo drum rolls signaled the end of the band's interim set. The drums were the only non-electronic instruments on the stage. The rest of the trio consisted of two keyboards and a maze of wires snaking around, all connected to myriad grotty-looking black boxes with lights, dials, and switches. I had no idea what they all did, except for the huge banks of speakers. Their function was eminently clear.

Detective Ricardo Simon and I were sitting in an uncomfortable booth as far from the stage as we could get, so we could converse without shouting at each other. We were here to talk with Gorgeous Gina. Why she hadn't been arrested yet, I couldn't figure, so naturally I asked.

"Why haven't you arrested Gina?"

Simon scratched his nose. "We think she can help us in other matters. I figure she'll be more cooperative if she's not in the slammer."

I nodded. It made sense. It also brightened the possibility I might get paid by the performer. I glanced around. There was only a scattering of patrons. Apparently Wednesday night wasn't a big night out for the boys. Simon had a glass of something that might have been gin, but I knew was only sparkling water with a twist of lemon. The strip clubs in Minneapolis don't serve booze. That way they avoided the more onerous licensing laws that prohibited public nakedness in liquor-selling establishments. I toyed with my rapidly cooling coffee. The place was a cavernous rectangular joint, with a stage against one of the long walls. Around the stage was a narrow, padded rail with chairs for patrons who wanted their action up close and personal. Behind them were tiny square tables with lots of chairs crammed into the spaces. Behind the tables but up a step were more tables and chairs. We were in one of the booths that lined the wall opposite the stage on the second level up. The place was called a strip club, but that was a misnomer. It was true that the dancers took their garments off. And they moved around on stage. But stripping, in the bygone definition, required training and a certain amount of athletic ability. Dancing. I'd never seen any here in the few times I'd graced this establishment.

The girls who worked in this club didn't dance and most showed little athletic ability. They mostly walked around and periodically struggled out of ordinary street clothes. To minimize the struggle to disrobe, some of them arrived on stage with almost nothing on. This show was more like watching a series of naked young women, usually two at a time, stalk around the stage looking bored. The place smelled of body sweat, heavy perfume, some sort of industrial-strength antiseptic cleaner, and smoke.

"So, Sean, it's your theory that Gina brought a john back to her place, and when they made it to the bed, she was able to use the air switch behind the bed to turn on the video recorder in Walker's apartment downstairs."

"Right. It allowed her to record the action without Walker being in his apartment."

"And you figured that she rewired the switch to blow the coffeemaker and fry Walker after they had a falling out?"

"That I'm not sure about." After I'd told Simon my theory, the cops had pulled the wall apart in Walker's kitchen. They discovered I was right. The switch had been recently rewired to send 110 volts through the coffeemaker. The air switch was designed to work in only one direction. When

Gina did her number in bed, the switch always turned on the recorder. But someone rewired the switch so that when the recorder was switched on by the pounding of the headboard of Gina's bed, it also sent a lethal charge into the coffee-making machine. Walker had stood at the counter and touched the machine while Gina was bouncing away upstairs. He grounded the circuit and zap. End of story. Or at least, end of Walker.

"It seems a bit random. Gina is the most likely to know when Walker would be in his place. But she could never be sure if or when he'd touch the coffeemaker." Simon scratched his nose.

"True enough. I figure that the circuit would function normally until somebody touched the machine when the connection was closed. Somebody wanted Walker dead and soon, but the timing wasn't critical. I just don't see Gina setting it up."

"I don't either," said Simon. "If Walker was doing the blackmail bit, with Gina as his partner, they apparently caught someone on tape with a powerful urge to eliminate the source of that someone's aggravation. Your visit and our coming to arrest Walker may have been true coincidence."

"How'd Gina take the news of Walker's death?"

"She was concerned but not broken up. She wanted to know how, and if we thought it was a burglar. She admitted a series of liaisons with 'generous gentlemen.'"

A drum roll interrupted Simon, and the house lights, already dim, got even dimmer. I looked around and discovered that the place had acquired a larger crowd. A few men were sitting at the stage rail. The rest had pretty much filled the tables and the booths along the back wall. There was more action back and forth from the bar by the two scantily clad waitresses. Several of the dancers were on the floor now, many talking with patrons in the booths. A few were sitting on stools at the bar.

At the entrance a large sign proclaimed:

NO DRINKING
NO ONE UNDER TWENTY-ONE
NO SHOUTING
NO ROWDY BEHAVIOR
NO TOUCHING THE DANCERS

Lots of prohibited behavior, but it was clear the no-touching rule didn't apply to the dancers, only to the patrons. The tables were too small for table dances, but personal writhings and other intimacies on the chairs and in the booths, as long as they were produced by the dancers or the waitresses, were apparently allowable. Such action allowed the women to make some money over their minimal salaries in the form of tips and outside liaisons.

An unseen announcer, in slightly distorted tones, exhorted us to put our hands together for a new dancer to the club. I didn't get her name. Like it mattered.

There was some desultory applause. The woman appeared, tottering in very high heels, wearing a full-length robe. She made a slow circle of the stage, actually moving in time to the music of the band, smiling and waving. I squinted through the smoky haze and estimated her age at something on the far side of forty. I waved at a passing waitress for a five-dollar refill of not-bad coffee.

The waitress offered me a generous view of her bosom while she exchanged a full cup for my empty one and removed Simon's foul-smelling cigarillo butts from the ashtray.

The noise level, an unhealthy combination of chatter from the audience and music from the band, rose still higher. There was another cymbal crash, a drum roll, and laser lights began to flicker across the space over our heads. The announcer introduced the headliner, Gorgeous Gina. There was loud applause and Gina, in an elaborate hat, big, round sunglasses, and a white, floor-length dress with many ruffles and a short train, appeared at the edge of the stage.

I blinked. The last two times I'd caught her act, it had been pretty ordinary, except for her athleticism. Clearly she'd improved her art by several levels.

I turned my attention back to Simon. We'd sent word to Gina that we were here to talk to her after her act, and we had to be ready.

"How do you want to play this?" I asked.

"She isn't going to change her story unless we can shake her up a little. Let's get her settled and then show her the pictures, Simon responded.

I nodded. "I have some additional pictures copied from recent magazines I want her to look at too. I'll lay them out after you show her yours."

Simon raised his eyebrows but nodded. Gina finished her act totally nude and departed the stage. I shifted to the other side of the booth so Simon and I would both be facing her.

After a short wait, Gina appeared in a surprisingly modest dress and sat down. She immediately whipped out a cigarette. I lit it for her. Drawing on it hard she looked at us and said, "So, what's this about?" Her hand shook slightly when she reached to the ashtray. Stubbing out the half-burned butt, she quickly lit another.

"We just want you to look at some pictures," Simon said. "If you've had any contact here or at your place with these people, we want to know it. Help us out here and we might be able to cut you some slack."

"A deal? Do I need a deal?"

Simon looked at her for a long moment and then said, "You figure it out."

Gina smiled and took another hit on the cigarette. "Yeah, sure. Well, let's see what you got," she said. She glanced around to see who might be paying attention, then bent over the table between us as, one-by-one, Simon laid a series of head shots in front of her. They went quickly through the stack. Gina tapped the few she recognized and shook her head when she didn't. Our knees were close enough that I could feel her leg jittering up and down under the table top. Once or twice the rhythm changed abruptly when Simon laid down a picture she said couldn't identify. It happened three times. Each time I nudged Simon's thigh. After he separated the ones she identified, he went back through the others. The same thing happened. It appeared to me that Gina wasn't being completely honest. Surprise, surprise.

"Is that it?" she asked when Simon picked up the last picture and put them all back in his pocket.

"No, Gina, I have a couple more I want you to look at." Actually, I had five. And I got a hit on the fourth.

"Sure," she said tapping a picture of Preston Bryce. "This one. He used to come in here a lot last year. Then Lucinda picked him up, and he quit."

"Do you know his name?"

"Nuh-uh. But Lucinda might. She's headlining the next show."

"Can I talk to her before she goes on?"

"No. She don't talk to anyone just before her show. I'll tell her to come see you after, if you want."

"All right, Gina, you do that," I said.

The show had progressed while we talked. Gina went to the dressing room and returned, assuring us Lucinda would stop at our booth. Then she left the club carrying a small satchel.

"What gives?" Simon asked. He had also recognized attorney Preston Bryce.

"Just a hunch, my friend, just a hunch."

"And now, ladies and gents, put your hands together for the star of our show, Lucinda the Luscious!" More applause and there was a sudden surge to fill the stage-side seats by men who obviously knew what was coming. Me, I was in the dark. Suddenly, we all were. Except for the dim exit signs at each end of the building, all the lights went out. Drum roll. Cymbal crash. There was a quick series of cracks like small caliber pistol shots. The lights flooded the stage, and there was Luscious Lucinda, front and center.

Whooee! Medium height and build, masses of dark hair piled high on her head. She wore a black, Lone Ranger mask, a black bra with cutouts over her dark nipples, a tiny black thong, and a pair of black shiny cowboy boots. They looked like Code West boots to me. No smile. At best it was a look of complete disdain for her audience. Coiled in her left hand was the source of the sharp cracks. It was a big, dangerous-looking, black bullwhip.

Lucinda pirouetted and snaked the whip out. In her hands it was a living device, shimmying and writhing across the floor. *Crack! Crack!* The sound was penetrating. I could almost feel it. A man stood up at one corner of the stage watching the performer intently. A cigarette dangled from his lips. The woman's move was so fast I hardly saw it. I don't think she really looked his way but the whip flashed out and took the cigarette away. She swung it again overhead and curled it around another man's shoulders.

"Heads down!" she roared in a deep, throaty voice. "Put your heads down, slaves!"

Around the stage every man save one obeyed. The show went on, as the woman dominated the room and the men in it. I glanced once at Simon. His mouth was hanging open.

Another man raised his head and reached to the stage with a bill in his fingers. Lucinda snaked her whip overhead to wrap around a bar in the dark up near the ceiling. She put her full weight on the whip handle and swung across the stage. She landed in front of the unfortunate man and dropped to all fours.

"Get your filthy hand off my stage." Her voice had dropped to a slithering hiss that penetrated to the far reaches of the room. She crouched almost nose-to-nose with him, and then stood, legs spread, raised one foot, and brought her heel gently down on the man's hand. Gradually she shifted more and more weight onto that heel. The man's fingers splayed out. I looked at his face. There was little question he was feeling a good deal of pain. Finally she relented and kicked the bill out of his trembling fingers.

For several minutes more Lucinda stalked the stage, cracking her whip and reviling her audience. She abused several other men at ringside. Then, as abruptly as she had appeared, the stage went dark and she disappeared. Thunderous applause followed.

"What do you think of that act, Simon?"

He shook his head slowly. "I think society is in trouble."

"You gentlemen wish to talk to me?" It was Lucinda, appearing beside our booth as abruptly as she had taken the stage.

I looked her over carefully. Still masked and wearing those expensive cowboy boots that still looked like Code West, she now wore a black shoulder-to-knee robe that covered her completely. I was relieved to see the whip was nowhere in evidence.

Simon cleared his throat and showed her his badge.

"Is there a problem? With the act?"

I noticed she didn't take ownership.

"I don't know about that," said Simon. "What do you call that? What you did?"

"I'm a dominatrix. I abuse my clients, sometimes with pain, sometimes with verbal abuse, sometimes both." She smiled. I thought it a cruel smile, almost a sneer. "You'd be surprised at the clientele I have. Small in numbers, but they pay well. So?"

Simon nodded and cleared his throat. "Uh-huh. Well, what we want is to know if you can identify any of these men. He laid five pictures on the table, one at a time. Twice he went through them.

Lucinda watched the pictures intently. Finally she sighed. "No, none."

But I knew she was lying. Her nostrils had flared just for an instant at one of the pictures. I would have missed it if I hadn't been watching her instead of the pictures. I wouldn't bet the farm on it, but I was sure. She knew Preston Bryce.

Chapter 18

THE NEXT DAY, when I retrieved my mail, I was pleased to discover that by mailing out invoices, I'd actually received payment on two outstanding bills. I made out a deposit slip and endorsed the checks. Then I stared at the wall for a while, visions of watermarks, whips, and a dead Magda Bryce filling my head. Last night's foray into the local sex industry had been productive, I decided. I was making progress but there were still too many missing pieces. I still couldn't make an intuitive leap to a coherent picture.

I decided to play for a while. Last year the Revulon cousins had convinced me that I had better become a player in the information age and computerize.

They'd set me up with a modest PC and I'd purchased a subscription to the Internet. I found the machine useful for certain kinds of research, although skip tracing wasn't my big thing. Belinda Revulon had devised a database program to help me to keep track of my cases, and the machine was fine for tracking billings and keeping notes, when I remembered to enter them.

At first, I'd been worried about security, so I tried the password ploy to protect the information. Unfortunately, I kept forgetting the clever passwords I dreamed up. Finally I just did all the work on disks, which I stashed elsewhere. It was easier to remember my little hidey-holes than some series of password codes. Anybody who broke into my hard drive would find applications but no useful information, unless they cared about the sorry state of my finances.

In the past, I'd always used a series of note cards to hold odd bits of information that I could shuffle to find connections I might have missed. The search and sort functions of the computer made that a lot easier. I was making more notes as a result of using the computer and by now I was reluctantly admitting it helped.

I fished out my Harcourt, Saint Martin, Bryce, et cetera disk and added last night's notes. I typed in questions. That was the hell of it. The questions kept mounting and the answers weren't keeping up. After a couple of hours of this, my neck began to stiffen.

I shut down the computer and got a book out of my desk. My current reading was a murder mystery by a Canadian writer, Alison Gordon. It's about a professional baseball team. I can read and think about a current case at the same time. I do some of my best noodling while I'm partially engaged in other activity.

It's like this. I have an inquiring mind, curiosity about a lot of things. Probably why I'm a P.I. I was curious about Pol-Polly. About the woman on inline skates. About Preston Bryce and his relationship with Lucinda the dominatrix. About the whip marks on the dead woman's rear. About…

The more I thought about it, the more Luscious Lucinda the dominatrix seemed to be a strong connection between Preston Bryce and his murdered wife. It also seemed to me that although Gina had entertained Preston Bryce, she was only tangentially involved.

Eventually the shooting pains in my neck and back became insistent so I put the book away. Then I called Catherine.

This person wasn't involved in the case at all. She is a masseuse. She gives me massages and she was teaching me shiatsu and Swedish massage. We are also exploring the uses and effects of different oils and lotions, the whole aromatherapy scene. Now why, you might wonder, would a hip savvy, tough if under-sized professional private investigator, and I'm nothing if not professional, bother with something sort of New Agey?

Just now I was more curious about my headache and my stiff neck and whether Catherine Mckerney might have a solution. Turned out she did have some ideas and was available in a couple of hours. So I met her at the house and we slipped into the hot tub for relaxation and conversation.

After an hour of heat and bubbles and meandering inconsequential talk, she dragged me out of the tub and onto my thick massage pad. Catherine is a small woman. She's very slender with almost no bosom, nice hips, and great legs. There's a faint sprinkling of freckles across her upper chest. At five-six she's a couple of inches taller than I am. She's a little bit of a thing, weighs no more than one-ten. But she's strong, works out, and her job helps keep her in good shape. Plus she knows how to leverage her weight and strength. In a slinky long dress and high heels at a black-tie affair like the Symphony Ball, she's a show stopper. I know because that's where I first met her a couple of years ago. She's also one of the smartest women I know. Now if you think it's usual to entertain your masseuse in your hot tub before you get a nice rub down and some intelligent conversation, don't go running off. It's not at all the usual thing. My relationship with Catherine is long-standing and special. She is a consummate professional in her regular massage relationships. But we have something special. It's probably due to my special personality.

Chapter 19

As I lay on my face on the massage pad in my hot tub room, Catherine went to work on my head and neck. In short order I zoned out.

A while later I awoke. Now I was on my back, a towel across my hips. Catherine was crouched over me, her fingers digging at my solar plexus. For a minute I just watched her face above me glide back and forth. Her concentration was total; she was completely focused on her work. I tilted my head slightly and watched the sway of her breasts under the loose cotton pullover she was wearing. I voiced something I'd been thinking about for several weeks. "Hey," I said. "Would you consider dating a customer?"

She stopped the massage and leaned back, squatting above my head and looked down into my eyes. "I never date my customers. It's unprofessional. Even my being here is a bit of a stretch."

"Let me put it another way. Would you consider dating me?"

Catherine blew out her breath, all the while holding my upside-down gaze. Then, in one sinuous movement, she rose and wrapped herself in the big white terry-cloth robe she always carried. "I think this session is over."

"What? Wait a minute." I sat up, alarmed.

"Put a robe on," she said, and padded barefoot out of the tub room onto the deck.

I mumbled under my breath and complied. Then I went out after her. Catherine was standing at the outer edge of the deck, staring at the undergrowth at the back of the yard. I reached out a hand and touched her shoulder. She shrugged off my touch and said, "You have rabbits."

"Yeah, I know. Would you like a cold drink?"

"I just saw one out there with something in his ear."

"That's Thumper," I said. "Somebody put a stud in one of his ears a long time ago."

"Yes, I would like a cold drink of water. Thank you."

When I returned with the tall glass, she hadn't moved.

"Sean, I'm not a rabbit."

"I know that. I got all the rabbits out here I can handle." I waved at the backyard.

"What about out there?" Catherine waved toward the city.

"No rabbits," I said. I remembered Gina and some others. "At least, not now."

Catherine had turned and was studying my face. "You have a strange job."

"Takes me out all hours of the night, sometimes."

"Dangerous, sometimes."

I nodded. "Sometimes. And if the work is undercover I can be gone for days at a time. That doesn't happen too often."

We moved to the chaise lounge and sat. Catherine carefully arranged the folds of her robe over her bare knees. "You associate with weird people, sometimes."

I nodded.

"You carry a gun."

"Almost never. Occasionally it's necessary."

"I hate guns. Do you ever shoot rabbits?"

I smiled a little and shook my head. "Never, only rabid predators."

"I'm taller than you."

"I noticed. You are also a real knockout."

Catherine smiled. "Ah, now comes the silvery tongue of flattery."

"Truth. Between thee and me, always."

"You'd have to stop being a customer."

"True, but if things work out between us, maybe we could, you know, provide informal massage for each other."

"Informal," she said and smiled a little.

A hopeful sign, I thought. "A mutually satisfying massage. From time to time." I smiled at her. Hopefully, I hoped.

She took my hand. "This is going a little too fast. Let's change the subject. What are you working on right now?"

So I sketched for her my clientless case, Magda the dead woman, and Gina the stripper, and Luscious Lucinda the dominatrix. I trusted Catherine Mckerney completely. Probably for the same reasons that I wanted her in my life as more than my masseuse.

When I finished my short narrative she nodded. "I know Lucinda. I mean, I know of her. We've met once or maybe twice. I've heard the stories. Some of them, anyway. There's supposed to be a small but very upscale group of people in the cities who go in for that sort of thing. Pain. Humiliation. S & M." Catherine shuddered. "I never understood the attraction."

"Me neither. I also don't know who all the players are. Apparently some local heavyweights are involved. Big law firms, perhaps."

"Whose?"

I shook my head. "Better you don't know. It isn't a matter of trust, but if you don't know names, other than the ones I just mentioned, no one will come looking for you."

"Who are the cops on the case?" I mentioned the two detectives, Simon and Holt.

Catherine tilted her head in that elfin way she has and looked at the now-dark sky. "I don't know them. And now I have to go."

"Got a date?"

She smiled, rose and glided toward the deck door. "Perhaps. Yes, actually."

I looked out at the darkening yard, wished I had a cigarette. When I returned to the front of the house, Catherine was already dressed, her massage things packed away in the small backpack she carried. We met at the front door.

"I am pleased," she smiled. "Flattered. Call me in a couple of days?"

"Sure," I said.

She leaned down and gently kissed my cheek. Went out the door. On the stoop she turned her head and said, "You keep a gun in the closet."

"Excuse me?"

"I can smell it." Catherine ran lightly down the steps and drove away.

Chapter 20

"HELP ME. PLEASE, help me." The voice slithered across my fogged consciousness.

"What? Jesus. Speak up, can't you?"

"Help me, you must help me."

I scrubbed open my eyes and peered at the cheap radio-alarm on the shelf over my bed. The numbers read 3:14. Was that *a.m.*? Logic said it must be since I was lying on my side in a dark room tangled up with bedclothes. As far as I could remember, after Catherine had left me at the door, I'd made some spaghetti and drunk a glass of wine. Well, several glasses of wine. I'm not a heavy drinker, never was, not even back when I smoked. But I never claimed a clean upstanding life. I can still go into a neighborhood bar where Minnesota's Clean Air Act is used for a target on the dart board and be perfectly comfortable among the gloom, the smoke, and the miasma of ancient and new odors.

Of course, I don't use that word.

Miasma. Anyone in the place who knew what it meant would be immediately suspicious, which, in my business, would be counterproductive. Not that I frequent such places. It has been my experience that, a raft of PI novels to the contrary, seedy bars full of suspicious-looking characters, cops, and what all are never where one finds answers to questions about whatever case one is working on at that moment. Too many people in such places are searching for answers, or questions. Answers to my questions are always in short supply in such places. But I digress.

It has been my habit when hitting the sack (always

wondered where that phrase came from) to set my voice mail to the shortest possible ring so I don't wake up. I almost never have cases that require sudden meetings after midnight. Apparently this night I'd forgotten to adjust the alarm. So now at three-something in the damn *a.m.*, I was answering the telephone. I have an extension by my bed. It's convenient, and once a long time ago it saved my life when some thug I never ever saw broke in through the sliding deck door. The thug woke me, of course, and I rolled over and dialed the local cop shop. They sent a squad in full cry. It arrived about the time the perp must have figured out where the bedrooms are. Lights and sirens in the driveway were a powerful incentive for him to split the way he'd arrived.

Anyway, the pleading fear-filled tones of the whispery voice sliding out of the earpiece dragged me awake. Mostly. I deduced it was a female voice.

"I can barely hear you sir, or Miss. *Whaddayawant-thishour?*" My usual polite manners desert me when rudely awakened in such a fashion. Besides, I had a headache, result of the wine I had earlier ingested. Headaches are the bane of my existence. I hate them. Even a small one virtually incapacitates me and I become, so I've been told, exceedingly surly.

The voice gasped in my ear. It gurgled and panted. My hackles raised. There was fear, and panic in that voice. Now, I am no knight, riding off in polished armor on a white horse to rescue damsels in distress. Or pledging faith to my liege, and some princess or other, whilst setting off on some grand quest. Not at all. I leave those chivalrous tendencies to my ancestors of yore. Such tendencies in our modern, more utilitarian, era are more than likely to get you maimed or killed. But the caller was in obvious terror from something. "Call 911," I muttered.

"Please, Mr. Sean. You must come." The voice stuttered a location. It was an intersection on the near north side of Minneapolis, a couple of blocks behind the Butler Building, a yuppified and modernized warehouse and factory building, that now held fern-filled bars and restaurants, along with architects, and other professionals offices, and a successful accounting firm or two. The five-story atrium held a lot of art. Big art.

"Please, Mr. Sean."

I was about to suggest the caller dial 911 again, but her second use of my name changed my mind. "All right," I mumbled. "I'll come down. Call me again in five minutes. I'll be in the car." I grabbed my Colt semiauto forty-five, my cell phone, and ran out the door. It was no more than a fifteen-minute drive. When I squealed onto 35W going south, mine was the only vehicle on that stretch of pavement. My headlights cut a swirling swath through the light morning mist but my wipers took care of the instant condensation. She didn't call again. I considered calling 911 myself, but I was almost there.

I roared up Washington Avenue and slid into a left-hand four-wheel drift onto First Avenue North. The streets were empty. Naturally there were no squad cars to be seen.

At Fifth I hung a hard right and dropped the still silent cell phone. I rolled into the cavernous gloom beside the parking ramp and skyway that served the Target Center and surrounding buildings. On my left, two blocks away, huge white plumes of moisture rose from the Minneapolis Recycling Center. In front of me, just inside the edge of my high beams, was the telephone booth from which she'd called. Or so she'd said.

Even from this distance I could see the booth was empty. I slammed the lever into Park, shoved the driver's door open, and simultaneously fell over in the opposite direction. I rolled out the right hand door to the pavement. Never read about Amos Walker doing that.

I landed on my rump beside the car, my gat squeezed tight in one sweaty hand. Listened. Nothing. Just the sounds of the city all around me in the middle distance. No gunshots, no cries or gurgles. I scuttled sideways away from the car, staying low to the ground. The telephone booth was positioned at the edge of an irregular plot of empty ground, too small for a commercial building. The city hadn't got around to landscaping so it was just uneven gravel, dirt and a few weeds. Behind me, a way off, a siren wailed. Now what?

I scanned the area around me. Nothing. Too dark to see much. The door to the booth was closed but the light was off. I straightened to my full five-three and dropped my hand with the gun to my side. Then I walked slowly to the booth, listening and skittishly looking about. Still nothing. I could see through the cloudy plastic sides of the booth that the receiver was hanging loose by its armored cable. Had I been suckered? If so why? It made no sense. I put my hand on the door of the booth to open it. Pause.

Whoa. Make a smaller target. I squatted, then pushed the door open. It didn't even squeak. I blew out my breath. Switched on the flash. Kept it low. On one side of the booth was a long smear of something that looked reddish-brown. I touched it with my little finger. Wet.

Smelled. Blood. *Damn it.* Touched it again in the same place to smear any possible print. Stood up and trotted back to my car, still watching warily. Since the street was empty, I maneuvered the car around so I could sweep the small plot of ground with my headlights. In the farthest corner, at Fifth and Second, my headlights picked up a lumpy mound. I yanked the car around and parked at the curb nearest the mound.

Scuttled out of the car again and flicked on my Maglite. *Shit.* No doubt about it, the lump on the ground was a body.

I got out and started toward the person. Suddenly I stopped. For no logical reason, my instinct told me the person in my headlights was dead. I back-pedaled to grab my cell phone and dialed 911. Two rings, then a connection. A moment later, red and blue lights flashed and a siren came to life. Only a block away. I might have searched the body, but I decided not to be found crouched over whoever it was, especially since I had a handgun with me.

The patrol car, first of several to gather like flies to a fresh-cut watermelon, arrived. I'd dropped the Colt on the front seat and stood by the hood waiting for the uniformed officers to arrive. In another few seconds, two officers were standing outside their vehicle looking at me.

"What've we got here?" asked the nearest uniform, watching me carefully. He hadn't drawn his weapon, but it looked like he wanted to. I knew this was a tricky moment and I kept still, my hands in front of me so he could see them. I opened my mouth to answer when the second uniform standing behind me on the other side of my car flashed his light into the interior and saw the forty-five.

"Gun!" He shouted and I heard him draw his own.

The older cop tensed and flicked his light in my eyes. "Yours?"

"Yes, officer. I'm a licensed investigator and I have a permit."

Three more patrols arrived almost simultaneously and they began to do what all cops do in such situations. But before they moved me to a patrol car, one of the officers turned his flash on the body.

Pol-Polly's dead eyes reflected tiny points of light back to us. I grimaced and the officer in front of me saw it. "You know her?"

"Sort of. I've encountered her once, maybe twice recently. If it's who I think it is."

An officer squatted beside the body and pulled back the coat she was wearing. "Wouldja look at this." We all turned and looked. She'd pulled open the coat enough so we could all see. The dead woman was wearing a bright, electric-blue bikini.

Chapter 21

"OFFICER. JUST WHAT are you doing?" The voice crackled with authority. We all looked up to see a brace of homicide detectives stepping out of their car. The uniform who had just disturbed the crime scene almost leaped away, muttering something I didn't catch. The two detectives looked quickly at the body and then began taking verbal reports from the two responding officers. Although I didn't know either of them, one of the detectives kept glancing in my direction and I heard him mutter the name Henry Holt.

He walked over and stood close, invading my personal space. "Mr. . . . Sean," he said. "My name is Anderson. I have a few questions."

"Sure," I said.

He put a hand on my shoulder and urged me over to stand beside their gray sedan, and I retold my story. His partner wandered off somewhere.

Someone from the crime scene came to us and said, "We're gonna test his weapon."

"What is it?" asked my detective.

"Colt .45 caliber semi-automatic."

"A large, heavy weapon," he remarked, looking down at me. A couple of the uniforms were standing by my car, smiling a little in the light. I had an idea what was coming. I'd heard it before. Starting when I was one of the smaller boys on the school or neighborhood playground. Bullies liked to pound on me. Later in high school, bigger bullies liked to pound harder on me. They also cast aspersions on my sexual prowess, due to my apparent size inadequacies. What'd they know? I learned to compensate, to protect myself. I learned to run fast and became highly maneuverable. For two years I did pretty well as a sprinter in the city league. I still knew how to run. Maybe the pistol was another compensation.

"Yes," I said. "It's large, and when the situation requires, it gets attention." I leaned back a little and looked up into the detective's eyes. "Being vertically challenged, as the saying goes these days, I occasionally find it useful."

"Occasionally?"

"I prefer more active means of protection."

"Such as?"

"I run. I'm very quick on my feet." I smiled when I said it.

One of the uniformed officers came over to us and said, "He checks out. Sean Sean, Private Investigator. Gets a pass from downtown."

"Okay, Mr. Sean," said my detective. "But you understand, we're going to take your weapon for tests. You'll get it back, eventually."

I shrugged. There was no sense arguing about something I couldn't change. They had no real reason to keep the weapon since it was obvious it hadn't been fired recently, but sometimes the people in charge do things without obvious reasons. Or just because they can. "Am I free to go?"

"Yessir, you are. But all the usual caveats apply."

That stopped me for an instant. Here was a cop who used the word *caveat*. Correctly, even.

It was late now. Really late. The adrenaline rush was gone and I needed to get some sleep. I drove home in a fog, although the earlier night mists had dissipated. That's about how I felt. Dissipated. I was barely able to drag my clothes off before I fell back into bed.

Later, much later, I woke to hot sun streaming through the blinds I had failed to close completely. Still feeling the effects of too little sleep, I showered, ate some cold cereal, and sat down to think about this latest development. Now there were two murders linked to Harcourt, Saint Martin, Bryce, et cetera. And linked to me, albeit tenuously. I'd encountered the dead woman three times in the recent past. There was no doubt in my mind. The first time brought up the most questions. That was last week when she'd skated by me on the Minneapolis street and slipped a note into my pocket . I saw her again at the Bryce mansion and then last night on that small empty patch in north Minneapolis.

Strange things were happening. It appeared I was caught up in something murky and convoluted. And right at a time when I wanted nothing more than to drift on placid water and work on my relationship with Catherine.

Apparently the goddess had other plans.

Chapter 22

THE TELEPHONE RANG. It jarred me out of my lethargy. Simon was on the line. "Hear you found a body last night. Or this morning, actually."

"So?"

"Hey, don't get testy with me, fellah. I'm just calling to let you know Detective Holt is being handed this one too. He thinks Magda Bryce and the Jane Doe are linked."

"Polly," I husked. "Her name's Polly."

"What? You can ID her?"

"Yeah, I know who she is. At least I know her first name. And she's definitely linked to the Bryce household."

"You better saunter on down here and talk to Holt."

"Yeah, I was on my way out when you called."

"Good. I'll let Holt know to expect you."

When I got downtown an hour later, I found Holt fuming in his tiny cubicle. "Ricardo said you were on your way. Where have you been?"

"Detective Holt, good morning. I hope you had a good night. I know I didn't. It's already hotter'n a cookstove out there, did you know that?" I opted for a few inane pleasantries to avoid snapping at the man.

He recognized my stratagem and accepted the implied criticism. Waved a big meaty hand at me to indicate a chair beside his desk. "All right. Sorry. You're right. What do you have for me?"

So I told him everything I knew about the case. I bared my soul, so to speak. Usually P.I.s don't do that, right? As I've pointed out, I'm not ordinary. I wasn't getting very far figuring out what was going on, but maybe the cops would do better. I even told Detective Henry Holt about the note Polly slipped me, about the watermark and how it had been stolen away. He was not happy. I was not happy. There wasn't much we could do about our unhappiness at the moment.

Oh, when I said I bared my soul? I didn't mean totally, entirely. I did hold back my suspicion that Luscious Lucinda the leaping and dancing dominatrix and mistress, had a closer connection to Preston Bryce than she would admit.

My head still hurt when I squinted in the sun so I slipped on my dark glasses after Holt was finished with me. I don't wear the dark glasses much, I think they make me look dorky. Since my destination was close to the cop shop, I walked the few blocks over to the strip joint. They were closed for the morning, although the noon show was supposed to start in an hour or so. I muscled my way in by slipping some greenish paper to the guy setting up the bar.

Upstairs, I found my way to a tiny office on the second floor, rear, of the place. Here I located the manager. He was cooperative, after I slipped him some more paper bills. Leaving the place, I considered that I was beginning to spend some serious money on a case with no client. The manager had given me the address for Lucinda the dominatrix. It was way the hell out in Eden Prairie.

I drove out there. I didn't call ahead, on the assumption that she mostly worked late nights or early mornings and wouldn't be running around this early. I knew she didn't have a noon gig at the club.

* * * *

THE PLACE WAS an ordinary split-level in a sea of split-levels in the older part of Eden Prairie. The streets curved, there were nice trees and cropped bushes around many of the lots; and lawns, acres and acres of green grass, mowed and edge trimmed to the nth degree. *Whew.* The address I was seeking was at the end of a winding street. There was a paved turnaround, and the house was separated on both sides by at least a couple of undeveloped lots. They isolated the house. I wondered if Lucinda owned them.

Lucinda-the-dominatrix dancer had a two-car garage at the end of a wide, slightly sloping concrete drive that fired the heat of the sun back into my face. My brain was having a hard time dealing with it. I pressed the bell button. It was a lighted button.

After a minute or two I pressed it again, and then I felt rather than heard movement inside. The door cracked open on its golden chain and one of Lucinda's dark eyes peered at me.

"Jesus, who're you and whaddaya want?"

"Morning Ms. Lucinda."

"Who you?"

"You don't recognize me?"

"No. And unless you state your business fast, I'm going to end this interview."

"Perhaps I should call you Mistress Lucinda. My name is Sean Sean and we met last night in the company of Detective Ricardo Simon."

She let out a gusty sign. "The P.I. Right?"

"Right."

"How'd you find me?"

"You gave it up last night to Detective Simon, remember?"

"Oh yeah."

I didn't figure she needed to know I hadn't told the cops I was coming to see her, or that I'd bribed the club manager for her address. "C'mon," I whined. "It's hot out here. I just need to ask you a few questions. It won't take long, Mistress."

Lucinda shut the door and slipped both chains off. I hadn't seen the second one a foot or so off the floor. By the time I'd finished groveling, she'd opened the door and smiled at me. "Not bad. I love it when men snivel like that. Come in."

I followed the thick-quilted robe she was wearing around the dog-leg into the living room. The place was fully air conditioned. The living room was large with thick beige carpet and a window that looked out at a nice back yard. Lots of grass, no garden, I noticed. I glanced around. No houseplants. Some nice framed prints on the wall. Coordinated furniture. Tasteful. A nice, upscale, but basically ordinary suburban home. A shelter for a nice, ordinary, suburban working woman. *Sure.*

"You live alone?"

"Why?" Her tone was neutral, giving me nothing.

"Idle question. No offense meant," I said.

"None taken. You don't strike me as a man who asks idle questions."

She had me there. "I'm investigating the murder of a woman whose body showed signs of having been whipped," I started.

"Magda Bryce."

"You knew her?" Maybe both husband and wife were into whipping.

"Personally? No, but I know she was around."

"Tell me about the S & M scene, Minnesota style."

Lucinda smiled faintly and crossed her shapely legs. When the robe fell open over her knees she modestly pulled the folds back together.

"Sure, but no names."

I was surprised she acquiesced so promptly. Maybe she thought she'd sell the scene to another client. Me.

"Basically, we're talking about control. It's a psychological thing. A surprising number of powerful men develop this need. They exercise a lot of control in their lives. They control their businesses, they control their families, particularly their wives. Their employees, their clients. Sometimes they want to give all that up for a short while."

"But why the physical abuse?"

"Oh, it isn't always physical. And even when it is, the pain is carefully controlled."

"How?"

"I'm good at this, Mr. Sean. We also have an arranged code word. When the client says the magic word, the pain stops. If it didn't, I'd lose my client. Since I can't advertise, I only get clients by referral, word of mouth. There are dominatrixes who won't allow their clients to have a code word. They prefer to operate with more control." She smiled and lit a long cigarette.

"You seem pretty relaxed and open about your profession."

"Look, Mr. Sean, I'm not embarrassed. I see what I do as a service. A lot of men abuse their wives. I think some of my clients would if they didn't use my services to get rid of their frustrations."

It sounded like a lot of psychobabble to me, but I wasn't going to say so to Mistress Lucinda. "Any women clients?"

"A very few. They would profile out about the same as my male clients." She shifted on the couch and took a deep drag on her cigarette. "Lots of personal control in their lives and few ordinary means of release. Usually they're unmarried, or divorced, and generally suspicious of the men around them, who they tend to see as weak or out to get their jobs."

"But surely not all powerful men and women turn to professional dominants."

"No, and not all use masochism. But a surprising number do. Others just talk to their shrinks. How's your health, Mr. Sean?"

"Fine. Why do you ask?"

"No heart problems? You don't smoke, I gather."

"Correct. I'm fine, I get exercise, lots of fresh air. My last physical gave me a clean bill of health. Why do you ask?"

She ignored my question, saying, "Would you like to visit my playroom?"

"That might be instructive." I wondered if there was some trick here. I had no wish to be enticed into some sort of ritualistic game. Lucinda had already explained that most of what went on was an elaborate game with safeguards to avoid serious injury. "So what you're saying is that if I saw someone with healed welts on her body, I'd be correct in assuming the game got out of hand or possibly that the individual has a high pain threshold."

"Correct. Come this way." Lucinda rose gracefully and led me to the back of the house and a door that opened on a stairwell. "There are people who can tolerate surprisingly high levels of pain. If they get into the masochism scene, they could be permanently marked before calling it quits."

"How widespread is the domination business?"

"Not very, but growing. Check the ads in some of the local free papers, like *City_Pages*. More and more dominants and submissives are starting to run ads."

"But you don't run ads, right?" I asked as we went slowly down the stairs.

"No. If you want more information, there are a number of slick magazines that cater to the whips-and-chains-crowd you can check out. Newsstands around town carry them."

"The what?" We reached the basement level and she turned right.

"Whips and chains. Part of the whole dominance-submission thing includes whippings, usually after the subject has been restrained, often in chains."

She switched on a series of pin spots that illuminated the walls on my right. I saw a series of shallow alcoves, each containing different paraphernalia. In one were shackles with light chain dangling from them. In another I saw ropes leading from wrist-shackles to a steel bar. The bar was connected to a rope-and-pulley affair hung from the ceiling.

"Here we are," she said. "Those are the bondage rigs, and here are some of my whips. I have an extensive collection." Lucinda slid a drawer open. Inside, neatly arrayed in the shallow drawer, were a dozen or more whips, ranging from feathered fronds to cracked birch wands to thin, black leather-wrapped steel rods. She told me they were steel.

"Quite a variety," I offered, searching for some quip or crack to lighten the odd feeling that was creeping over me.

Lucinda smiled slightly and slid the drawer close. "Now, here, this is the cage." She turned and led me down four steps into a lower level of the basement. The ceiling rafters and boards were painted a dull black, giving a feeling of even greater height. In the center of the space hung a tall tube of dark rough fabric. My guide unzipped the fabric and it fell to the hard tile floor. Suspended on a short chain was a crudely welded metal cage, a little taller than a good-sized man. It hung two feet off the floor. I touched the cold, flat steel.

"See the hinges?" Luscious Lucinda smiled. A trifle cruelly, I thought, but it might have been my imagination. "The side opens here, but it's jointed so the occupant is always restrained by the cage. The occupant can't crouch, even should their legs give way. It's not even possible to draw a full breath when you're secured in the cage."

"What happens once you're in the cage?" I thought my voice was a little ragged, but Lucinda seemed not to notice.

"That depends on the client. A scenario has already been agreed to. Sometimes it's a torture scene, with cold water sprays, or lashings. Other times a client wants to be humiliated or embarrassed."

"What about sex?"

"Some of this is very sexual, sensual, really." I have a client from out of town. He periodically arranges to be confined in the cage over night. He's naked. The next day, I parade a small group of strangers past him. They are instructed to make disparaging remarks; they throw overripe fruit on him. He's masked, of course, and so are the strangers."

"No, I mean sex. Intercourse."

"Prostitution is illegal, Mr. Sean."

"Come on, Mistress Lucinda. You've been very forthcoming so far. Are you telling me none of this is illegal?"

"I'm very careful. I'm not interested in having sex with my clients and besides, most of them are far more interested in being dominated, a form of humiliation. I may dress in revealing costumes, but my clients never touch me, unless I command them to. Perhaps you'd like to try the cage?" she asked in an abrupt change of subject.

"Uh, no thanks, not this morning."

"Here are some other techniques that might interest you. This is the leather and rubber room." She unlatched a door and I found myself in a room peopled with black empty husks of various body parts. There were latex arms, legs, gloves, feet, and even full-body armor. And masks, partials, and full headpieces, some very elaborate with all kinds of zippers on them.

"I think you should try one of these, just to get an idea of the sensation. Here's a mask that should do the trick."

I didn't like the idea much, but right then I couldn't think of a good reason to just say no. She sat me down on a low stool and placed a wide latex strap around my temples. It wasn't particularly tight, but it wasn't loose, either. Then she buckled on a wide black collar that held my head and neck in a tight grip so I couldn't look around without moving my whole upper body. I raised my eyes to the mirror across the room and saw a stranger with a strange black leather and latex rig on his head looking back. Behind me I saw that Lucinda had shed her robe and was now clad in a black two-piece outfit that appeared to be made of leather.

"This is the helmet that fits over your head." She held it in front of me so I could see it. "Still okay?" Without giving me a chance to respond one way or the other, Lucinda fit the carapace, really a soft leather helmet, snugly over my head and smoothed it down over the collar. A strap fit under my chin from side to side. It forced me to keep my mouth closed. A front zipper and a back zipper secured the helmet to the collar. When my hostess zipped them closed, my head was even more restricted. In the mirror, I saw a stranger's eyes, mouth, and nose. They looked like my nose and mouth, but on a stranger wearing an odd black device of leather and latex. I was beginning to think this had been a bad idea.

"All right, Mr. Sean, we're down to the final piece." Her voice was muffled by the sides of the helmet pressing against my ears. "You won't be able to hear or see anything once I put this on you, so listen carefully." While she talked, Lucinda ran another zipper across my throat which attached the front of the mask to the collar. "I'll secure this last piece and zip the mouth shut."

"What're these tubes inside the mask used for?" It was difficult to articulate clearly because of the straps restricting my jaw.

"In a minute. After the mask is on I'll leave you sitting right here for a couple of minutes so you can get used to the sensation. Then I'll help you stand up and turn around in a circle, and sit down again. After that I'll remove the mask. If you feel any real discomfort or start to panic, pull this tab."

She put the fingers of my right hand on a flat leather loop hanging just below my right ear. "If you pull it, three of the zippers open immediately. All right?"

"Yes, Mistress," I said. "But what about the tubes?"

Lucinda took hold of the final piece in both hands, positioning herself directly in front of me, standing between my knees. Since I couldn't look down, she raised the piece to eye level. "The tubes are for breathing. When the mask goes on, the tubes go into your nostrils a little. Signal me with a raised hand if a tube misses. Ready? Close your eyes."

I tried to nod, but couldn't. So I bowed slightly from the waist. Lucinda smiled and raised her hands, and darkness descended. Two soft balls of foam pressed against my eyelids. With nimble fingers, she smoothed the front of the mask up onto my forehead. I felt the zipper vibrate across my brow when she zipped it shut. The mask pressed tightly against my cheeks. Now I was sure this was a bad idea.

The breathing tubes, each about one-quarter inch in diameter, fit gently against my nostrils. I could hear no outside noises, only the roaring of my breath, and behind that, the faint rhythm of blood pulsing in my veins. My heart rate was elevated. I opened my lips slightly and breathed in. Then I felt Lucinda's fingers on the mask and a zipper roared again in my brain. She had closed the flap over my mouth and now the only life-giving air came through the two breathing tubes set against my nostrils. I sat quietly, listening to the internal, secret rhythms of my body. When I sensed Lucinda moving back away from my stool, a powerful sense of being isolated swept down on me. It was oppressive, saddening, like a weight had settled on my shoulders. I was very much alone.

I lost all sense of time passing. Sat there, on my stool, breathing through my nose, deeply, slowly. Hands suddenly grasped my shoulders, urging me to my feet. Obeying the pressure of the hands, Lucinda's, I assumed, I was turned about, then forced to sit again. It didn't feel like the same stool. My mental picture of the room and my position in it disappeared. I was drifting, disoriented. In my left nostril came the smell of lemon, then roses, then over the next several moments I was treated to a succession of pleasant scents, always in my left nostril. Suddenly, with no warning, the tubes were pinched off or capped, and I discovered how really tight the hood was. Unable to open my mouth, I was totally dependent on the tubes remaining open to breathe. To stay alive.

I flailed out with my hands, but grabbed only air. My body was captured in a hard grip that made it impossible for me to maneuver in any direction. If the tubes weren't uncapped, I'd pass out in moments. I struggled to suck in another lungful of air. I got a little around the tubes in my nose. Then just as suddenly as they had been capped, the tubes were open and sweet, warm air flooded my lungs.

The roaring sound of the zippers on the headpiece being opened filled my ears. Light came next as Lucinda expertly worked the pieces of the device off me. In moments my eyes were open and the nose tubes were gone, and my head was released from its prison. I squinted at the sudden wash of light.

"Look at yourself," commanded Lucinda in a soft voice. She held a big hand mirror before my bleary eyes. I saw a face with tousled hair, droopy eyelids, and slack mouth. My cheeks and forehead bore pale pink marks where the leather and rubber had imprisoned my face.

"Now," she said. "How do you feel, right now? Would you do almost anything I command you to do to avoid being returned to the head cage?"

I nodded, working my throat. "Why did you cut off the air?"

"I wanted you to experience the loss of control. Suppose you had been in restraints, unable to move any part of your body? How would that have made you feel?"

"Powerless," I whispered, my throat working.

"Exactly. This is a very dangerous device. Suppose you had a bad heart? Even if I didn't cap the breathing tubes, just moments without sufficient air could raise your anxiety levels to cause a heart attack. Upstairs, I observed that you breathe through your nose, not your mouth, so I knew your nose was clear and covering your mouth wouldn't damage you."

"You seem to take a lot of precautions."

"That's my point. That's why I agreed to talk to you. I don't accept just anybody as a client, and I always do an extensive background interview. I don't have many clients."

"But I'll bet you charge them plenty." By now she'd removed the rest of the head piece and I stood up to loosen my muscles.

Mistress Luscious Lucinda just smiled. "Here are some other devices you might wish to examine." She slid open another drawer in the tall expensive-looking, oiled-wood cabinet. In this shallow drawer, laid out neatly on the felt, were small chains, black-leather-and-steel wrist and ankle shackles, and studded collars.

"What are those?" I pointed at a pair of gold-colored clips linked by a short chain.

"Those are nipple clips. Some women claim they enhance the sex act if they wear them during intercourse. Some men agree." She slid the drawer closed and opened one below it. "You've probably seen women and men with pierced ears."

"Of course."

"Have you noticed people with multiple piercings?"

"Sure."

"We humans have a penchant for adorning ourselves with ornamentation. We always have."

"Like tattoos."

"Yes, and wearing earrings is an acceptable form of adornment in our society. But what if you run out of space on your ears? Women now wear jewelry attached to many parts of their bodies. Part of my business is offering a piercing service." She pointed at various devices in the drawer. "I have done tongues, nipples, noses, genitals."

"It must be painful at first and later uncomfortable. Why do women do that?"

She smiled. "It makes them feel special. They have a secret they only share with special friends. But it isn't just women, and there's historical precedence. Various kinds of mutilations have been practiced for centuries. In parts of Africa, women's genitals are still mutilated through circumcision as a means of control, of domination.

"In an earlier century, English explorers reported that men in some tribes in Africa put ivory bells in their foreskins. During mating rituals, the women chased the men in the dark by listening for the sounds of the tinkling bells. The more bells, presumably the more desirable the man they were chasing."

"A distortion of natural selection."

By now we'd made our way back upstairs to the living room and to the front door. Lucinda gave me her hand. "Mr. Sean, many people think of all this as aberrant behavior. It can be dangerous and of course that adds a little spice for some people. But I've never whipped anyone so hard it left permanent marks. What I do is play mind games. There's no lasting harm to my clients."

I wondered about that, as I went out into the hot sun.

Chapter 23

I HAD A LOT to think about on my drive back from Eden Prairie. If people wanted to put rings or studs into their bodies, tattoo themselves, and perform other mutilations on themselves, that was okay by me, I guess. I wouldn't do it. Even the idea gave me the shudders, and I wasn't so sure about the mind games Luscious Lucinda insisted she was playing, particularly her statement that there was *no harm done*. Even if there were no lasting effects, one might wonder about the stability of one's financial manager, say, who had to get a humiliation fix every so often.

The other piece of it was the things such people did to each other. If you beat on your wife with a split birch rod, however gently, was it an act of love or were you a closet sadist? And what about Magda Bryce? Had she rebelled against the pain and humiliation and been killed for her rebellion? Or was there something else? Was someone covering up a thrashing gone too far? There were rare cases of multiple murder of the same victim. It was done to try to confuse the authorities. I resolved to ask Detective Holt whether the ME thought the last beating and Mrs. Bryce's murder were directly related.

I also wondered about the relative ease with which Lucinda had revealed her basement of treasures and games. Was it her attempt to lead me down a winding path with no end and away from the truth? Perhaps. One thing was certain. I never got to ask her the questions I had about her relationship with Preston Bryce.

I thought back to the way I had looked in the mirror

when she had released me from the head prison. The pale pink marks on my face from the restraints bothered me for some reason, but I couldn't grasp it. I made a mental note to check with Detective Holt and ask if Magda Bryce had pierced ears, or pierced anything else.

I went to my office and made some notes. Detective Holt wasn't in when I called the cop shop, so I decided to set that all aside for something more pleasant.

Catherine Mckerney picked up on the first ring. "How do you feel about dinner tonight?"

Her low laugh tickled my inner ear. "Why, Mr. Sean, the rule book says I should never accept an invitation on such short notice."

"Really? I guess I'm not a rules kind of guy."

"Nor am I. At least, not those rules. Where and when?"

We decided on the St. Paul Grill in the venerable Saint Paul Hotel, if there was room. There was and I called her right back.

"Ah," she said, "promptness. I like that in a man."

That early evening I drove to South Minneapolis to Catherine's pad, an apartment complex near Powderhorn Park. The city had razed a huge swath of older homes and apartment buildings to make room for the upscale apartments.

Security was tight. Cameras scanned me and my vehicle when I stopped in the driveway. I glanced at the camera over the door, resisting an urge to thumb my nose at it. When I went into the outer lobby and stopped at the intercom panel, I had the strong feeling the camera eye had followed me. It hadn't, of course; the door and its frame were between us. I couldn't see a second glass eye but I'd bet the farm I was still under surveillance. But hey, I wasn't wearing my red Keds, and I was wearing a nicely fitting linen suit, white shirt and dark conservative paisley tie. I'd left my straw boater in Roseville.

I found CM's number and picked up the handset. They didn't have any cheesy wall-mounted speaker-mike in this place. I pressed the button and moments later I heard the warm sound of Catherine's voice in my ear. Clear as a bell and distortion free.

"Yes?"

"'Tis I," I said, "World traveler, man-about-town, *bon vivant*. Sean Sean, his very self." I sometimes overdid the palaver when I was feeling good, and tonight I was feeling quite good.

"We have time, would you like to come up? For a drink?"

"Delighted, delighted, I'm sure m'dear," I said, switching to a nasal drawl.

"Take the elevator to the fourth floor, turn left. At the first crossing, turn left again. I'm all the way at the back of the building. But leave W. C. Fields behind, if you please."

I laughed and she buzzed me in. It wasn't an ordinary buzz. It was a ding-dong, a two-note chime that repeated itself until I pulled the heavy glass door open, cutting the circuit. I wondered how long it dinged before self-canceling if the door was never opened. I wonder about such things.

The elevator was posh as well. It had a nice carpet, what looked like hand-rubbed wood walls and polished brass rub-and-handrails. I touched "4" on the control panel and we began to rise. At least I thought we did. There was no sound or discernible movement. I inspected the brass rub-rails. No scratches, gouges or repairs. I'd bet they'd never hauled anything heavy or bulky in this cage except tenants. There had to be a service or freight elevator somewhere else. The door slid open and I exited, turned left, and sank into the deepest, softest short-pile carpet I'd ever experienced. It was a pale rose in color and went very well with the heavy papered walls. Beyond that, it was an ordinary apartment corridor. The walls went straight up and down, the ceiling had recessed shadowless lighting behind acrylic panels, and there was an occasional framed unremarkable print attached to the wall. Lots of nice carpet, though.

I slogged my way along the carpet toward the middle distance. Fifteen or twenty feet along, (I wasn't measuring), I came across an opening to another corridor that headed off in what I figured must be a southwest direction. I hung a hard left and way down at the end of the corridor, a door opened. There was bright light behind that door, and then, framed in the door, my date, the object of my attentions. It occurred to me that if old Shell Scott never stopped working on the case of the moment for a little recreation, Luiz Mendoza and a few others did, so I was feeling very much all right.

Now that I'd drawn near enough to make out distinguishing features, I could see that Catherine was wearing a very nice black cocktail dress that drew my attention to her slender figure, her high heels, and her exceedingly trim ankles. She waved one hand and stepped back inside, leaving the door open. When I arrived on her doorstep, she came to meet me with a heavy cut-glass container in her hand that carried a nice dollop of a very good scotch, a couple of ice cubes, and a tiny splash of water. All my senses are well-honed, you see. She was drinking the same.

"Quite a place you live in."

"I like my creature comforts. After years of struggling, living in too-small, too-drafty, inconvenient rooms and apartments, I made myself a promise. When I'd saved enough money and my income was steady enough, I would indulge myself. I was very frugal for several years. So," she gestured with one slim, bare arm, "this is the result, or at least, part of the result. Would you like to see the rest of it?"

"Of course." More scotch slipped warmly down my throat, and I followed Catherine down a short hall to the farthest and smallest of the three bedrooms. It wasn't all that small.

"I had the carpet removed and a pad put in to dampen the thumps on the floor." She waved at the room that contained several exercise machines, some of which I didn't recognize. "Over here is one bath, there's the guest bedroom, and here's the master suite."

Now this was very nice. Her bedroom was large, carpeted, had big windows looking west and north over the city, a king-sized bed, and two separate dressing rooms. The bedroom alone was larger than some living rooms I'd been in. Off one dressing room was the bathroom. It had a sunken tub, a Jacuzzi big enough for a peewee baseball team, a multihead shower, and all the other important stuff. "Very nice," I murmured. "I'm surprised. I didn't realize the massage business paid so well."

Catherine laughed. "It's like any other business. Properly managed, it is profitable. Massage got me started, and I have several clients, who, like you, only know me for the therapy side of my life. But there's another side. The other room over there is my office."

We were back in the living room, which was plenty large enough for seven or eight couples without crowding. Catherine sat on a large padded footstool affair and curled her legs under her. I sank to the comfortable sofa a couple of feet away. Now we were eye-to-eye.

"By the time I'd finished training and got my license as a massage therapist, I realized I didn't want to go through life working for somebody else. My dad left me a reasonable inheritance, and I saved my money, trained to become a teacher, and made some wise investments. Have you seen today's paper?"

"Well, I skimmed the front page and the Metro section."
I shrugged.

"This piece about your client was in the business section." Catherine stretched over the back of the sofa. It gave
me a nice view of her bosom and hips in the black fabric.
She turned back and handed me a section of the *Strib*. Below
the fold was a story about a multimillion-dollar merger between a tobacco company and another corporate giant. The
successful merger had been led, according to the story, by
local merger star, attorney Preston Bryce of Harcourt, Saint
Martin, Saint Martin, Bryce, et cetera.

"They'll make some big bucks for pulling that one off,"
I said and tossed the paper on the sofa. Catherine smiled
at me over the rim of her glass. We finished our drinks and
went to the door.

She picked up her purse and opened it. With a tiny smile
she fished out her cell phone and placed it on the table by
the door. "I don't think I'll be wanting this tonight."

Chapter 24

THE ST. PAUL GRILL has floor-to-ceiling windows that look out on the valet-controlled entrance and over Rice Park. From our booth we could see the richly glowing lobby of the Ordway Music Theatre, St. Paul's major performing arts venue, a block away. I ordered scotch and Catherine switched to a dry white wine.

"Wine before dinner, interesting."

"I told you I don't always follow the rules." She smiled over the glass rim. Her smile was a little crooked, as was her nose.

"Pardon my asking, but I'm curious. Did you break your nose once?"

She held the smile for another moment. "I knew you were observant, but that's pretty good. Yes. My ex hit me in the face with a book. Not deliberately. Truly, Sean," she insisted, reacting to my expression. "He swung around abruptly with a book in his hand. I was just standing too close."

"How long ago was that?"

"Um. I've been divorced for about five years, so it must be seven or eight since he smacked me. Have you been married?"

"Never. I've never found a woman who'd put up with me for very long. It's my profession, my height, my mug." I shrugged and adroitly switched subjects. "Why'd you decide to go out with me?"

Catherine leaned forward a little and ran her fingers over my hand where it rested on the table between us. I felt a frisson of excitement at her touch, so different from the touch of the professional masseuse. "I know quite a bit about you from the conversations we've had during your massages. I already knew that I was attracted to you and I decided that if you ever asked, I wanted to get involved."

"Involved."

"With you."

"With me." I sat back and exhaled, held her gaze. "You mean you want us to have a relationship, an affair?"

"A relationship, yes."

"Ah, hm." I was at a sudden loss for words. Rare for me. Catherine's smile got wider.

"Am I scaring you? Going too fast? Do assertive women put you off?"

"No, no. It's just...Well maybe Travis McGee has all these gorgeous babes falling all over him, but I don't. I never expected..." My voice trailed off and I gulped at my scotch.

Catherine sat back and took her fingers away. I wanted them back. "There's a difference. How long have we known each other?" She answered her own question. "Almost three years. As I said, I know a good deal about you. I know how you think, and how you feel about some important things, like crime and children, and about rules. I have a pretty good idea how you feel about what you do for a living, and I think I have a clear picture of what kind of person you are. I probably know more about you than a lot of women know about their fiancés just before the wedding." She smiled. "We are definitely not playing out a scene from a Mike Hammer novel."

I looked at her across the table. My usual suspicious reflex seemed to be on vacation. The waiter brought our dinners, grilled salmon for Catherine and bay scallops for me. They were tasty, I guess. I don't remember much about that dinner. My mind was occupied with the woman across the table. I'm no virgin. I've had various kinds of relationships with different women over the years. Those relationships were important at the time, but I always had a sense of impermanence. Vagabond, kiss and run, that was more my style. Was I changing? All of a sudden, never mind three years of history with this woman, I seemed to be softening my attitude. The dating game, if that was the right label, had never held much fascination for me. Men and women in the small circle of people I called friends had sometimes seemed obsessed with finding and marrying the right person. Not me. But now....

"So, Mr. Sean." Catherine had abandoned her light teasing tone. "What do you think? And please don't be afraid to say *no.*"

"I'm at a loss for words," I managed. "I've always assumed the role of aggressor fell to the man." Suddenly I was choosing my words carefully. Thinking first and talking second, not always my forte. Why? Suddenly it was becoming important that I not screw this up. Careful, Sean, I cautioned self. Neither trapped nor trappee be.

"And? Have I disturbed your view of things?"

"And, I'm startled. I was pretty excited when you agreed to dinner, but this is more than I expected."

She cocked her head and smiled again. "I'll take that as a *yes.* Or at least a *maybe.*" I got the feeling she was enjoying my discomfiture. "Shall we go? Or are you interested in dessert?"

We went. At the entrance to the hotel we waited, hand-in-hand, while the valet brought my car around. He left the driver's door open and hustled around the hood to open the door for Catherine. I handed him a tip as he crossed between us and the car. My outstretched hand made him hesitate just slightly. It saved my life. He bent toward me, reaching for the bill, when his hat was snatched from his head and flew over Catherine's head. A second shot exploded the left rear window. My reactions were pretty good in spite of the booze and food I'd had. I grabbed the valet's wrist and yanked him to the ground while I reached my other hand for Catherine. The valet fell into her and knocked her to her knees. Her mouth was open in her white face and a soundless scream echoed in my head. Behind us, at the door, others screamed aloud and tried to flee.

I had no idea where the shots had come from. I didn't care. Getting us out of there whole was my only concern. I hauled Catherine through the passenger-side door of my car after me and slammed feet on the brake. I think I bent the shift lever jamming it into Drive. With no one ahead of us to block my way, I sent the car screaming out of the driveway, made a fast right around the first corner, tires smoking and sliding on the red stone paving. The open doors slammed shut. A short block later, I ignored the red light and twisted another right onto St. Peter. An apt name. At the end of the block was an empty no-parking space. I pulled up and killed the lights.

"Catherine?" My shaking voice mirrored the tremors in my hands. "Are you all right?" I looked over. She was holding herself, arms crossed over her chest, hair tousled, eyes wide, staring at the windshield. "Catherine?"

"Yes, yes. Okay, I guess. Bruises, scrapes, but that's all. What about you? Are you okay?"

"Yeah. Could use that cell phone about now, though." We stared at each other.

"Was that a warning?" she whispered.

I shook my head. "No. Somebody tried to kill me, possibly you too."

"You sound so sure."

"Instinct. Maybe our getting involved with each other right now isn't such a hot idea."

She took a deep breath, then another, then turned her face to me. "Shh-h-h." Catherine leaned toward me. "Did you know you seem to have a limited vocabulary when you're in a high-stress situation?"

"What?"

"Over and over, you kept shouting 'Goddamn, goddamn, goddamn.'" She was starting to smile. "Over and over, until you stopped the car." Her smile widened. I smiled. She clapped a hand over her mouth and started to laugh, and suddenly we were clinging to each other, laughing and sobbing by turns.

After a few minutes, my internal warning mechanism began to beep and I raised my head, scanned the dark streets. "We better not stay here, or the cops will be all over us. Did you see anything? Hear the shots?"

"Nothing, Sean." She shook her head. "But I'd like to go home now. This is more excitement than my dates usually provide."

Chapter 25

I STARTED THE CAR and we turned onto Kellogg toward the freeway that would take us back to Minneapolis. As we passed the first intersection I glanced right and saw numerous flashing lights as St. Paul's finest responded to the call of shots fired.

The drive home was mostly silent. I didn't even turn on the radio, but my mind was busy. The central question of the moment, how did the shooter know we were at the Saint Paul Grill?

As we exited the car in her underground garage, Catherine said, "I hope that valet is okay. Can we find out?"

"Yeah. I'll call from your apartment, but I don't think he was hit." I knelt on the concrete and peered under the car.

"What are you doing?"

There wasn't much to see, so I got up, went to the front of the car, and repeated my peering. "Somebody knew we were at the Grill. I don't go there regularly, so either I'm being followed or somebody is tracking me some other way."

"Some kind of homing device?"

Sharp, this lady, I thought. By now I'd moved to the rear of the car. "Exactly. And look what I have here." I'd found it wired to a tie-down ring on the frame. It was a small box with a tiny wire antenna. I ripped it off the car and stood up. I looked at it for a minute and then yanked the antenna out of the plastic box. I didn't want some thug tracing the box to Catherine's apartment if they weren't already out there watching. We took the disabled transmitter upstairs, and I diverted to call the hotel. No one would or could tell me anything. Whoever I was badgering wouldn't even admit shots had been fired. He did agree there'd been some kind of altercation, but that was all I could pry out of him. Sure. Finally I contacted an acquaintance in the St. Paul PD who assured me the reports of the incident had not mentioned any gunshot wounds. I told Catherine what I'd learned when she returned from removing her soiled and torn dress, swathed in a bulky dressing gown.

I examined the small box. "It looks like a homemade job. See here? Whoever built this thing glued the cover on this plastic box after it was assembled."

"Is that important?"

"Possibly. I have a friend in the electronics business. He'll tell me either this is just an amateur job, or it was put together by somebody whose work he might recognize. If he doesn't know the work, it will be impossible to trace. There's probably a nine-volt battery in it along with a few components that send out a fairly weak signal." I put the transmitter in my pocket and looked at her.

"Brandy?" She turned toward the small cabinet that housed the bar.

"Yes, please." I sat on the sofa across the room and stared out the big picture window at the distant lights of the Minneapolis skyline.

"Here, try this." Catherine handed over a small balloon of brandy and sat beside me, drawing her legs up under her. "What kind of trouble are you mixed up in, anyway?"

I sipped the brandy and felt the fire go down my gullet and into my belly. "I'm not working on anything at the moment that could possibly lead to being shot at. It must be this business with Magda and the Saint Martin firm. *Dammit*. I should go back to the hotel and see what I can dig up."

"No you shouldn't. Sean, the police are all over it and

whoever fired those shots is long gone. What can you do now?"

"I could talk to people, find out what anybody saw."

Catherine leaned closer. "But not tonight." She took a serious swallow of her brandy. Set it on the table at the back of the sofa. Brought her hand back and smoothed my hair. I looked into her face, at the serenity there, put a hand to her cheek. My pulse was galloping along. As many times as I had considered what it would be like to be intimate with this woman, now that it was happening, I was feeling a bit nervous. Part of it was the aftereffects of the adrenaline rush, I had no doubt, but that wasn't all of it. I wanted to be especially good with her, and I was suddenly a tad unsure of myself.

As if she'd divined what I was thinking, Catherine smiled and leaned forward until our noses touched. Her tongue came out and touched my lips. We slid into a long, languorous kiss that ended with us reclining on the couch among the pillows. She took my hand and directed it into the neck of her robe and I discovered she wasn't wearing a bra. I felt her hands on my head, pulling me closer, and then her fingers slid around and she began to undo the buttons of my shirt.

We toyed with each other for a few minutes, increasing our breathing and our desire. Then she blew softly in my ear and whispered, "C'mon, we'll be more comfortable in the bedroom."

* * * *

THE SUN THROUGH the partly closed blinds had a distinctly downward cast. I peeled open one eye and squinted at the small clock on the bed stand. Nine-fifteen. I couldn't remember the last time I'd slept that late. I was alone in bed, but I could hear the shower running. I rolled over feeling the pull of pleasantly sore muscles in my thighs. The shower stopped and a few minutes later, a cloud of steam billowed out of the bathroom. Catherine appeared at the bedside, wearing only a towel wrapped around her hair, hands behind her back. Gorgeous, I thought, stunning. I hope she's happy with me.

Catherine was expressionless. For a silent moment she just stared at me. Then with a sudden movement, she drew one hand around her hip. It came into view holding a small cup. With a widening grin, she dipped the fingers of her other hand in the cup and tossed cold water on my face and bare chest.

"Yikes!" I hollered, springing up from my prone position.

"Up, old hoss. You can't lie there all day." More cold spray.

"*Yow, woman! Stop!*" I scrambled naked out of the bedclothes across our rumpled king-sized playground to the opposite side. Then realizing she'd used all her ammunition, I started back toward her.

Bad move. She squealed a high laugh and whipped the damp towel off her head, twisting it expertly into a terry cloth rope. In my present state, I was vulnerable.

Laughing, I skipped out of her way but her aim was true. As I bounded around the bed and into the bathroom, she snapped a smarting thwack on my bare rear end before the door closed.

I glanced around, found the fresh towels and new toothbrush she'd laid out for me. "Hey," I called through the door, "nice shower." It was indeed, with its three heads, a flexible hand-held tool, and, I was to discover, an ample supply of hot water.

Catherine was already dressed by the time I finished my shower and skinned into my clothes. In the kitchen she was whipping up soft scrambled eggs and crisp bacon. Following her directions, I located a grapefruit, sliced it in half and

THE CASE OF THE GREEDY LAWYERS

made some toast. We lay breakfast on the kitchen bar and sat on tall stools across from one another.

Catherine grinned at me and shoveled her food into her mouth. She was no dainty eater, picking at the food; she acted more like a hungry farmhand appreciating both quantity and quality. After cleaning her plate, she sighed and picked up her coffee mug. "Last night was really fine, sweetie. You are one terrific lover."

"Well, there were two of us there. I thought *we* were awesome."

"I know. Let's do it again. Real soon."

My pulse went from a canter to a trot. "Amen to that."

"What's on your agenda today?"

"I better call the Minneapolis cop shop. They've still got my weapon, and I want to talk to Detective Holt about last night." I went to the telephone in the living room while Catherine cleared away the dishes.

In the underground garage Catherine said, "Call me to-night?"

I nodded, we touched noses and drove out to go our separate ways.

* * * * *

THEY'D TOLD ME Holt was expected back in the office around eleven. I left a message I'd be in shortly to see him. I got downtown to the station and was walking toward his cubicle when I heard a familiar voice. It was Ricardo Simon talking to Holt. So I stopped just outside Holt's office space. Maybe I'd pick up something worthwhile.

"As I mentioned before, Sean is okay."

"Yeah? He's due in anytime. Said he wanted to see me and pick up his weapon."

"I've known him for several years. He can be stubborn, but he'll play it straight. Sort of a pit bull when it comes to people he cares about. He's careful of his rep, but he won't screw around with you."

"Seems more like a terrier, or maybe a Chihuahua, to me." I could hear the grin in Holt's voice as I leaned closer. "I'm not wild about sharing anything I don't have to with a civilian."

"Well, he won't tell you everything, either, but you can count on what he does say."

After that ringing endorsement, I cleared my throat and rapped on the cubicle opening. "The pit bull is here."

Simon turned with a smile and said, "Howdy." Then he walked out. Holt looked at me and waved at the chair beside his desk.

"I settled myself and said, "Nice to see Minneapolis's finest detectives pulling Saturday duty. Detective Holt, there was an incident in St. Paul last night. A shooting attempt on me. I expect you can verify the particulars from the St. Paul PD."

"You wanna tell me about it?"

I related the circumstances and gave Holt Catherine's name and telephone number.

"You sure the shooter was after you?"

"Based on everything I observed, yes. I'm not working on anything right now that would provoke such an attack, so it must be connected to the Magda Bryce thing."

Holt stared at me for a minute, pulling on his lower lip. "We aren't getting anywhere with her murder. Just a bunch of loose threads and dead ends."

"There's another element to this case." I went on to tell him about my encounter with Luscious Lucinda the dominatrix.

"Why do you think she's involved?"

"She knows Preston and Magda. Remember, Magda had whip marks on her and I get the feeling this is tied to the murder of that woman, Polly."

"Polly La Famme," Holt volunteered. "What's your basis for that?"

"No basis, just a gut feeling."

Holt grunted and reached into a desk drawer. "We probably know about this Luscious Lucinda. I'll check. Here's your weapon." He pulled out my .45 and the clip and slid them across the desk.

I picked up the weapon and checked the chamber. I do that automatically. Then I saw that the clip was also empty. "Where are my shells?"

He shrugged. "I couldn't give you a loaded weapon in here."

"All right, but those bullets are not cheap."

He shrugged again. "Big weapon."

I looked at him. Could see the smile lurking in his eyes. Ignored it. I've heard it all before. "It stops people when I have to use it. I like the solid feel of it."

"Still. I carry a Chief's Special. I get the feeling that Colt's sorta like compensation, or something." The grin threatened to break out on Holt's face.

"What for?" I shrugged. "I've used several different handguns over the years. I like this one."

Holt gave up and changed the subject. "You ought to lay low until this is over. Let us handle things."

"Look," I said, "I've been slugged twice, shot at, and friends have had their office door smashed. I'm a little pissed off. So I think I'll just keep poking around, if you don't mind. Even if you do mind."

"Be a shame if someone else gets hurt."

"Yeah," I said getting out of my chair. "You got that right."

Chapter 26

THERE WASN'T MUCH doing the rest of the day. I touched base with Catherine and we had a pleasant early supper downtown in a little bistro I knew about. "What's on for tomorrow?" she asked.

I'd just finished telling her that nothing much had happened all day, that I'd retrieved my Colt semiauto again. I decided not to mention that Holt thought the real reason I favored such a large weapon was compensation for my small size in certain areas.

"Would you like to come to my place tonight?" I said.

"Yes, I would, very much. But I can't. Not tonight, sweetie. I have to take care of some business matters."

"Tonight?"

Catherine looked at me with a level gaze. "That's right. And it'll probably take most of the evening."

I nodded. If she didn't want to include me, it was her business. I wasn't one of those men who had to know everything, every minute about my friend. If she decided it was my business, she'd tell me, right?

She smiled and then looked over my shoulder. I glanced back to see a man in a conservative suit approaching our table. He didn't look like trouble.

"Excuse me for interrupting," he said softly. "Mr. Sean?"

"That's me."

"Mr. Saint Martin, Senior, asked me to give you this." He held out an envelope with an instantly recognizable imprint.

Now why was old Ephraim himself reaching out to me?

Did it signal a shift in our relationship? "How'd you know I was here?"

"Chance, Mr. Sean. I was asked to deliver this to you as soon as possible. I've been to your office and your home. I was informed you sometimes eat here. I was taking a short break for supper when I saw you and the lady come in."

"Why didn't you just drop it at my office?" I don't like clients, even lawyers, running around my Roseville neighborhood, and chance or not, Eppy seemed to know an awful lot about my habits.

"My instructions are to deliver this envelope personally."

"I see." I took the envelope and ripped it open. The messenger didn't leave. "Something else?"

"Yes, Mr. Sean. I'm to take your answer directly to Mr. Saint Martin."

I nodded and glanced at the heavy paper in my hand. The note was very short. It requested my appearance at the home of Ephraim Harcourt Saint Martin, anytime between eleven and three the next day. Hell, another trip all the way out to Minnetonka. Why at home and not his office in the IDS? I'd go, of course, to satisfy my curiosity if nothing else.

I looked up and saw the messenger staring at the neckline of Catherine's blouse as if he was trying to penetrate the cloth. I cleared my throat and looked at him so he'd know I'd caught him. "Tell Eppy I'll see him Monday morning, if that is acceptable."

"Thank you, sir. I'll relay your response." Messenger turned and left.

I handed the paper to Catherine. "He was staring at your chest."

"I noticed. If I had anything to show, I'd probably have leaned forward a little, given him a peek." She smiled and took the paper. "Poor Sean. You need a voluptuous blonde to be around to distract the bad guys at crucial moments.

Isn't that what all PI's have?" She read the note.

"Yeah, I'm really disadvantaged. No big-chested blonde, I'm short, and I carry a big gun."

"More compensation for Miss Flat Chest of the year, here." Catherine started to laugh.

I shook my head, smiling widely. Then we were both laughing in each other's faces while nearby diners looked at us in wonder.

"I don't have anything particular going on Monday. Would you like some company?"

I thought about that. Yes indeed I'd like her company, anywhere. But did I want to drag her any closer to this situation? I voiced my thought.

"Sweetie, anyone with any connection to this case must know by now you and I have had two dates. For all you know, they could have been misreading our relationship for a long time. More than one man has been accused of having an affair with me. 'Sides, if I'm with you, you won't have to be worried about me."

She had a point, but I was getting the feeling she could take care of herself, and probably me in the bargain. "Okay, deal. I'll pick you up around ten and we'll motor on out to the upper crust."

On the way out of the bistro, I was paying the cashier and looking idly at her sweater when I felt warm breath in my ear and Catherine whispered in a low throaty voice, "I think I'll run out and buy me one of those specially designed push-up wonder bras."

I almost choked on my laughter, to the mild consternation of the cashier, and we went out into the hot night.

Chapter 27

MONDAY MORNING DAWNED hot and clear, like a lot of Minnesota summer mornings. I showered, fed myself and the cat, cleaned and reloaded my sidearm, my gat, then locked it in a drawer in my bedroom.

At ten I was in my car waiting at the front of her building for Catherine to appear. Today she appeared dressed in new-looking pressed jeans, a short-sleeved white shirt and Top-Siders. Dark glasses and a long-billed white cap completed her ensemble. It all emphasized her slender build and the grace with which she moved.

She slid into the seat beside me, leaned over and kissed my ear. "Good morning. How's my personal private eye this morning?"

"Good. Slept well, no dreams, not a care in the world. You look ravishing this fine morning." I put the car in gear and we headed west toward Minnetonka. In spite of my occasional gripes about the distance to that up-scale suburb, I knew the freeway system would get us to Saint Martin's in plenty of time. We were working against heavy morning go-to-work traffic still coming into the city.

"What do you think this meeting's all about?" asked Catherine.

I looked a question at her.

She shrugged. "I'm just trying to get a handle on what to expect. It's a habit of mine. A long time ago, I went to get a business loan to buy one of the training schools I own. The banker asked a lot of questions I couldn't answer. I was embarrassed and I promised myself it would never happen again. Now I always try to prepare for my business meetings. Don't you?"

"I don't see this as a business appointment. Thinking about it, I guess I don't prepare much at all, for interviews or meetings. I go with my gut."

"Different strokes," she said smiling.

"Let me amend myself. I do review what I know about a case, but reports to clients are always written. Almost always. Anyway, I like to leave myself open to suggestion."

We reached the outskirts of Wayzata and I hung a left on Bushaway Road. Driving south we crossed the bridge between Wayzata Bay and Grays Bay on the northern end of Lake Minnetonka. The lake was already populated with a scattering of white-clothed sailboats scurrying lazily across the blue water. Not everybody went to work on summer Mondays in these affluent suburbs. We lost sight of the water as we wound through Woodland and into Deephaven, always angling west, back toward the lake.

Here the trees and underbrush grew thick and close along the road, hiding the walls and fences of the large homes that faced the water. Residences of the lawyers, the big-time owners of major Twin Cities commerce and industry. From time to time we glimpsed the rooftops of some of the houses through the screen of trees. This was an exclusive part of the metro area, peopled by those who valued and protected their privacy.

I missed the discreet number etched on the stone pillar beside the Saint Martin entrance. The last time I'd been here, I hadn't entered from the street. We backtracked a quarter mile and I swung my car into the paved entrance, drove through a heavy steel gate that stood open and up a long curved driveway that opened onto a vast green lawn. There was a wide parking and turn-around space beside the house, mansion, really, all stone and glass, one of the more modern homes in this part of the world.

I parked and switched off. "Are you carrying?" asked Catherine.

"What?"

"You know. Do you have a gun?"

"Really, Catherine. You've been watching too many second-rate movies. No, I'm not carrying a weapon. You'd have smelled it if I was."

She nodded and got out of the car. "There's that, I guess."

"I rarely go around armed. Loaded guns cause more problems than they solve. I rely on my feet." We walked up the broad stone steps and I lifted the heavy door knocker. No lighted bell button here.

"Meaning?"

"Somebody pulls a weapon, I usually run," I said, as the door opened on a dim hall. I recognized the woman who answered, Mrs. Saint Martin, wife of Sir Ephraim Harcourt Saint Martin. Eppy.

"Yes? Mr. Sean, is it?"

No unnecessary ostentation here. "Yes, I'm Sean Sean." I saw her glance at Catherine. "This is Catherine Mckerney, my...associate."

"How nice to meet you both," she said softly. "Won't you come with me please? Ephraim is on the back lawn." She turned and led us through the silent house and down a hall I vaguely remembered, toward the lake. I felt the hairs on the back of my neck prickle.

We entered a large sunny room with one glass wall on the west side and a sliding-glass door that led onto a broad stone patio. At the end of the patio, in front of the strip of grass edging the big swimming pool, sat a figure in a white lawn chair beside a small white table. The pool was empty. So was the lawn.

Mrs. Saint Martin led us onto the patio and bid us wait. She went forward and leaned over the shoulder of the man in the chair.

"Empty, lonely," murmured Catherine. "Do they have children?"

"Yes, but they've all grown and have mansions of their own, I expect."

Mrs. Saint Martin straightened and turned to beckon us forward. As we walked across the patio, she came toward us and said, "Would you like coffee?"

"If it's no trouble," responded Catherine.

We walked onto the grass and wheeled around in front of Saint Martin. "Mr. Sean, thank you for coming. I apologize for sending a messenger but . . " He looked up and saw Catherine beside me.

"Mr. Saint Martin, this is Catherine Mckerney, an associate."

"Ms. Mckerney. Pardon me for not rising. Doctors orders." Mrs. Saint Martin reappeared with two folded lawn chairs that matched the chaise Saint Martin was in. "I wasn't aware you had expanded to include an associate. Business must be good."

"I'm not a detective, Mr. Saint Martin, I handle other aspects of Mr. Sean's affairs," Catherine lied smoothly. Then I decided it wasn't a lie at all.

I examined the lawyer. He looked considerably less vigorous than he had the last time I saw him. His legendary voice had lost some of its force. Or maybe he was holding back. Conserving his energy. I didn't think his color was good either.

"In spite of what my partners believe, I'm aware that the professional relationship between our law firm and your agency has been long and successful. Fruitful for both of us, after a rather unfortunate beginning. In all the years, you have performed well and with utmost discretion."

I nodded my acceptance of his statement, masking my surprise. Saint Martin was known for the depth of his knowledge, a veritable Perry Mason at times. But I hadn't expected him to be so well informed about our ongoing relationship.

"The firm is proposing to take on a new out-of-town client, one who will provide a significant volume of new work. However, I have some reservations and questions about this client. His business is all outside Minnesota. Cleveland, Ohio, is his base.

"I require a discreet, thorough, background check. But it must be separate from the work you do for our firm on other matters. I do not wish this to go through regular channels and I intend to pay you from personal funds. No one at Harcourt, Saint Martin, Saint Martin, Bryce must become aware of your work on this matter."

I'd almost added the "et cetera" out loud. I looked at the old man, keeping my face expressionless. Then I nodded to let him know I understood what he was saying. "Go on."

"I expect you'll have to go to Cleveland. I know it's the general practice to hire a local investigator to do some of the work. I'd prefer you not engage another, but if you must do so, I can't emphasize too strongly that the client must never become aware of your investigation. Is that quite clear?"

"Certainly, but I can't evaluate the project and give you an answer until I have more information, especially the name of your client."

"Proposed client," Saint Martin corrected. "I understand. However, I'm not prepared to reveal that information at the moment. You needn't decide immediately, but I do require an answer within forty-eight hours. I'll pay your standard fee plus a fifteen percent surcharge because of the nature of the assignment, in addition to all reasonable expenses. Here is a financial statement on the client with names removed. You may be able to figure out the name of the subject, but I doubt it's worth your while to do so, if you don't accept my offer."

I took the sealed envelope and said, "How much time would I have to complete this assignment?"

"Not much. I require that the matter be attended to as quickly as possible. At the same time, I want a thorough and exhaustive report. There is another matter I wish to broach."

During the exchange, Catherine had sat silently beside me, watching both of us and occasionally glancing at the house. Mrs. Saint Martin returned with a tray and a silver coffee server, two china cups, and matching sugar and creamer. Saint Martin took no coffee. She handed him a small glass of water with a single ice cube.

He sighed and said, "Even though your links to the killing of Magda Bryce are tenuous, I understand you've been assaulted twice and someone tried to shoot you recently. I hope you realize that your continued inquiry may be extremely hazardous." His tone of voice was flat, emotionless, but I could tell the subject was painful. I was not surprised that he was fully informed on everything tied to Magda Bryce's murder. He probably had better contacts at the cop house than I did.

I leaned forward and raised my voice slightly. "Are you telling me to butt out? I remind you I wasn't involved at all until those things happened. I don't like getting knocked on the head and shot at. I like it even less when people close to me come under fire. I think the best way to end this is to find the killer. The police don't seem to be making much progress, so if you know something I don't, I think you should tell me right now."

Saint Martin shook his head slowly and stared into my face. For a moment I saw that famous predatory spark in his eyes. But it faded and he looked away. "I'm as puzzled as you at this juncture. But if you turn up information you think I should know, I hope you'll confide in me."

"Who was Polly La Famme?" I asked bluntly.

"A woman who worked for Magda and Preston Bryce. She lived at Preston's. I'm not entirely sure of her position in that household, but she was merely an employee." He looked out and contemplated the expanse of lawn running down toward the lake. "I don't mean to denigrate her, or her unfortunate demise. However, I think she has nothing to do with either Magda's death, or this project." He gestured to the envelope I'd laid on the table between us.

I decided not to ask about his son's connection with Luscious Lucinda; I'd save that for another time. I looked at Catherine. She was regarding Saint Martin with something like sympathy. "Was there anything else, Mr. Saint Martin?"

"No, Mr. Sean. I will await your decision on the assignment. Thank you for coming out here."

In the car I looked at Catherine while I fished for the ignition lock. "What do you think?"

"I think he's dying. I suspect he hasn't known it for very long. I also think he knows, or suspects, something connected to his family that disturbs him greatly."

"Absolutely. And I bet it has to do with Magda Bryce's murder. He may not know who shot her, but I bet he knows a lot about why."

"Is that offer of a contract legit, you think?" Catherine asked.

"Probably. But it may also be his devious way of trying to make me too busy to spend more time nosing around the murders."

"Is this why you brought me along?"

I smiled at her as we rolled serenely back toward Minneapolis. "You have to be a pretty good judge of character in your business, so your impressions are helpful. That's one of the reasons. Mainly I invited you along because I enjoy being with you. Lots."

"Oh yeah. We still do a lot of outcall business. Strictly legit, but you know it's hard to keep our reputation clean. I try to evaluate our clients very carefully. Our masseurs and masseuses as well. We were being watched, Sean, back there."

"Excuse me?"

"Watched. The whole time we were at Saint Martin's. There was a woman at an upstairs window looking at us. I saw her again at a front window just as we drove off."

"Huh. Describe her."

Catherine did, describing a woman I'd known as Magda Bryce.

Chapter 28

THE SUN SENT slanting golden rays through the dusty half-closed Venetian blinds, making a barred pattern on the tile floor of my office. It was a hot, still afternoon. I'd just finished another short session dealing with bills, some record keeping and other mundane sidebars of my business. Air conditioners hummed and fans listlessly stirred the air, but the building was almost silent, drowsing in the heavy heat.

On my desk lay the brown envelope Saint Martin had given me earlier that day. It was still unopened.

On the floor about ten feet from my desk, in the middle of the barred pattern from the sun, was a black hat. It wasn't a battered fedora.

It was a cheap cardboard top hat. A year ago I'd been to a costume ball and worn the hat and a rented tuxedo. I don't know why I kept the hat.

Footsteps passed my door, hard heels tattooing the floor. I flipped another playing card at the hat. Missed again. I'd read somewhere that old-time detectives, when they had to think about a case, sat in their offices, nipped at the bottle of sour mash stashed in a desk drawer, and flipped playing cards at their hats to help their concentration.

I had no bottle. Instead, I had a Travis McGee and an Alison Gordon novel. I wasn't thinking about my case, either. I was concentrating on trying to get the cards to sail into the damn hat. Tipped on the two back legs of my chair, one of my size 6-1/2 B feet on the edge of my desk, I wasn't doing so hot. Second time through, the floor around the hat held more cards than the hat.

Came a rapping at the door.

"Nevermore," I muttered. "Come," I called.

The door opened. It wasn't a raven, but a man, a squat man in a cheap brown suit that didn't fit him. He didn't have a hat but he did have a bad haircut. He came in and shut the door behind him. His eyes skittered about, taking in my office in quick, darting, weasel-like looks.

I dropped my foot off the desk and clunked forward onto all four chair legs and my feet found the box under my desk. "Yes?"

He glanced at the cards scattered on the floor and came forward, then sank onto the hard chair on the other side of my desk. "You're Sean. I hear you been lookin' for somebody." My unknown visitor reached into the inside pocket of his jacket and my buttocks and thighs tightened in reaction. He slowly withdrew his hand holding a pack of cigarettes, the unfiltered kind. He shook one out and stuck it in a corner of his mouth. He found a kitchen match in a side pocket and scratched it alight off his thumbnail, then lit the cigarette. His eyes never left my face during this maneuver, his weasel-like darts having ceased.

I eased open my desk drawer, found an old ashtray and slid it across the desk in his direction. The man sucked in a lungful of smoke, burning down at least a quarter of the cigarette in one long hit. When he exhaled, smoke poured out of his nose, but only from one nostril. The cigarette stayed in the corner of his mouth.

"We've never met. Am I looking for you?" I was being polite. So far as I knew I wasn't looking for the man across my desk, but maybe he knew somebody I was looking for.

He said, "You been askin' around, lookin' for a big man, hired muscle, maybe." Ashes dropped to his jacket lapel and scattered down toward his lap. He ignored them.

He was right. I had put out the word after the cops

found the car I'd shot at.

"You been lookin' for the guy who jumped you at your place. A big guy, wide shoulders. Real wide, goes maybe two-sixty, two-eighty."

"Could be," I said, flashing back to that evening at home when a large thug had battered down my screen door and slammed me up side of the head.

"Dark brush-cut hair. Beetle brow. Big eyebrow right across his forehead?"

I nodded, realized that I could remember more about what my assailant looked like than I had thought.

"Gotta gimp. Has a little hitch-along walk. Not much, though."

I'd missed that. We hadn't spent a lot of quality time together, that thug and I. Then my visitor went on to describe the car. I'd seen the car the cops had impounded up close and he described it to a T.

I leaned forward slightly. "Maybe you were driving for my visitor?"

Cheap-suit didn't respond to my thrust. He bobbled the cigarette and blew more smoke into the thick air. "You still want 'im?"

"Do you know where he is?"

"He's around. Hangs out at the Watering Hole."

"What's that?"

"'S a bar out on Nicollet."

"Why are you telling me? What's in it for you?" I expected him to ask for money or some other kind of help. He stood up, peeled the cigarette off his lower lip and dropped it in my ashtray. A thin line of smoke trailed upward between us.

Cheap-suit didn't respond. He just turned around and went out the door. It closed quietly behind him.

I heard the elevator stop on my floor and then fade away. I stubbed out the still-smoldering butt, then went to the door and looked up and down the empty hall. Very odd. Then I reached out to Detective Holt.

"D'you think it's a legitimate tip?" Holt asked.

"I don't know. If it isn't, what's the point?"

"Maybe it's a set up. They could be trying to take you out again."

"Well, I thought of that. Do you know this place, the Watering Hole?"

"Yes. It's nothing special, just a smallish neighborhood-type bar. What do you plan to do about this tip? If it is one?"

"I thought we could make a few visits from time to time, see if it checks out."

"We, huh." Holt's sigh came through the phone.

"If it pans out, that guy who slugged me might help us with some answers."

"But of course you deny wanting to get your hands on the guy because he slugged you."

"Of course. I'm not the revengeful type, Detective Holt. If I were, I wouldn't be telling you about this tip. I'd go down there with my gat and politely knee-cap the son of a bitch."

Holt grunted in my ear and said, "I'll pass along this location and ask the patrol cars to check a little more frequently. You and I can have a drink there sometime tonight."

* * * * *

EIGHT O'CLOCK CAME and I drove across the city into the setting sun. I found the bar. Holt was right, it was nothing special, just a bar, sandwiched between a Thai restaurant and a small appliance repair shop. The block had seen better days, but it wasn't run down. I found a parking spot on Nicollet where I could observe the entrance and take a gander at the people walking by. There weren't many on the street and they all appeared to be minding their business, going from someplace to someplace else. No loiterers.

Detective Holt appeared half a block away and I watched him saunter down the street. His tie was askew and he had his hands in his pockets. He looked nowhere in particular and turned into the door of the Watering Hole without hesitating. I gave him five minutes and went in after him. It was a cat's whisker after nine.

It was an ordinary neighborhood place, just as advertised. The bar ran partway down one side of the long room on my right. The back-bar had the usual stuff—signs, a smudgy mirror and assorted bottles of cheap whiskey. There were booths along the other wall, and a few tables scattered about. Toward the back was a single pool table with worn green felt on the edges of the bumpers. Behind the table, up against the cheap wood paneling was a silent jukebox. Like most of these places, the lighting was dim but you could see well enough. The miasma of odors in the air combined body, old booze, age and disinfectant. A door in the back wall carried a faded sign lettered RESTROOMS. I assumed it also led to a back door.

Two men sat on bar stools, hunched over, nursing their drinks. I didn't see Holt. I hopped up on an empty stool at the inside end of the bar so I could see the door if I looked to my right. I fished a fiver out of my jeans. The bartender, fat, almost bald with a dirty apron wrapped around him, sauntered over.

"Gimme a Bud."

"Draw or bottle?" he responded. One hand held a damp rag he pushed around the bar top in a lackadaisical sort of way.

"Bottle," I said. He turned around and pulled out a cold wet longneck and uncapped it. He set it in front of me and flicked up the five. No glass.

I took a long swig of the icy brew, heard movement and a door behind me banged. Holt's voice said over my shoulder, "My man, let's move to a table."

I scooped up my change, leaving a dollar tip and followed Holt. He selected a table across from the bar, taking the seat so his back was to the wall and he could see the whole room. I sat opposite, facing him. There were ratty framed sports prints on the wall above his head.

For the next hour we sat and sipped our drinks, talking about the Twins, the Vikings' prospects for the coming season, and other riveting topics. People continued to drift in and out, and gradually the small crowd grew. Holt kept up a running conversation, interspersed with terse descriptions of the new arrivals.

Around ten a tired waitress showed up and began to circulate among the tables and booths, filling orders and chatting with the regulars. Another half-hour passed.

"Nobody has paid us any particular attention," said Holt, downing the last of his first beer and signaling the waitress. I stretched and looked casually toward the back of the bar. Two bearded men in plaid work shirts and jeans were putting balls on the pool table and selecting cues. "Are you wearing a gun?" asked Holt after the waitress left.

"No."

"Good. If your man shows and things go wrong, I don't want to have to explain you shooting some bystander." There was a burst of noisy talk and the door whammed open. It sounded like a crowd. I restrained myself from looking around.

"Three men, one very large," Holt said. "He's not with the first two. Could be your guy. He's in the middle of the room by the bar directly behind you. Seems to have a slight limp. Now he's sitting on a stool. He looked the place over very carefully."

I saw Holt ease his chair back just slightly. One hand had disappeared from the table. My scalp started to itch. I tried to ignore the feeling.

"Hey, bartender, gummier a Bud, Goddamit!"

I knew that voice. "It's him," I said, looking straight at Holt.

"All right, just take it easy. The uniformed guys will be here any minute now. When they come in, you get up and head for the bathroom. We'll take him then." We waited tensely for another couple of minutes. Then the door opened and I looked around to see two uniformed officers step into the room.

I shoved back my chair and stood up, turned to my right and started toward the back. Our target must have looked around at that same instant. I took three steps and the familiar voice bellowed, "Hey! Hey you! Shorty!"

I stopped in mid-stride, conscious that conversation and movement in the bar had gone still, like a freeze-frame in a movie. I straightened and looked over. My Neanderthal, dark beetle-browed and brush cut, was leaning toward me, half rising from his stool.

"What the hell are you doin' here?" People were sidling away from him, and from me.

"Hold it!" Holt had stood, his left hand holding his shield out in front of him. "Police. Keep your hands in sight and freeze." Holt's other arm was hanging at his side.

"Fuck if I will," bellowed our target. He slid off his stool, both hands reaching for his belt.

"Freeze," shouted one of the uniforms. Beetlebrow's eyes shuttled back and forth between the patrolmen and Holt. His hand came out from under his shirt holding a pistol. As he drew the weapon, it tangled in the tail of his shirt and he squeezed off a single inadvertent shot that drilled into the floor. Then Holt shot him in the chest. There were screams and shouts. Both patrolmen had their guns out. The pistol in Beetlebrow's hand clattered to the floor and he let out a loud wheeze. His knees buckled and he sagged to the floor, knocking over a bar stool. Holt and I, followed by one of the patrolmen, rushed the man. I put my foot on the pistol and knelt on the dirty floor.

Beetlebrow gurgled and husked, "Son of a bitch." We watched while life went out of his body.

"Get the door," ordered Holt and took out his cell phone to call in the troops. "We want statements from everybody in here." He looked at me. "Damn. We got some information from Cleveland after you and I talked. They said if he was our guy he wouldn't go easy."

I stood up and looked back at Holt. "Another dead end. I wonder who really was the patsy here."

Chapter 29

IT TOOK HOURS to complete statements, satisfy department protocols, and interview witnesses. I dragged home at around two the next morning, in no mood for anything other than bed.

My cats had alternative ideas. Somewhere I'd acquired a second critter. He'd just shown up at the door. Apparently there's a cat telegraph that let's 'em know about soft touches.

Since they'd run out of their regular fare, they'd gone on the prowl for other comestibles. Usually it isn't worth their trouble, but while I'd been gone, the little buggers had managed to pry open several cabinets in the kitchen, leading to boxes of dry cereal, some popcorn, and the under-sink garbage pail.

There was an unpleasant odor emanating from the kitchen and when I stepped in, I neglected to turn on the light at first. My foot encountered something soggy and slick. I flicked on the overhead light and found a brown banana peel stuck to my shoe. One glance surveyed the disaster that had once been a kitchen. Uncooked oatmeal, popcorn, corn flakes, and garbage littered the floor and slopped over into the edge of the dining room carpet.

I swore a fearsome oath that sent both cats scuttling for the dark corners of the living room behind the sofa. Then I reached for the broom and dustpan, although what I swept up could hardly be dignified by calling it dust. A pail of water and the mop came next.

While I worked, I thought about Catherine. Where was our relationship going exactly? More to the point, where did she want it to go? It was already obvious we fit well together. Our views of the world weren't that divergent. Our professions were similar in many ways.

I'd been in past relationships in which the woman had never completely understood why I sometimes didn't get home until very late or not at all, or why I didn't call when I was going to be late. Or why I seemed, upon occasion, too eager to ride out in defense of some low-life or other. To be fair, I was never receptive to suggestions that I change occupations.

By now I'd completed the kitchen mop-up and put the contents of the cabinets back to rights. "Miserable pests," I muttered. I was too irritated to hit the sack immediately so I snagged a beer from the refrigerator and went onto the deck. It was warm and still and dark.

Overhead, the stars glittered, a million points of light, filled with immense knowledge, answers to all my questions if only I could figure out the code.

My relationship with Catherine hadn't reached the plane of intimacy where we talked about the next step. It was pretty early for that. Those past relationships that had even touched on questions of marriage, or children, had always foundered on the sharp reefs of uncertainty—my uncertainty. My unwillingness to consider other possibilities, other professions. What else would I do?

Oh sure, I'd worked in security, I'd even been in charge of training security persons—you could hardly call them guards—for a short time in a past life. I hadn't liked it much, although the regular paycheck was attractive. I sat back on the chaise and looked into the sky, beyond distant galaxies, back in time while I contemplated my future. Then I fell asleep.

* * * * *

THE CHEERFUL RUSTLE and wakeup calls of the backyard critters, that and the newly descended dew, woke me just before dawn. I staggered inside and dragged myself to bed, not forgetting to set the perimeter motion alarms I'd installed a few months earlier.

The world was hustling toward noon when next I returned to conscious thought. Still out of sorts from last night, I showered and decided to forego a home-cooked meal. I did remember to feed and water the animals, and headed out to my office. On the way I stopped at a small Central Avenue eatery I'd discovered years earlier that served up great burgers if you got there at the right time. I got there just at the tail end of right and was able to fortify my inner-man with a juicy bacon-burger and fries, lettuce, and two slices of tomato, if you please. About the only thought in my head, apart from pleasure at the meal, was the nagging question of whom did Catherine spot spying on us at Saint Martin's?

I was feeling pretty positive about life, all things considered, when I parked the car and started in the back entrance of my office building. That's where fate, at least the fate of the day, caught up with me. Fate, in the form of Belinda Revulon jiggling across the tiny lobby from the elevator.

"Oh, God, Sean, I'm glad I caught you. I was going to stick a note over your mailbox, but I wasn't sure you'd see it. And I didn't know what to say to warn you—"

"Hold it, hold it. Stop the train and tell me what's going on."

Belinda stopped, nodded, and took a couple of deep breaths, meanwhile flapping one hand at her face in a vain attempt to cool her flushed cheeks.

"He's back. He's upstairs now, talking to Betsey. We saw him standing by your door and when he noticed us he came down to talk to us."

"Who? Who's back?"

Belinda stared at me for a moment and then said, "That guy, the one who wouldn't tell us his name."

"The detective with no name?"

"Yeah, him."

"Okay, thanks. You go upstairs. Forget you saw me. When he leaves, you go to your office window and wave. I'll watch for you." Belinda nodded and I pushed her gently toward the elevator to get her moving again. I didn't think the snoop was dangerous. At least not to the Revulon cousins. He'd been too open, so both women could identify him. So I sent her back to her office to act as my forward observer. I went out the door and moved my car so I could see the lobby and the window of the Revulon cousins' office. I had a fifty-fifty chance the guy would come into the back lot, instead of exiting to Central Avenue. I could see through the small lobby, so both doors were visible, and it wouldn't take me any time at all to whip around the end of the building and onto Central.

Ten minutes later, Belinda appeared, almost filling the window frame, and waved enthusiastically. I blinked my lights and focused on the lobby. In a few minutes, a tall, very thin man in a dark brown suit and hat appeared in the lobby from the direction of the elevators. I was sure he was my target. Tall, and thin to a fault. I gave him time to get out of sight and rolled around the end of the building to the intersection. I ran the risk he'd turned my way, but If I'd been doing his job, I'd have parked somewhere downstream at least a block away on the same side of the street. He stopped at the intersection, glanced both ways, and crossed the side street, going away at an easy gait. From this distance, the man appeared to be so thin a strong breeze might dismember him.

I eased far enough into the intersection to see down

the sidewalk. On my left, the afternoon traffic steamed by, hell-bent for who knew where. It would be difficult to find an opening to get into that traffic stream. On my right, I spied Tall Brown Hat getting into a late model Chevy Caprice. Already in my hands was the small expensive pair of Nikon opera glasses I carry in the car. As TBH eased into traffic, I stared at the bronze trunk of the Caprice and the Wisconsin license plate. Then I made a space for myself in Central Avenue traffic and followed. By the time I'd reached the end of the block, I was wearing large plastic sunglasses and a dark blue, long-billed, fishing cap. Tailing people is also something I'm good at.

We headed west and then south down the interstate until, inevitably, we encountered Bloomington. At I-494 my target turned west and, like the dutiful caboose, so did I, maintaining a four-car separation. By now I'd doffed the fishing cap and was wearing a pale green baseball cap backwards.

At Normandale Road, the Caprice headed north and then got off at the Edina Industrial Center, where there were a couple of hotels. Sure enough, the Caprice slid into the Holiday Inn lot and my man went inside. I was right on his heels. Well, not literally.

In the restaurant, sprinkled about with a few late lunchers and coffee drinkers, I saw TBH walk down the outside row of booths. He now had his hat in his hand. He disappeared into a booth near the end of the row. There was one person already seated with his back to me. At least it looked like a he.

Now what? I didn't see any way of getting close enough to slip into the next booth with a chance to overhear their conversation. I assumed one or both of the occupants would recognize me on sight. After checking back-of-counter reflections, I took a seat at the counter among three other men toying with their coffee cups. At least I'd learn who the nosy parker had come all this way to meet.

An hour later I was no wiser but considerably more uncomfortable. I'd managed to down two glasses of water and three cups of coffee. Pressure was building up in my lower regions. If something didn't happen soon, I was likely to make an embarrassment. I looked around to figure the shortest route to the men's room. I'd just about decided I'd run out of time when Preston Bryce slid out of the booth and turned toward me. I was facing the other way, of course, watching Bryce's wobbly reflection in the polished steel accent piece behind the counter.

As soon as Bryce cleared the room, I bolted for the restroom.

Chapter 30

THE SKY, REFLECTED in the windows of the building across Central Avenue from my office, turned bright, bloody, arterial red from the sunset. I looked blindly across shimmering asphalt rooftops softening in the sun, thought I saw fetid, polluted air rising on thermal currents into who-knew-what higher atmospheres. I imagined it was something like second-hand cigarette smoke; humankind's effluvia gone off to foul someone else's environment. But maybe I was wrong, maybe gravity kept it all in our own planetary orbit, hanging there, overhead, gradually squeezing the life out of us.

Now that I knew Preston Bryce, husband of the dead woman, had hired a detective to scope me out, I had to decide what that meant.

Since the guy had been on the scene early, right after Magda Bryce had come to see me, that meant that Bryce could have known about her visit to me. Had he suggested it? No, she'd told me Ephraim had suggested it. Or had she? I replayed her few words, and after them, Saint Martin's from our confrontation in his office. She'd suggested that I was recommended, along with some others. He'd expressed surprise that my name was on the list.

I mumbled under my breath. Did I need to know who'd supplied the list of investigators Magda had? So then I thought, whatever happened to the reason Magda Bryce came to see me in the first place? Did it go away because she was dead? Maybe, but maybe not. I slid open my left-hand desk drawer, the one that locks. The one where I sometimes keep my weapon.

Looking up at me was that ten-by-twelve-inch brown envelope I'd received from the hand of Ephraim Harcourt Saint Martin. It was still sealed.

"Ah, hmm," said I. I said it aloud. We detectives do that sometimes. I was getting a tingling in my toes. Some people call them premonitions, others call them hunches. I call them gut feelings. I have no reason to call them that, I just do. I had this gut feeling that maybe Magda's problem and Sir Harcourt Saint Martin's problem were connected. Perhaps was even the same problem. That possibility enhanced my natural curiosity about what was in the envelope.

I had until tomorrow morning to give my answer to Saint Martin. Since I'd pretty much decided I didn't want the job, I'd curbed my raging curiosity about what was in the envelope. I could have steamed it open and then re-sealed the envelope, I suppose, but that seemed unethical.

But now things looked different. So I did the obvious and tore the end off the envelope with a flourish. No sirens, no thunderclaps, just the sound of the envelope tearing. I peered inside and shook out several pieces of paper.

According to one piece of paper, a copy of an IRS form, my target was named Donald R Sant—something. I couldn't read all the letters in the sprawling signature. The printed name on the label at the top had been whited out, as Saint Martin had warned, but whoever was trying to cover up the name of the target had forgotten to white out the signature. On such small slips are battles won and lost.

The person was, according to the form, a plumber and he made a healthy salary, well into six figures. I concluded after scanning the form that Donald R. Sant was either a working fool who did his plumbing seven-days-a-week, twenty-four-hours-a-day, or he charged absolutely astounding rates. A plumbing contractor is what he was. In Cleveland, Ohio.

I looked at more of the stuff from the brown envelope and concluded further that he owned trucks. There was a picture of a good-sized showroom behind several trucks. A publicity shot. There was another picture which led me to conclude that the guy was a happily married man. This one was of a large beefy guy with a handlebar mustache and a wide-open grin, a large but not beefy blond wife, two boy children and one girl. They were all smiling in the picture, which had no date on it.

I fired up the computer and began to see what there was to see. My Yellow Pages program told me there was a plumbing contractor in Cleveland, Ohio, with a fleet of trucks and an address in the upscale part of Cleveland's commercial district. It also told me his name was Santangelo.

Another little program gave me a different name in Cleveland that might turn out to be handy. This program was just a simple database in which I kept virtual information about investigators I had encountered over the years who might one day be useful. Or not. I searched the database for Cleveland, Ohio. I got a hit. I had once met an investigator named Alain Russol. We'd met at a law enforcement convention in the Midwest somewhere. I'd been impressed by his erudition, his panache, at least that's what my database reminded me. If he was still in business in Cleveland, perhaps I could hire him to investigate Donald Santangelo, plumbing contractor. So I called him.

"Russol Investigations. How may I help you?" The voice was pleasant, professional. Alain Russol must have progressed in the world to afford a receptionist. On the other hand, it could be a professional answering service.

I gave my name and explained my business. Pause, then a well-modulated bass voice entered my ear. "Yes? This is Alain Russol. Sean? Long time no contact. How are things in the frozen North?"

"I can assure you, things are not frozen at the moment. You've heard of pavement hot enough to fry an egg? Well, it's that hot and humid to boot."

Russol's deep chuckle came through the phone. "What can I do for you?"

"I have a local long-time client who wants a very confidential investigation of one of your local citizens. Very hush-hush. The client mustn't tumble to the inquiry. Are you available?"

"I am. Do we know why the covert inquiry? Not that my people are indiscreet, you understand."

"I don't know why. My client is playing this one very close to his sunken chest. And that leads me to the other aspect of this. There is a certain air of urgency and I'd appreciate it if you'd handle this personally."

Russol laughed again. "Just in case things get nasty, you can assure your client you handled things the way you were directed. Am I right?"

"There is that. It is also that this may be tied to a couple of murders up here." For a moment the line was silent.

"I see. How far do you want me to go? Wiretaps? Surveillance? In addition to the usual? What's the target's name?"

"Nothing out of line, Alain. Just a thorough backgrounder. The target's name is Santangelo, Donald. A plumbing contractor."

"That he is. One of the biggest in town. A civic leader. No scandal that I recall."

"I'll fax you what I have."

"Good. I'll get on it right away, Sean. Changing the subject."

"Why?"

"Still with the smart mouth. Are you still a jazz fan?"

"Absolutely. Why do you ask?"

"My lady and I have reservations tonight for Riverside. It's a hot jazz venue just outside of Cleveland. Headliner tonight is the Tony Fennelly quartet. Really good acoustic jazz. Some people think Fennelly is Brubeck's heir."

"Really? Brubeck is a favorite of mine. Who's in the group?"

"Burl Barrer is the drummer. One critic called him the saint of the brushes. Bass man is a guy named Jerry Heale. I don't know much about him. The other side man is Michael something. They're a very tasty group. If they ever get up your way, try not to miss 'em."

"Got it," I said, jotting a note on my pad. Thanks for the tip."

We made the financial arrangements and disconnected. I then called Saint Martin. He was not at the office. Naturally I called his home next.

"Mrs. Saint Martin. Sean Sean here. May I speak to your husband?"

Her voice sounded wan. "I'm sorry, he's sleeping right now. May I take a message?"

Sleeping in the afternoon? That didn't sound like the dynamo attorney I was used to. Catherine was right, the man must be ailing. "I'm sorry to disturb you. If he's not feeling well, I can leave this message with you."

"I'll be happy to convey your message."

"Tell Mr. Saint Martin I will take the assignment we spoke about when I came to see him. I'll start immediately. He can expect a contract in the mail in the next day or so."

"Thank you, Mr. Sean. He'll be relieved. I know he hoped to get that project under way as soon as possible."

"I wonder, Mrs. Saint Martin, if you could give me a little insight into this investigation. It might help me, you see, to have more background. And if you can tell me anything, I can avoid disturbing your husband."

There was a slight hesitation, and then she said, "I'm sorry, Mr. Sean, if you need any further information, you will have to talk with my husband."

Well, I'd tried. She hadn't denied someone else was in the house, and the implication that Saint Martin's illness was serious was also evident. I was also pretty sure she knew more than she was willing to tell me about the Cleveland investigation, reinforcing my sense that it was tied to recent unfortunate events in the family or the law firm.

I went off down the hall to the Revulon cousins' office to fax the Santangelo information and a contract to Russol in Cleveland, Ohio.

Chapter 31

THE REST OF THAT week oozed by in the oily summer, uneventful days, thank God. No hitting, no shooting, no car chases. No dead bodies. Not unusual for me, regardless of my caseload. I like that word. Caseload. It makes me sound professional.

I'm not like the housewife who stumbles over a neighborhood dentist having illicit sex and then murdering her patients, or the medical examiner who is threatened by a new serial killer every month or so. Most of my cases are, in a word, boring. A client needs some information and I provide it. An employer decides their in-house security folk aren't covering all the bases and employees are stealing the company blind. I go in undercover and ferret out the culprits. Or one of my insurance clients decides they need to surveil a claimant. Enter Sean Sean, complete with vehicle and pee can. Like I said, boring. Pays the bills, though. Allows me to have a pretty nice life. A life that was becoming eminently more satisfactory. My relationship with Catherine Mckerney was progressing in most positive ways, and tonight I was going to demonstrate to her my not inconsiderable culinary talents.

Just something else I'm pretty good at.

Dinner consisted of *Mousse d'Omble*. It's a delicate specialty developed by the chef of a restaurant near Lyon. That's in France somewhere. One makes this particular mousse from arctic char. The recipe requires whole milk, eggs and careful preparation. Sinful in this age of politically correct diets. Too bad. One also creates a sauce of fresh truffles and butter, and serves the creation with a very crisp, very fresh, green salad, and a quite dry, icy cold, white wine.

Dinner was quite successful, if I do say so. We'd avoided talking about the Saint Martins the entire evening. Since the humidity and temperature had dropped, I suggested we adjourn from the dining room to the deck for more wine and conversation, diverting Catherine from trying to participate in kitchen cleanup.

While we settled ourselves, across two yards we heard a low growl and then several deep-throated barks.

"Neighborhood dog?" queried Catherine.

"Yep. I call him the *dog that barks in the night*. Never have seen him in the light of day. For all I know, it's a high fidelity recording."

Catherine chuckled softly in the darkness. In the simple black dress she wore, her form was just discernible, reclining on the chaise only inches away. I took a healthy sip of wine and said nothing. This was usually the time when I made a move on my companion of the evening, if I was so inclined, usually the case. But in spite of our previous intimacy and Catherine's stated interest in developing our relationship, I discovered I was uncertain about how to proceed. I guess I was afraid to offend this woman in some way, do or say something that would make her think less of me.

Her slender hand came toward me in the dark, holding out the glass in an invitation to give her more wine. While I retrieved the bottle from the floor and filled her glass, I thought about my feelings. Why was I uncertain? A couple of flip comments came to mind but I had the good sense not to voice them. Then it came to me that the rest of this evening could be the reef on which our relationship foundered, or it could be the tide that swept us together into an exciting future.

"A wonderful meal, Sean."

"Thank you, my lady."

"My lady? What a proper label. Surely that's not how you think of me, is it?" There was a slightly tipsy, tone to her voice. I knew she hadn't had enough wine to cause that. I couldn't see what she was doing but I heard a sudden inward hiss of breath.

"What?"

"Cold wine," she said. "You know, Sean, this French wine is very good chilled like this, but it is also excellent when warm."

"Really?"

"Body temperature releases the essential essence of its nose."

"Really?"

"Yes, really, and I think you should come over here and experience that essential essence. With your nose." Was she giggling?

I slid over beside her on the chaise. When I leaned down, I discovered she'd pulled down the top of her dress to expose a tiny indentation over her breastbone into which she had poured a teaspoon of wine. I bent my head to inhale the sweet aura of her body, and my lips touched the warm wine between her breasts.

Catherine murmured, "You know, my dear, you haven't shown me your bedroom yet, and I think now would be a very good time."

* * * * *

I ROLLED OVER and flinched to the shooting pains in my thighs. When I tried to sit up, other muscles I'd long since forgotten about protested. I was going to have to start a new exercise routine if I wanted to keep up with Catherine. I already knew she was no shrinking violet in the bedroom, but she'd obviously been holding back on our first encounter. I said as much.

"Well, lover, you demonstrated ample willingness to participate, but you men have this funny psyche. You seem to want passion and love and sex all tied together, but only as long as you're in charge. Even thoughtful lovers usually want to be in charge."

"Yeah, I suppose that's so. But—"

"No buts. Passion and love are one thing. I think sex is another. Oh sure, they're linked but you know as well as I that sex is basically a funny proposition, especially the way most of us practice it. You know, with the lights out, under the covers, eyes closed." While flinging these words at me, she was rooting around under the covers, tossing pillows about and straightening the wrecked bed without actually getting out. "Here, lift your butt."

I lifted and she slid the sheet around. Finally one slender bare arm and her eyes under tousled hair appeared over the quilt. "You're good, lover. More to the point, we're good together. But you've got a ways to go before you're very very good." She smiled and wiggled her toes in the soft pit of my stomach. "And you need some exercises. I felt those thigh muscles trembling last night."

I opened my mouth once or twice, like a fish out of water, but couldn't think of a single retort. I'd just taken several hits to my fragile male ego and suddenly realized it didn't hurt the least little bit.

"What's on your agenda today?"

I thought for a moment. "Not a whole lot, worse luck. I mean to say, it's too soon to expect a report from Russol in Cleveland and I'm running out of people to interview. How 'bout you?"

"I have appointments this afternoon, but nothing pressing this morning." Catherine sat up a little straighter and pulled the sheet around her torso, leaving smooth shoulders bare and gleaming in the pale golden sunlight. She ran her slender fingers through her hair, pulling and prodding it toward its usual shape. "Could I persuade you to make some coffee?"

"You bet." I scrambled out of bed and belted on a short robe. I started for the bedroom door.

"Not so fast, Sir Lancelot. I want a goodbye kiss."

"I'm just going to the kitchen."

"Call it a good morning kiss then." Catherine puckered her lips and leaned forward. The movement sent the sheet sliding lower on the upper curves of her bosom. I scuttled around the end of the bed and planted a moist, noisy kiss on her upturned lips.

When I returned, the sheet was bunched at her waist and one smooth leg was bare, from toe to hip. I gurgled, trying to balance two over-full mugs of hot coffee without spilling the contents down my front.

"Hold it, lover. I just want to fix this image in my mind." I stood before her for another minute while she pointedly ran her gaze up and down my body. Her tiny pink tongue slid out and touched her lower lip. "Very good. Just put the coffee down for a minute."

As I did, she reached out and tugged at my belt. Later I had to make fresh coffee.

Chapter 32

ANOTHER BEASTLY HOT and humid Minnesota summer day. Catherine had gone off to do her business and I was standing on my front step, contemplating the four-wheeled oven, otherwise known as my car, in the driveway in front of me. Behind me the telephone rang.

It was Detective Holt. We arranged to have a small lunch together at Williams Pub, just down the block from the department's great gray granite home. On the top of the rocky pile we commonly called City Hall was a four-sided clock tower with a carillon. Some years ago when the city decided to sand blast the accumulated grime off the old building; they'd also fixed the clock which had been inoperable for decades. Now it kept pretty good time. It boomed out a noontime song as I parked my car and fed the meter.

Holt was already occupying a corner booth when I shoved through the door. I stepped over and dropped onto the vinyl cushion which wheezed and gasped under my weight. I like to avoid padded booths whenever possible. The dimensions are always designed for people with longer torsos and I end up resting my chin on the tabletop. Believe me, a waiter may take a damp rag to the tabletop every so often, but clean they ain't. The smell is something to avoid. I glanced around. The place was largely empty but the small bulbs in the red-shaded sconces on the walls gave the impression there could have been a lot more people there if only you could see better.

"Take a load off," he offered as I slowly began to disappear behind the table. He grinned at me.

"Is this a power lunch? Are we going to have a big resolution now?"

Holt just smiled and took a hit on his beer. "I was gonna ask you if you've come up with anything new."

"I'm afraid not. I can't get around my hunch all this weird shit happening to me is tied together somehow, but I'm blamed if I can figure how. Either I've become uncommonly dense in the last few days, or there's still some pieces missing that will explain a lot. Maybe everything."

A waiter sauntered by and disinterestedly took my order, a club sandwich, which I knew from experience would be edible even though I wanted a hamburger, and a bottle of Sam Adams ale.

"Here are a couple of pieces you may not have," Henry Holt said, surprising me. His willingness to share information could only mean the cops weren't getting anywhere very fast either. "We found George Cassidy's apartment."

"Beetlebrow?" I asked, biting into my sandwich.

"Right. He had a walkup a couple of blocks from the Watering Hole. Do you know a private investigator named Noble?"

I thought about that. "No, not that I recollect. Should I?"

Holt shrugged and took a bite of his pastrami sandwich. "Nathan Noble. I thought you might have run across him sometime. He's from out of town. Detroit."

"What's his connection to our party?" I was beginning to think detective Henry Holt was playing a little game with me.

"He's an ex-P.I. Before he lost his license and moved to Detroit, he lived in Cleveland. That's in Ohio."

"Uh-huh." My scalp prickled. I don't much believe in coincidence.

"We got a description, because this Noble came and went a few times from Cassidy's rooms. Noble is short, thin, always wore a brown-checked suit and smoked cigarettes constantly."

"And he lit 'em with kitchen matches that he flicked with his thumbnail," I said and swigged my ale.

"Right. Recognize him?"

"Sure, just like you do. The putz I called Cheap-suit, the guy who turned us on to Cassidy's favorite bar. What else? I have the distinct notion you wish to tell me some other goodies, Detective Holt."

Holt smiled and took another bite of his sandwich. "Cassidy had another visitor, neighbors said. But this one only came once or twice. He was a tall guy, very thin. Ring any bells?"

I shook my head and stuffed more sandwich into my mouth. So, Cassidy, or Beetlebrow as I preferred to call him, and Cheap-suit were not only linked to each other, but they also knew the nameless detective who'd been hanging around. He, in turn, knew Preston Bryce who, presumably, had hired him. The stew was definitely thickening.

I looked across at Holt who had grown quiet. "Something?"

"*Quid pro quo,*" he said.

"Oh, I see. You laid out the *quid* and now you want my *quo*, is that it?" He nodded.

"Okay. The tall lanky guy is probably the same individual who's been lurking around my office the past week or so."

"Lurking?"

"Well, he questioned the women who have a small business down the hall. About me. They described him as very tall and quite thin. He refused to tell them his name. He was back there just yesterday. Belinda intercepted me so I was able to follow him to the Holiday Inn out in Bloomington."

Holt nodded and swigged his beer.

"My hunch is he's the one who slugged me."

"Slugged you? When did that—wait a minute. Seems like you've left out a few things along the way." Holt leaned in and stabbed me with his look. You know the one. The back room look. The I'm-about-to-get-out-the-rubber-hose look. All homicide dicks cultivate it. They probably practice it in front of the mirror, just like I practice my eyebrow wiggle. I held up a hand. Then I told him about the disappearing note, the whack on the head, and my suspicion that this tall, thin detective might have been responsible.

"You got any proof he hit you and stole that note?"

"Nope. Just my gut feeling. My experience."

"Sure. What else?"

I didn't have much else. I reminded him that there was a connection between the strippers and Preston, but that seemed to be a dead end. I didn't tell him about Saint Martin's request for information on the Cleveland plumber. No connection, right? Sure there wasn't.

"What else is that I think I've been unconsciously working around a central character in this little soap opera."

"And that would be?"

"That would be the deceased, Magda Bryce. I had no reason to get involved in this mess, even after Beetle-brow attacked me, but I've decided to get a little closer to the deceased."

Holt shrugged and suggested I share anything untoward that might bear on her death. He finished his beer and lunch and left me there to contemplate my own as well as the sins of others. What had become increasingly clear to me was that I'd made a couple of mistakes that had contributed to at least one death. Although I couldn't prove it, I was morally certain Polly La Famme had slipped the note into my jacket that morning, and my less than attentive subsequent actions had not only lost the note but contributed in some way to her murder. Whoever lifted it from my desk probably recognized it right off and must have figured out the source right after that. *Shit.* She hadn't expected me to be so damn careless with the note. Well, I owed her for that. One other thing I'm good at is paying my debts.

* * * * *

"SO YOU CAN'T tell me anything at all about Mrs. Bryce?"

"No, I'm sorry. She served as a member of the board for six years. She was faithful in her attendance and contributed as we expected." Alissa Johnson, executive director of the Johnson Foundation (no relation) smiled at me from across her big desk. She was holding the thick minutes book, a record of all significant actions of the foundation board. "Her term was up this year and she might have been reappointed, but we had the impression she was ready to be replaced."

I rose from the soft beige chair where I'd been sitting and took her fingers in a perfunctory touch. I nodded my thanks and took myself across her beige carpeting and into the outer office where a secretary in a light gray suit with a brownish tinge smiled a polite goodbye.

The public library had provided a list of Magda Bryce's civic and social activities and I was making my way through the list. Next stop, Orchestra Hall and someone from WAMSO, the Women's Association of the Minnesota Symphony Orchestra. They're active in providing financial and other support for the orchestra. Every year they stage a big elegant Symphony Ball. It's one of the few really dress-up affairs left in society these days. It was at the Symphony Ball a couple of years ago that I met Catherine Mckerney.

Minneapolis's Symphony Hall is not like many others. Probably not like any others. The design is something I'd call functional modernity. Or maybe modern functionality.

The office in Symphony Hall was just a couple of blocks

away over on Nicollet Mall, so I strolled on over. The office staff was busy with ringing telephones, people scurrying here and there, and no one important in charge.

I sort of oozed around the small office and pulled up my most ingratiating image. After all, we Minnesotans tend to assume *nice* first. And here was this short, slender, pleasant-appearing fellow who just popped in for some casual commiseration.

"It certainly was a shock. Magda Bryce has always been one of the nicest, hardest-working people around. It got so we almost always called her first." The speaker was a short blonde woman who'd been sitting at the desk nearest the door when I sauntered in.

"Until about six months ago," countered a very young man with a small ring in one ear as he hurried by.

"Oh, Kevin," said the short blonde, grinning and covering her mouth. "Just because you had a little tiff with her." She stopped and covered her mouth again. It was the third time she'd done it since I arrived. I wondered if she had bad teeth.

Kevin returned from the other side of the office. "It wasn't that at all. She'd just turned into this moody bitch. At least sometimes."

"Kevin, right?" I asked. I stuck out my hand but he ignored it, kept both hands on an untidy pile of papers he was carrying.

"I read she was murdered. Is that right? Hardly any one will talk about it. Do they know who did it? I bet it was her husband, that big-time lawyer."

"Kevin-n-n..." warned the blonde.

"You're correct," I said insinuating myself around the corner of the desk so as to partially block the blonde's view. "She was murdered all right. What do you mean, she turned moody?"

"It's just that she seemed to have mood swings all of a sudden. And she'd forget stuff. One day I called her to get her opinion on a letter and she just hung up on me."

"Why was that odd?"

"Well, up to then, she'd been a perfect lady. I mean she was always so sweet and even-tempered, never complained. Maybe she was doing drugs." Kevin shrugged elaborately and turned away.

"Kevin!" The short blonde acted shocked. Gossip about the volunteers was discouraged in some quarters. "Mr. Sean? What did you say you wanted?"

"I wanted to talk with your director of volunteers. But you told me she's out of town." I smiled down at her. "So I guess we could say you can't help me with my request."

My next stop was North Memorial Hospital in Robbinsdale, an aging, inner-ring suburb, northwest of Minneapolis. Magda Bryce had been active in their volunteer program too. The director, a chubby, no-nonsense woman with black hair and intense black eyes took me to her office and shut the door as soon as I announced my mission.

Mrs. Hilger, she said her name was. The plastic tag on her ample bosom said Carly. "Now, exactly what is it you wish to know, Mr. Sean?"

Here was a woman with no hesitations about my name. She'd probably seen dozens of oddities in that department. "I'm a private detective, Mrs. Hilger. I've been asked to look into the circumstances surrounding the unfortunate death of Magda Bryce. This visit is merely background." I tried to sound stern, a little weary, as if I'd made the same speech hundreds of times before. It was a little difficult, considering that if Mrs. Hilger had leaned forward, she'd have smothered me to death in her bosoms. After a moment of thought, she went around her desk and sank into the chair, gesturing me to another beside the desk.

"Ask your questions," she said.

"Is there anything you'd care to tell me about her? Any general comment?"

"No." Mrs. Hilger leaned forward and rested her bosom on the desktop. Stared at me. I figured she'd answer any questions that didn't violate her sense of privacy and the stringent legalities of the hospital trade. But after all, I wasn't asking about a patient, was I?

"Was Mrs. Bryce ever a patient here, that you recall?"

"Next question."

"How often did she volunteer here?"

"Ten to fifteen hours monthly, like a lot of our volunteers."

"What did she do at the hospital?"

"She was not a candy-striper, so she didn't work on the medical floors except to run errands. She did telephone service, answered mail for patients, some office work."

We went through a series of questions, most of which Mrs. Hilger answered. The ones she rebuffed were those that dealt with specific relations.

"She was a pleasant, efficient volunteer, reliable, dependable. She always called in at least two days before her scheduled work."

"And can you recall when she last worked at the hospital?"

"I don't have to recall it, my records are detailed and complete. As it happens, I do recall." Her eyes flicked to a calendar hanging on the wall behind me. "Mrs. Bryce was assigned to the front office for two half days, July sixteenth and July twenty-second." Suddenly her professional mask slipped a little. She looked down at her clasped hands and sighed. "She was a good person. I really liked Mrs. Bryce. That's why that last day was so odd."

I waited. Finally, after several seconds of silence, I asked, "In what way was it odd?"

"She seemed different somehow. She forgot where the supply cabinet was. And she wasn't as warm. She was remote, distracted, as if she had some heavy burden on her mind. Perhaps she just wasn't feeling well. But I did mention it to Mr. Bryce when he came by to pick her up at the end of her shift."

"Did he do that frequently? Pick her up?"

"No. As a matter of fact, that was the first time that I can recall. But I don't always see the volunteers when they leave. I mentioned to Mr. Bryce that I hoped Mrs. Bryce would be feeling better."

"What was his reaction?"

"He just smiled and nodded, said it was probably the medication she was taking."

Really? I thought. There'd been nothing in the medical report or anywhere else that Magda Bryce had been on any kind of medication. Not even aspirin.

"Thank you for your help, Mrs. Hilger." Mrs. Hilger smiled her professional smile as I let myself out of her office.

Chapter 33

THE PHONE RANG, disturbing the afternoon calm, and Alain Russol's voice penetrated my mental stupor. No, no. I don't do drugs and everybody knows I rarely drink to excess. But I'd just spent several hours in what to me are mind-numbing routine office tasks. When I stop to think about it, which is almost never, I bet most people who dream of opening their own businesses, never mind what in, wouldn't if they knew they'd spend almost as much time doing the business of their businesses, instead of the real business, if you take my meaning.

Where was I? Oh, yeah, entering data in the computer. The telephone buzzed and it's my Cleveland connection. "I have a preliminary report," informed Mr. Russol.

"You going to fax it?" I asked.

"Sure."

"My fax ladies have gone home. I don't want the report sitting in their office overnight." The chances of anyone finding it were so remote as to be nonexistent. But it went against my natural instincts to leave confidential information floating about, even in someone's locked office.

"You have a fax-modem on your computer, right?"

"Yeah, I think so," I said cautiously. "Can't you just send the fax tomorrow?"

"I'm going out of town later tonight. D'you want to wait until I get back?"

"Not really. But—"

"Look, Sean, you can do this. Besides, you need to get into the twenty-first century. I'll talk you through it."

I sighed. "All right. I'll give it a try." And so, with a few false starts, I managed to receive my first-ever fax, right there in my computer. I even saved it on my hard drive. After Alain and I separated our computers, we reconnected by phone while I scanned the report. "Santangelo looks like a clean, upstanding citizen."

"That's my reading. It's only been a couple of days, but I can't find anything that isn't strictly on the up and up."

"Guy was really poor starting out."

"Poorer than dirt, as they like to say around here."

"I noticed from the family picture my client supplied that they have only one daughter. But you report she was a twin."

"Right. In the section on Santangelo's family, you'll discover Ellen Santangelo had twin girls. The one in the picture was named Magda."

"Geeze, you're telling me Magda Bryce was a twin?"

"Correct. That's the only real tragedy in the Santangelo's entire married history."

"Did the other one die a baby?"

"Nope. The twins were their first kids. The Santangelos married real young. Ellen wasn't married when the twins were conceived. The story is that in order to avoid having both kids taken by the welfare system, they turned over one of them to a relative. But they never got her back."

Russol recounted this sad story in a matter-of-fact voice, but I was getting serious warning prickles.

"What sort of family is the Santangelos?"

"Close. Supportive. A lot of fun to be around."

"Odd," I said.

"Do you have something I don't know?" Russol was quick to pick up on me.

"I'm not sure," I said. "But doesn't it seem odd to you that a close supportive family, according to your finding, would give away a baby, no matter how poor they were? And, unless the baby died, why were they never reunited?"

"Yeah, when you put it that way, it is a bit strange. You want me to do some more checking on the Santangelos?"

"Definitely. And Alain, concentrate on finding that twin girl or what happened to her. I'll take anything else that comes along, but that's now my main question."

"Uh, okay, but it'll have to wait until next week. I have a little vacation planned."

"Double your usual rates if you put off the vacation a few days." There was a pause, then Russol sighed through the phone.

"Geeze, my wife is gonna kill me for postponing this trip, but you got it, Sean."

Yes! I silently high-fived myself, thanked Russol, and put the phone down.

Chapter 34

IT WAS TIME to call my client and make a preliminary report. Long ago I'd discovered it was a mistake to take on an assignment and just go off and do the job. I lost a couple of plum contracts early in my P.I. career because I didn't contact my employer to make progress reports. Now I always do, even when there isn't anything substantive to report.

I'll call the client and say, "No problems, nothing to report, just calling to let you know I'm on the job." Total waste of time if you ask me, but the client is king. I'm a quick learner, especially from my mistakes. I never run into dark alleys, especially with good-looking women in high heels.

Except when I forget.

So I called. Not Harcourt, Saint Martin, Saint Martin, Bryce, et cetera. First, I didn't think the old man would be there, and second, I remembered he was handling this investigation outside the office. I also remembered I hadn't gotten a retainer or a contract.

A small oversight there.

So I called the mansion on the peaceful shore of Lake Minnetonka. A strange female voice answered. "Saint Martins."

"This is Sean Sean. May I please speak with Mr. Saint Martin?"

Long pause. "I'm sorry, that isn't possible. Mr. Saint Martin ... junior ... is not available."

I was surprised. I hadn't known that Saint Martin had a son named after him. "No, excuse me, I mean senior. I want to speak with Mr. Saint Martin, senior."

"What did you say your name is, sir?"

Breeding, culture, a good education in that voice. But who was she? "My name is Sean Sean. I'm doing some work for Mr. Saint Martin."

"Work? You mean here at the house? Are you a contractor?"

Exactly, I thought, but not the kind you probably mean. "If Mr. Saint Martin isn't available, may I speak to Mrs. Saint Martin?" I wasn't about to tell some stranger why I was calling or what kind of contractor I was.

"Hold on, if you please. I'll see if she's available."

I heard the kind of knocks and noises you get when someone carelessly sets down a receiver. I listened intently. With the line open, there was no telling what kind of incautious remark I might pick up. I was disappointed. Nothing, just the sounds of silence, of an empty room. After several minutes a new voice. "Yes, Mr. Sean, this is Mrs. Saint Martin."

"I have a preliminary report for your husband on the matter we discussed a few days ago. I'd like to talk with him or run out there, if he prefers. I thought you could tell me which would be better."

"I'm so sorry, Mr. Sean. Neither is possible. You see, my husband is dead. He died of a cerebral hemorrhage early last night."

"My God. I'm very sorry, Mrs. Saint Martin."

"Thank you. In a way, it was a blessing," she said obscurely. "I ... I'm not clear on the protocol of these things, but I expect I shall wish to receive your report at some point." Her voice, which had wavered badly over the facts of Ephraim Saint Martin's death, was firming up with every word. "Mr. Sean. Please keep all of this very confidential ... yes, thank you for your condolences. It's a great shock to everyone." Her voice changed again. Apparently someone had passed within hearing. "I will contact you. Goodbye, sir." She hung up.

I placed the receiver back in its cradle. More questions. She hadn't wanted someone there to know who she was talking to. Why? Did she know the purpose of my investigation? Should I give her the report? After all, *she* wasn't my client, Saint Martin *was*—had been.

Shit. I felt as if I'd taken a hard jab to my gut. Ephraim Harcourt Saint Martin and I had never been friends. Hell, we weren't even friendly enemies. But I knew I'd miss reading about the old man's courtroom exploits, about his successes. The city had lost an icon, a defining member of its ruling class.

I felt the way I felt after attending my fifteen-year high school reunion. Now there was a mistake I'd never repeated. Most of my classmates had gone on to college, but I went on to work. And after college, most had begun building stellar careers, if they were to be believed. And why not? I think one of my classmates was even employed by Harcourt, Saint Martin, Saint Martin, et cetera. I looked around sometime during the evening and realized that the people who hadn't shown up for the reunion were probably those who hadn't been so successful.

Maybe they had bad marriages. It was too early for the missing to have died, that would come later. I'd pretty much enjoyed myself in high school, even if I hadn't made the football team. Or the honor roll. I'd had music and photography and a few close friends. None of them had shown. The bankers, young insurance execs, a couple of government bureaucrats, even a politician, they all put in an appearance. Doing the power dinner. Me, I was a private investigator. I quickly discovered I owned a kind of parlor game when I answered the question about my career. What would the reaction be? Everybody had some kind of reaction. But the essence of the reunion had unsettled me. I thought I was pretty good at what I did and was getting better. But it was clear my classmates didn't agree. The classmates I had never really known wouldn't be calling for a casual drink, or an invitation to dinner. Not that they'd done so before the reunion. A mournful sense of isolation and being looked down on had crept over me.

Now a similar feeling had coalesced into a sense of loss. I hadn't had much of a relationship with Ephraim Harcourt Saint Martin in the past. With his death, I never would.

Chapter 35

THE MORNING OF Ephraim Saint Martin's funeral arrived as a clone of several previous days. It was hot and humid early. I contemplated changing my mind about leaving my air-conditioned home and briefly considered skipping the funeral and the cemetery service. When I stepped outside to collect the morning paper, it felt as if I'd been shoved into a blast furnace. To say the sun was oppressive is to understate the case.

Catherine called to suggest that we meet at the church, so we'd have separate transportation after the ceremonies. Since the funeral would be held in a Lutheran church in Minnetonka, burial in a cemetery even farther west, and Catherine had a business appointment later in Chanhassen, separate cars was the most convenient arrangement.

I arrived at the church after a long, hot, sweaty trip across Minneapolis. Something had gone haywire with my car's air conditioner, so I was already in a bad mood. Funerals always put me off anyway. I'm not sure why. Perhaps it's the sight of all those insincere people gathering to celebrate the passing of an enemy, or a competitor. Yes, I understand that for many people it's a chance to say goodbye, to create closure, but sometimes the public displays of grief are too much to be believed.

Never mind. I parked the car a good two blocks away. On the sidewalk I looked up and spotted Catherine coming from the opposite direction. The sun was already stifling and we hadn't even entered the church.

I was a little surprised that the funeral was sited at such

an out-of-the-way location. Considering the prominence of the man, I suspected there'd be hordes of people turning out to pay last respects, or to gloat. Hell, just the partners and associates at Harcourt, Saint Martin, Saint Martin, Bryce, et cetera, alone, would overflow a small-town church. Still, this was the family church, I supposed, and who was I to question the location of the service?

Catherine slid her arm into the crook of my elbow and we went up the broad stone steps to the large, dark-wood doors. I discovered my first observations were off the mark. A clever architect had laid out the church so that its size was minimized when seen from the street. The land itself was a sloping greensward that ran down to a small bay at the southernmost end of Lake Minnetonka. It was a long, narrow bay that hooked to the left just before it opened into the main lake. The bay wasn't even named on most maps.

The main sanctuary was laid out parallel to the street. We entered the main doors and were directed left down a long, stone hallway of warm, golden-hued granite to the far end of the sanctuary. When we went through the wide doors, I discovered a vaguely Gothic design of arching overhead wooden beams of a lighter hue than the beams I was familiar with from pictures of old European churches. The room was large, long and light. Lots of windows with religiously themed stained-glass designs let in a lot of light.

The place was not air-conditioned. Big pedestal fans scattered through the hall noiselessly moved the water-weighted air about.

We stopped about a quarter of the way down the central aisle. I looked around and realized the building was shaped like a traditional cross with the raised altar at the junction of the arms and the body. We were standing in the nave, facing the altar and the chancel which lay along the main stem of the design, behind the public side of the altar.

"Where shall we sit?" Catherine murmured from my side.

"Someplace where we can see most of the people who show up, but without being too obvious," I replied.

Above my head, a speaker affixed to the ceiling popped and snapped. The hum and sibilants of murmured conversations died away and people already seated looked around as if expecting an announcement. There was an air of anticipation that died quickly when nothing else happened. I looked at the dais and the raised podium. To the right and left at the foot of the four broad steps leading up to the altar and the nave the layout had been modified from the traditional. Instead of rows of pews fixed to the floor, there were rows of chairs set at an angle to the altar and the main rows of pews. We discovered that when we went to the last chairs farthest from the altar, a slight turn of the head brought almost all the congregation into view.

"Why do you suppose they have these chairs?" whispered my companion.

"Look at the floor," I whispered back. My keen powers of observation, honed by years of activity, had immediately noticed that instead of the carpet in the central aisle, we were now on a parquet floor. "I imagine that for some activities they clear out the chairs and use the space for some kind of performances."

The place was rapidly filling and the unseen fingers of an organist began to softly add atmosphere with her somber tones. We fell silent, and for a time addressed our private inner beings and watched more people coming in. The immediate family was seated across the central aisle from our position, all except for the smallest children—grandchildren, I supposed—wearing appropriately subdued suits and dresses. I recognized Preston Bryce, but not his male companion. P. Hall, the firm's receptionist, appeared toward the far side of the church, and farther back I glimpsed a veiled woman in a black hat. She must be hot, I thought.

The widow, Mrs. Saint Martin, appeared from a door somewhere down the wing opposite our seats and sat down. She too was veiled but I could clearly see her face when she raised her head after being seated and looked directly at me. If there was a telepathic message there, my receiver must have been out of order.

The service or ceremony went about as expected, except it went on for a while. A great many people had decided to pay their last respects and had made an appearance. The group of dignitaries, politicians, and sycophants included the mayors of Minneapolis and St. Paul, a senator and a congressman, a couple of police officials, the president of the Minnesota Bar Association, several lawyers I recognized and a few I didn't, et cetera, et cetera. Unfortunately, most of them felt constrained to eulogize the deceased. That and their dress was how I knew the strangers were lawyers. It made for a long afternoon. The rising postmeridian temperatures and the mass of packed humanity added to a general feeling of intensifying discomfort. The odor of human perspiration and the chemical masking attempts became a noticeable presence in the church.

Eventually we were released. As Catherine and I made our way slowly out of the church, we encountered some of the attorneys who worked at Harcourt, Saint Martin, et cetera. Some ignored me; several, whom I knew only on sight, seemed to make it a point to come over and shake my hand. I decided they were really interested in getting closer to my lovely companion. After all, my companion was wearing shoes with modest heels, but they still added to her height advantage.

We weren't invited to any of the after-funeral soirees, but we went to the gravesite for what became an overlong and fulsome consecration of the ground and its next inhabitant. Standing on the edge of the smaller crowd, I had a better chance to observe, so I didn't mind. The graveyard was still, the birds and critters stunned into drowsiness by the sun flaring out of a cloudless, windless, sky.

After several minutes of not listening to the service, I noticed a tall, middle-aged man approaching, slowly working his way through the fringes of the crowd. He stopped close in front of me and said softly, "Mrs. Saint Martin appreciates your presence. She wonders if you could arrange to see her at the house sometime in the next few days."

I recognized him as the same man who had found me in the restaurant and delivered the invitation to visit Saint Martin not too many days before he died. "Of course. I'll call and arrange an appointment."

The man nodded and moved off heading in the same direction he'd been going when he stepped beside me.

"I've seen that woman before," said Catherine suddenly. Her right hand squeezed my elbow.

"What woman?"

"The one in the heavy veil. She's standing across from us beside that big oak."

"You mean the one from the church?" I'd commented as we left the church that it must have been hot under the veil.

"Yes, but that's not where I mean."

"How can you tell? Her face is completely obscured by that veil."

"It slipped aside just a minute ago when she turned her head. I caught a glimpse of her profile."

"That's hardly—"

"There's more, Sean. I thought she seemed familiar somehow when I saw her at the church. Her hands, her way of moving. You know I always look at people's hands."

I nodded. "What's your point?" I knew she had one, we weren't engaging in idle chatter here.

"I have the feeling I've seen her some other times before, but one of the times was at the Saint Martins. She's the woman I described who looked just like Magda Bryce. The one who was watching from an upstairs window."

"C'mon," I said, and snapped a glance toward the woman in question. She had moved, still across the gravesite, now she was sidling unobtrusively through the mourners at the rear of the crowd.

I took Catherine's hand and we started our own sidle, toward a small planting of bushes beside a huge oak that shaded part of the family plot. I turned around to guide Catherine back a few steps between two people. When I turned back, the woman had reversed her direction and now she moved back across the gentle slope where we stood, in the direction of the road and transportation. Her back was to us and I watched the way her body moved as she made her way more quickly now, to the road. Without causing a scene, we hurried as fast as possible back toward the gate and the line of waiting cars. I lost sight of her. I waved Catherine around the gravestones to her left while I made a circle to the right. There were plenty of stones high and wide enough to conceal the mysterious woman in black, and we spent several minutes trying to catch a glimpse of her or figure out which direction she'd gone. Unfortunately for us, those extra minutes gave the woman a longer lead. I heard the snarl of a high-powered engine starting out in the road. I bolted toward the sound but I was too late. A black Porsche Spider convertible with its top up pulled out of the line of cars and went by the gate to the Saint Martin plot while I was still yards away. As the car went by, I caught a glimpse of the driver's profile.

"Did you see her? Was it Magda?" Catherine's panted

questions whistled past my ears. Sweat dripped down my face. I shook my head and threw a glance back at the gathered mourners. None I could see were paying the least attention.

"No, officer, sir. No ID and no license plate. Nada." I favored Catherine with a moist smile and dragged out a handkerchief to mop my damp forehead. Here's the intrepid investigator at work, I thought, laid low by the heat and humidity.

Chapter 36

QUESTIONS, QUESTIONS, questions. The list of questions was still outdistancing the list of answers. There was another consideration. Who paid? Where was the money? I'd been running up a lot of time and other expenses. Like the bill that would soon arrive from Russol in Cleveland. My attention to cases pending, as well as calls to my list of contacts to remind them of my exceptional detecting skills and availability, were all on the neglected list. I was going to have to get some money coming in or file bankruptcy.

A heavy knock sounded at the office door. When it opened, a Federal Express delivery person stood there with a flat package. I signed and she left. Since the package was flat, I didn't see how it could contain a letter bomb. I ripped it open. It was the report from Alain Russol in Cleveland.

He had reached a dead end in tracing the Santangelo's missing baby. Apparently, local authorities hadn't been involved. The nearly destitute parents had somehow relieved themselves of the responsibility for one of the two girls shortly after birth. According to the report, a family member had agreed to take one of the twins on a temporary basis, sort of a limited-term daughter.

Russol's report indicated that a lot of his information was assumption, speculation and inference. Hearsay. I'd expected that because he had to stay away from talking to family members. The story was that after two years away from Cleveland, during which Santangelo got on his feet, they returned to their roots, now with an infant boy as well.

But when they went to claim their daughter, the family, temporary daughter and all, had disappeared.

Russol suggested there were faint rumblings about some kind of illegalities involved, but he emphasized that's all they were, rumblings. In any case, the Santangelos had never ceased to search for their child. Russol concluded his inquiries when he'd been tipped that the Santangelos had learned about his investigation.

Great. Innuendo, inference, and supposition. But it was a report, together with the business and personal information on Santangelo that I'd been tasked to provide. Now, if I could find a receptive client, perhaps I'd get the money promised. Then I could stay in business for another month or so. I called the Saint Martin ranchette.

Yes, Mrs. Saint Martin was in. Yes, she said, she'd be pleased to see me in an hour or so. I thought about Catherine while I drove west to Minnetonka. It occurred to me that I'd been doing that more and more. Whenever Catherine was away from me, I'd start wondering where she was, what she was doing, who she was with, and if she was thinking about me. Getting a bit obsessive, I thought.

Again, or still, the gate to the Saint Martin home was open and I wheeled in without pause. There were a couple of automobiles in the forecourt that I didn't recognize. As I started up the steps, the door burst open and an upset-looking Preston Bryce stalked out. He favored me with a single glance I would only describe as malevolent. A young woman in jeans and cutoff tee shirt stood at the open door. She let me in. I turned to ask her for Mrs. Saint Martin, but she went out on the snap of her gum and shut the door behind her. I turned and saw Mrs. Saint Martin coming toward me across the hall.

We greeted each other formally and went to a corner of

the living room. Mrs. Saint Martin didn't bother to explain who the girl was. The place we settled had floor-to-ceiling windows on one wall and the drapes were pulled back to give us a nice panoramic view of the lake and the lawn leading down to a narrow strip of stones that passed for a beach at the water's edge.

"Would you care for some coffee or tea?" Mrs. Saint Martin asked softly.

"Thank you, no."

"I'm not sure of the protocol or legalities in this matter, but let me say this and then your conscience may guide you to the right decision. Although it was my late husband who appeared to employ you to make certain inquiries, in fact, Mr. Sean, it is I who am your employer in this matter. It is my private trust on which the check would have been drawn to pay your charges, and it would have been my signature on that check. We decided, Ephraim and I, it was the best course to conceal that small fact from you until you had completed your investigation." She smiled a tiny meek, smile. "I am quite wealthy in my own right, Mr. Sean, and I am the one who desired to employ you. Against my husband's initial advice, I might add. He insisted that he be the one to interview you, even though it took a good deal of his waning strength to do so."

"I see." Did I see? How was I to know if this was truth or dare? She could be scamming me in order to get her hands on the report. I decided I didn't think so.

"Let me explain a bit more. It is of course possible that my husband discussed this assignment with me before his death, which is why I know the details, but again, you'll have to be the judge of that."

She paused a moment and looked away, organizing her thoughts, I assumed. "You were employed to do a background check, using the utmost discretion, of a certain family in Cleveland, Ohio. That family is named Santangelo. Am I not correct?"

"So far, you're spot on." I sometimes use phrases that belong in the mouth of someone from another place. No particular reason, it's just part of my detective mystique, whatever that is.

"I am aware, Mr. Sean, that you haven't been paid and since I believe you have a report, preliminary though it may be, I wish now to reimburse you, at least partially, for your expenses to this time." With that, Mrs. Saint Martin, turned to the small table at her elbow. She flipped open a flat leather case which turned out to be a check book. She picked up a fine-looking pen, wrote out a check, blotted the ink, no common ball-point for this lady, and with a subtle flourish, offered it to me. It was for the nice round sum of five thousand dollars.

I had the strangest feeling I should genuflect or bow to this woman who was growing larger in stature by the moment. The feeling quickly went away. Instead I merely nodded and said, "Thank you very much, Mrs. Saint Martin, this will do nicely until I'm able to tote up the final bill. I'll provide details, omitting only the name of the operative I employed on your behalf."

Her eyebrows went up. "Was that wise, to bring a third party into this? You were asked to treat this matter with utmost secrecy."

"I've known the man for years. He's thoroughly reliable, and a complete professional. It took much less time than if I'd gone there myself. He was discreet and stopped as soon as he detected some interest in his investigation by the target parties. As far as he knows, I'm the client. Your husband's name didn't come up. There was another factor that influenced my decision."

"Explain yourself." Again the lifted eyebrow. She maintained eye contact, sitting upright in her chair.

"Frankly, I couldn't decide if this was a legitimate contract or not. I've been involved in several ways with the murders of Magda Bryce and Polly La Famme. I considered it a strong possibility that I was being diverted with a job that would take me several days, weeks even, if I went to Cleveland."

"You could have rejected the job."

"Yes, that's so. But I decided to take a middle ground when I found out that the man I employed was still active in Cleveland."

"I see. How long has that young woman been in your employ?"

"I'm sorry, I don't—" *Oops.* Mrs. Saint Martin was talking about Catherine.

"Perhaps I should be asking a different question. How long have you been involved with Ms. Mckerney?" She smiled at me.

Observant lady, I thought. "Maybe you'd like a job?" I said. "I've known Catherine long enough to become quite attracted to her and to trust her. But I think we should get to the report I have for you." I took the report from its Fed-Ex envelope and held it. "The target family, Santangelo, is a hardworking, upstanding part of the community. Santangelo himself owns and still operates a very successful plumbing business, and he and his wife are active in civic affairs of various kinds. Their three children were apparently well behaved and, unlike their parents, well educated. It wasn't always like that. Their first and second children were girls, identical twins, apparently. Their third was a son, who became active in the business." I paused to see if I'd shocked or at least startled her. All Mrs. Saint Martin gave me was polite interest. "Santangelo was poor, desperate, probably shocked to discover they were saddled with two kids, not just one.

"Apparently they decided that to give everyone a better chance, they'd temporarily give up one of the girls."

"You mean to say they placed one of the twins for adoption?"

"No, although that must have been an option. Instead, they asked a cousin to take one of the baby girls on a temporary basis, until they could work themselves into better circumstances."

"Fascinating, Mr. Sean. How much of this is factual and how much mere suspicion?"

Astute lady, Mrs. Saint Martin. "Good question. The facts are twin girls were born and one disappeared shortly, with no official record of what happened. I mean, there's no recorded death of the baby and nothing to indicate adoption or even placement in foster care. There was no police investigation, either. We assume therefore, she's still alive. The story we've pieced together is that Santangelo moved out of Ohio to Pennsylvania for a few years, leaving one of the twins with a relative.

"Santangelo worked hard and began to have success. Five or so years later he returns to Cleveland and establishes a plumbing business. But when they try to retrieve their infant daughter, the cousin and his whole family have disappeared. They just dropped out of sight. In spite of years of looking, the Santangelos have never found a trace of that missing daughter. They are still looking for her. They must have spent a small fortune by now."

Mrs. Saint Martin was silent, looking inward. Finally she stirred herself and I came back into the moment. "Excuse me, Mr. Sean. This is a very sad story you have brought me. That poor girl, and her parents. Never to have learned the fate of their child. I wonder. Do you suppose it would be possible someday to tell them, the Santangelos, assuming one somehow found out about that child, but to do it anonymously?"

I looked steadily at her for a moment. "Possible? Certainly. But assuming that the recently murdered Magda Bryce is one of the Santangelo twins, it might be kinder not to say anything." I leaned forward, watching for her reaction.

"You are making an interesting assumption, Mr. Sean." Her gaze became firmer, I could almost feel it.

"Tell me, Mrs. Saint Martin, did the Santangelo's attend Magda's funeral?"

"I'm not—there were a great many people present."

"Easy enough to check."

She glanced down and then returned her gaze to me. "Of course. You are correct, both in your facts and in most of your assumptions. Magda Bryce was a Santangelo twin and her parents did attend the funeral." I became aware of someone approaching. Mrs. Saint Martin glanced over my shoulder and then returned her gaze to me. "This matter may not be finished, but my time is. I presume that our conversation today has been quite confidential. I expect we may need to talk again."

"Have no doubts on that score, Mrs. Saint Martin. I'd have no business if I wasn't closemouthed. If I can be of additional help, please call." I rose and took her offered hand, pressing her fingers lightly. Then I gave her the report.

As I turned to leave, passing the oncoming shorts-and-gum-snapping person, Mrs. Saint Martin said to my back, "Thank you for coming, Mr. Sean. You have been most helpful."

Chapter 37

"I'm in my office, hon." Catherine's voice floated to me as I entered her digs. She'd made me a gift of a key a few days earlier. We'd talked about it. We weren't ready to move in together. Yet. She was justifiably proud of her place, it was a sign of her success and independence and she liked living in town. I, on the other hand, had lived in the city and was happy with my suburban location. Besides, the house in Roseville had been a gift from a very satisfied client a few years back, and I felt a certain obligation.

There were other considerations. We could afford two places. Mine was paid for, after all. The implications of moving in together were a little more than either one of us wanted to deal with just then. It meant giving up a certain amount of independence and even though I was pretty sure I would never feel about a woman the way I felt about Catherine Mckerney, moving in together would necessitate several adjustments for both of us. What would I do with my guns?

Her present to me of her apartment key was as far as she was willing to go at the moment. I'd never before favored one of my lady friends with the key to my house. Turn about is fair play and I knew this was something I wanted to do in return. I'd stopped at a locksmith on the way in from the Saint Martins. I was about to present her with my house key As with her key, it would come with small limits. No dropping in. No showing up unannounced, no prowling around each other's abode when the owner wasn't in attendance. We were going to go to careful lengths to stay out of each others' personal space—except at certain, mutually agreeable times. My key was in a little box, wrapped in gold paper. A gift, as it were, a small token of my love and esteem.

I kicked off my loafers and padded into the bedroom-cum-office where Catherine sat at her computer, scrolling through some document or other. When I looked at the side of her head I stopped. "Well!"

"What?" She glanced at me and then back to the screen.

"You've cut your hair!"

"Yes. Like it?" Where it had been shoulder length before, her hair was now in a shaggy cut that tapered from her ears to a point that rested at the nape of her slender neck. Now she had raggedy bangs that hung over her forehead and brushed the round narrow-rimmed glasses perched on her nose. "It's a lot easier to take care of."

"I guess. It's just a bit of a shock. I liked your hair the way it was."

"Well, I just wanted a change. It'll grow back." She threw me a quick smile.

"Okay, I guess." I approached her chair. "What're you doing?"

"Remember a long time ago I told you, I'm a mystery buff. I like to read crime novels." She waved one hand at a crowded bookcase behind her. "I subscribe to a couple of mystery news groups on the Internet. This one's called Dorothy L. You know, after the writer, Dorothy L Sayers. All of us who subscribe share an interest in anything to do with mysteries."

"Uh-huh."

"There are librarians, writers, policemen, fans. Well, we're all fans. It's a lot of fun." She was scanning and scrolling through an apparently endless series of messages.

"Okay." I put the small gold-wrapped box on the desk beside her left hand and put my hands on her shoulders. I started to gently knead her smooth skin. Did I mention she was wearing only a skimpy pair of silk panties?

Catherine arched her back. "Umm. A little lower. Harder. Feels good."

I continued to knead her back and shoulder muscles. I leaned over and kissed the top of her head. She smelled sweet with a faint odor of dried perspiration.

"Been working out?"

"Yep. Oh, right there, on my left shoulder. You know, lover, I should teach you massage. You've got good hands. Good instincts, too." Catherine canted her head up and favored me with another smile. "Then I wouldn't have to go to one of my people. What's in the box?"

"Open it." My voice caught and I cleared my throat, continued to rub her back. She reached the end of the messages on the screen and closed the file with a deft click of the mouse under her right fingers. Her left hand picked up the box and she tore off the wrapping. When she bent her head and opened the box to take out the key, I stopped, left my hands resting lightly on her shoulders. I watched in silence as her strong slender fingers traced the jagged outlines of the key.

"Ah, yes. Thank you, my dear. Keys representing trust." Catherine arched her head up so I could see her face. She puckered her lips, inviting my kiss, which I was only too happy to present. What started out as a quick buss lengthened until our tongues began a more intense play.

When we broke, a breathless minute later, my pulse had elevated noticeably. "Come in the living room and give me your news." Catherine smiled and tugged my hand. She snagged a blue chambray shirt from a chair and slipped it on as we went down the hall to the living room couch.

"Games," I said. "There are games going on amongst the Saint Martins and the law firm. Mrs. Saint Martin is determined to sort things out. I bet on her. She is one strong lady." I told her about my interview and the report from Russol. When I had finished, Catherine nodded.

"What do you think now?"

"I think Preston Bryce, the dead woman, Polly La Famme, maybe Magda Bryce, and the mysterious woman at the funeral were all involved in something that got the two women killed."

"What about that domination woman, what was her name?"

"Lucinda, Luscious Lucinda," I said.

"Right."

"Suppose," I said, leaning back on the couch and lacing my hands behind my head, "suppose both Preston and Magda Bryce got involved with Lucinda. Suppose further that Polly was also involved."

I stared at the beige carpet. "I just remembered something. When I went to see Lucinda and she put me in that head piece, I looked in the mirror after. There was a reddish band across my forehead where the strap had pressed."

"Yes, you told me about it."

"An hour later, I could still see the faint band. Now I remember that when I interviewed pasty Preston Bryce, he had a similar mark on his forehead. I remember it because he was so colorless otherwise. And I'm sure Lucinda recognized his picture when we showed it to her at the strip club." My voice rose slightly as some of the pieces began to fit together in a discernible pattern.

"Proof? Supposition?" said Catherine. "And how does Magda's death fit?"

"No proof, but a bit more now than just wild supposition. Hooks, snags, places to go and wiggle the structure to see what falls off. As for Mrs. Preston Bryce, remember Magda had whip marks on her body. If she was an unwilling participant and decided to blow the whistle, that might have got her shot."

"That seems extreme, but back up. What structure?"

"Oh, there's a structure all right. I can't describe it all and I realize there are missing pieces, but I can put my hands on part of it. The part that could be motive. If I'm right, a firm like Harcourt, Saint Martin, Saint Martin, Bryce, et cetera couldn't stand the notoriety of an important partner being involved in something most people think is aberrant behavior."

"Preston Bryce? Who's ever heard of him?"

"Few outside the corporate world. He's not a high-profile trial lawyer. He never appears in court, but he's a key player in that firm, in other ways. He does civil stuff, tort law, mergers, acquisitions, due diligence, stuff like that. It'd be a major problem if he turns out flaky."

"What's due diligence?"

"Fact finding. A firm being acquired or merged has to reveal all, and the process is referred to as due diligence. It's an important part of any merger. In a big deal, like a takeover or the acquisition of Pillsbury by Grand Met, due diligence is vital. Relies heavily on the reliability of the attorneys, their expertise. Mega bucks are usually involved. That's Preston's specialty. He does acquisitions and mergers all over the country. All over the world, probably. A freaky reputation would kill him."

"Poor choice of words. With Ephraim dead, who do you tell? Mrs. Saint Martin?"

"Well, the big revelation is that Magda Bryce is a Santangelo from Cleveland, Ohio."

"So?"

I went on to repeat the essence of my report to Mrs. Saint Martin. "My suspicion is that Magda's missing twin showed up here some months ago, maybe years ago. Why else did Saint Martin ask me to run a check on the Santangelos of

Cleveland? Particularly at this particular time and in this particular secret fashion?"

"Did you discuss this possibility with Mrs. Saint Martin?"

"No. I'm not sure why. Mrs. Saint Martin knew Magda was a Santangelo, but she didn't know Magda was a twin until I reported to her."

"Are you going to tell her? This could be very important."

"Yes, I'll tell her, but I have to think some more about the structure. I wonder if the domination scene is expensive. It must cost a lot more than just popping in to some strip club from time to time."

Catherine stood up and walked to the window.

"I don't think I have all the people and their relationships clear in my mind."

"How long will that take?" Catherine was still standing at the window.

"I dunno, a couple of days I guess. Why?"

"Meanwhile, what do you think Mrs. Saint Martin will be doing?"

"Mrs. Saint Martin?" I glanced at Catherine. There was something in her voice that wasn't there before. "I suppose she'll be doing what she does, recovering from the death of her husband, settling affairs of the estate, talking with members of the firm. The usual. Why?"

"Since you don't yet know who's responsible, isn't that a little dangerous for her?"

I nodded. "Sure, it could be, but she's a smart woman. I assume she'll be discreet."

"Does she know everything you know, and everything you suspect?"

"Mostly. We've never discussed the whipping or the connection between Preston and Lucinda the dominatrix."

"Don't you think she should be told?"

"Catherine, what's your point?"

She whirled around to face me, the tails of the shirt flying out from her body. "Sean! You have to tell Mrs. Saint Martin your suspicions right now. Who else knows? Magda and that woman Polly are dead, probably because they found out some of what you suspect. What if something Mrs. Saint Martin says makes the killer believe she's onto him? If you're right about the connection, Mrs. Saint Martin could be in danger! You can't just leave her to probe this on her own and hope she'll be safe!" I'd never seen Catherine so agitated.

"Hold on. This is all just supposition, with very little fact."

"And you should tell the police. You don't know what they know. They may have some information that'll help. Sean! Don't you see?" She whirled around again, and stalked away from me a few steps, jammed her hands on her hips.

"I can't, Catherine. Not yet. Soon, but not right away. If I start talking about this now, I might blow any chance of finding out the rest of it. If I say anything to Mrs. Saint Martin, she could let something slip. I have to have time to do some more checking. Just a few more days, hours, even." Catherine stood there, feet spread, every line generating outrage. I stood up and faced her.

"More time! You're putting an innocent woman at risk. How can you do that?"

"Catherine—"

"Is the case more important than those people's lives?"

"Of course not. But I have to have more time." Both of us had raised our voices.

"Why, just to inflate your fee? Oh!" She clapped a hand over her mouth and stared at me, wide-eyed.

I stared back. I took a deep breath. "I hope you didn't mean that," I said.

"I—maybe you'd better leave. Before I say something I'll really regret."

I raised my eyebrows at that. What more could she say? "Catherine, please. This is my job. My profession. I do know what I'm doing. It's not just giving somebody a back rub," I snapped.

She stared at me, unblinking, almost as if she'd never seen me before and said, "Just—go. Just leave now. Please."

For a moment, I stood in silence, feeling the chasm between us growing by the second. Then I stepped around her and went to the door. When I looked back, she was still standing as she had been, back straight, an unyielding barrier.

I opened the door and touched her key, safely nestled in my pocket. Then I went out and shut the door quietly behind me.

Chapter 38

CLACK. THE GREASY playing card nicked the edge of my desk and sailed frivolously across the room. I uttered a wordless sound and threw the rest of the deck in a whispered splatter across the room, swept the nascent game of solitaire onto the floor with my arm. *Shit.* I rubbed the bristle on my face. The telephone ringing with a wrong number had roused me from sleep at the ungodly hour of seven that morning. I'd forgotten to set the answering machine. It was two days since I'd seen or talked to Catherine Mckerney. Our split weighed heavily on my mind.

Last night I'd called her, but when her recorded voice came on, I hung up without leaving a message. I was restless, couldn't sleep, even after a couple of cold beers. So I went for a walk. I walked down the road toward the water at Lake Johanna, a mile or so north of my place. It was dark, soft, and I was alone. What should I have expected at one a.m.?

The public beach was at the edge of a medium-sized park. There was a long crescent of sand, a concrete-block concession and lifeguard building, picnic tables, swings, and all the usual accouterments one finds at most Twin Cities public parks. I trudged along the hard wet sand of the crescent, just off the wavelets feeding soundlessly at the lake's edge. Occasionally I stopped to stare at the dark water or reached down and snagged a soggy fragment of wood to pitch back into the lake; and I replayed over again that scene in Catherine's apartment.

In this part of the world, a lone figure, dimly seen striding up and down a public beach, particularly one with homes nearby, isn't likely to be alone for long. A car, with its high beams brightly shining, cruised around the bend in the street, slowed, and descended the short slope into the gravel parking lot behind the beach. I heard the tires scratch the ground. The engine shut down. I thought I heard the whine of a heavy-duty generator before the engine died, but I wasn't sure. The headlights pointed at the lake. They illuminated nothing more substantial than rising vapors from the calm water. I looked around, mindful that I'd been shot at in the too-recent past. The headlights shone over my head, so maybe the occupant of the intruding vehicle wasn't sure of my location. Or maybe he wasn't even aware of my presence. I stood there indecisively for a moment, then backed off a few steps to ease into the darker area of beach.

I wasn't armed; in fact I wasn't wearing all that many clothes. I'd come down to the beach with a vague impulse to skinny dip, but hadn't gone in the lake above my knees. Now what? I dropped to my knees, scuttled sideways, and crawled up the beach toward the lifeguard's shack, until I could make out the outline of the vehicle behind the lights. A car came down County E behind the lot and turned away, toward the south. In the moment the vehicle in the lot was between me and the lights, I saw some rounded knobby things on the roof.

I realized I was peering at an official vehicle, most likely a Ramsey County Sheriff's patrol car. Somebody in one of the dark houses had seen me prowling the beach and called the cops. Not wanting to startle the officer, I slid back down the beach and walked into the center of the headlight spread. Then I walked slowly up the incline again, brushing damp sand from my chest as I went. When I got near the car, a young-sounding male voice said, "Park's closed, sir." As I stepped closer, out of the headlights, the officer pinned me with his flashlight.

"Yeah, Officer, I know. I live up the road, just past County D."

"Got some ID?"

"No, sorry. I've just been walking, thinking, sorting out some issues I'm dealing with right now."

Pause. "What street you live on?"

I told him. Another pause. Apparently he figured he'd take a chance with me, since I seemed to be familiar with the area. "Better take off, Mac. Park's closed." He started the car and I heard the whine of the heavy-duty generator. The officer backed around, flicking off his flashlight as he went.

I shrugged and shoved my hands in my pockets, then started slowly up the gentle hill that took me away from the beach, the lake and back to my empty house. When I crossed New Brighton Road and turned down D, I glanced to my right. About fifty yards from the intersection, a Ramsey County patrol car was idling on the gravel shoulder.

That was last night. Yesterday I'd decided Catherine was right, so with a lot of circumlocution and use of elliptical statements, I informed Mrs. Saint Martin of my concern that she could be vulnerable if she started any action based on the report from Cleveland, or asked the wrong kind of questions, based on our conversations. She pushed me for more but I successfully resisted. Interestingly, Mrs. Saint Martin never threatened to go ahead if I wouldn't answer her questions. We did agree I should have an opportunity to talk with the partners and other employees at the law firm. Mrs. Saint Martin suggested she would call the remaining partners and the administrative manager, somebody named Holmgren, and clear the way. We'd never met, but Mrs. Saint Martin assured me he was easy to pick out of a crowd since he was almost seven feet tall. I didn't recall seeing such a tall man at the funeral, but he must have been there.

I still hadn't heard from Catherine. On the other hand, she hadn't heard from me, either.

I deposited Mrs. Saint Martin's check, which made my banker happy. I paid a few bills, which made those creditors happy. I tried to stay busy with routines that required little constructive thought. It didn't help a whole lot. I was in a funk, no question. Since I couldn't decide what to do about my relationship with Catherine, and I wasn't going to get into the law firm today, I called my friend, Detective Ricardo Simon.

"Hey, my frien' how they hangin'?"

"Ricardo, stop trying to sound like a gang banger," I said. He laughed in my ear. We arranged to meet for a drink at a small bar on Hennepin Avenue, near the Metro State University Minneapolis building. I was on my third beer when Simon made his appearance.

"I suppose you want to know about Walker," he grunted, settling himself in the booth across from me.

I lifted my eyebrows. Actually, I haven't thought about that DB for days."

"Well he's still dead, and we aren't anywhere near closing the case, much less making an arrest."

"Have you checked out that dominatrix, Lucinda?"

"She's on my short list. Maybe you'd care to tell me if you've turned up anything that might help."

"Has your buddy Holt turned up anything on Polly La Famme?"

"Do I look like a sieve? I thought we were gonna just get together for a friendly drink. You're beginning to act like a reporter. Or my boss." Simon drained his glass in one long swallow.

"Another?"

"Sure. Actually, Sean, if you hadn't called, I would have called you."

I signaled the waitress to bring us another round.

"We've discovered a connection between Walker and

La Famme. Another resident of his apartment building thought he recognized Polly from a picture spread. She appears to have visited Walker several times. She's also been seen with men going into or coming out of Gina's apartment."

"You're kidding."

"We think blackmail and its aftermath are the reasons for both Walker's and La Famme's death."

"Which could link somebody in our very prominent law firm to murder."

"Exactly why we're going slow. Busting some low-life's chops on a supposition is one thing, getting arrest warrants for a member of a big-time law firm is another." Simon nodded at his own words, pursed his lips, the way he did when he thought he'd scored a good point.

"Equal justice under law," I murmured to myself. *Right.* The beer was cold and felt good going down my gullet. A lot better than I felt about my life at the moment. I set down the glass and slid my eyes to Ricardo Simon beside me. He was staring into the back bar, at an untidy sea of half-empty bottles and a mirror. "Have you interviewed anyone connected to Harcourt, Saint Martin, et cetera? In connection with Polly L.?"

"Of course. She was living with Preston and Magda Bryce. Naturally we talked to the family."

"Anybody else in the house?"

"No."

"What about Ephraim and Mrs. Saint Martin? They're practically family."

"Well, we went very cautious there. The Saint Martins had their attorney present. We stayed pretty much with confirmation questions about what we were told by Bryce." Simon looked at me, waiting. I wondered if he was holding something back.

"Look, what I may have is pretty iffy. But when I put it together with what you just said, there may be real substance. That dancer, the domination one, Lucinda? She knows Preston. I'm sure of it. Ephraim and Mrs. Saint Martin were concerned about a problem involving the law firm in some way. My gut tells me it's that problem that got Magda and Polly killed."

"And now you're gonna tell me what it is." Simon's tone belied the words.

"No, because I don't know what it is, yet. But it must be connected to Beetlebrow and his attacks on me."

"Who?"

"Sorry. That thug, George Cassidy from Detroit, who mugged me at home and then got killed when Holt tried to arrest him. This all ties together somehow and that law firm is right at the center."

Simon looked at me for a long, silent, minute. "Madre de Dios. Thugs, mugs, two murders, prostitution, and domination. One of our big-time corporate law firms. There must be a lot of money floatin' around in this stew somewhere."

"I wouldn't bet against it."

"When the flag goes up, the stuff is really going to hit the fan." Simon slid off his stool and laid a hand on my shoulder. "I hope you've got a heavy raincoat." He raised his hand and started toward the door. I watched him go, thinking I'd rather just drown in the flying shit if Catherine has disappeared from my life. I had two more beers and went out to find a florist. I would send her roses. Red roses.

Chapter 39

THE ELEVATOR DOORS noiselessly opened. I was on the forty-ninth floor of the IDS. There directly ahead of me were the massive double doors that led to Harcourt, Saint Martin, Saint Martin, Bryce, et cetera. And here I was. Once again poised to breach the walls of the inner sanctum.

I was well set up this morning. I'd had a good breakfast, two fried eggs over easy and four slices of thick bacon with a slice of oat bran toast on the side. Cranberry and raspberry blended juice and lots of strong black coffee swirled through my system.

I'd even paid some attention to my wardrobe. I was wearing pressed Levi's. Black. I wore a black silk shirt open at the throat under a dark blue herringbone jacket. My briefs were also silk. Catherine had turned me on to the slick feel of silk against the skin. I'd even pulled out a brand new pair of my red, high-top Keds, the ones with white soles, to go with the arctic white athletic socks. I was dressed for bear and ready for anything.

I opened the big door and went in. The firm's receptionist-cum-lifeguard, P. Hall, looked up. He had a bland expression on his face until he took in my whole persona. Then the expression on his face changed only a little.

"Hi," I said. "I'm Sean—"

"Yes, sir, Mr....Sean. You're expected. Right this way. We've made a small conference room available. It's down this hall." He rose, gestured down the hall and I followed, remembering to raise my feet so my shoes didn't drag on the thick carpet. We passed the massive door to Ephraim

Harcourt Saint Martin's office. A small loop of black ribbon was stuck to the wood above the brass knob. I would have preferred to drop in on the people I wanted to interview, but since they'd gone to the trouble of arranging things...I mentally shifted gears, so to speak, and decided to play it as it lay. Never mind I haven't touched a golf club since high school.

"I have the list of interviewees from Mrs. Saint Martin. Whom do you wish to see first?" P. Hall was being the ultimate of politesse, but I could tell by the set of his big shoulders he wasn't happy with my presence.

"I'll talk with Ephraim's factotum, Ms. Day, isn't it?" She was the one I'd insulted in Ephraim's office a few days earlier.

P. Hall nodded. "Press that button on the table when you are ready for the next person. If you will indicate who that will be, I'll alert them ahead of time."

"Thanks, but you just trot on down here when I buzz and I'll tell you who's next."

"It's not a buzzer, sir, it's a light at my desk."

"Whatever. I buzz, you come." P. Hall's mouth twisted and I had the impression he was leaning in my direction. I suspected he'd have liked to put his thumbs on my Adam's apple. But he just went out and I walked around and sat at the end of the richly polished oak table opposite the door. Short as I am, the tabletop hit me at mid-chest. I'm sure I made an unprepossessing figure at the end of that long polished table. That suited me just fine.

The door opened and P. Hall ushered in Ms. Day. I gestured to a chair and she sat down on my left, leaving two places between us. I looked her over for a minute. The silence didn't put her at ease.

She finally spoke. "The police have already interviewed all of us you know. I don't see what I can tell you—"

"Tell me about what?"

"Why, about poor Magda—Mrs. Bryce."

"What makes you think I'm here about Magda Bryce?"

"Why, why, I just assumed—"

"Did you know Polly La Famme?"

"Who? Oh." Ms. Day bit her carefully made-up lower lip and looked at her hands resting on the table. When she saw them trembling, she slid her hands into her lap. "Oh, dear, we—I just assumed—" she broke off.

I lowered my gaze and made some marks in the notebook I'd laid on the table. Then I looked back up at her. She looked rattled. "Well? Did you know her?"

"Uh, not really."

"Try to be more specific. When did you first meet her? What were the circumstances?"

"It must be two years ago. She never came to the office. I suppose it was at a social occasion. Either at the Saint Martin's or perhaps Mr. Preston Bryce's. Mr. and Mrs. Bryce shared the firm's social obligations with Mr. and Mrs. Saint Martin. He was—is—a senior partner. Mr. Bryce, I mean."

"Is he back at work?"

"Yes, Mr. Bryce comes in most days, part days, I guess. I don't really know."

"What are you doing these days, since your boss died?" She blanched and fished out a crumpled tissue.

"When one of the firm's partners retires, Mr. Holmgren collects the files. Then we review them and determine reassignments. We're doing that now with Mr. Saint Martin's cases."

"It must be more difficult when someone dies suddenly. Are you responsible for going through Mr. Saint Martin's personal effects?"

"Yes. As his personal assistant for over ten years, I probably have more direct knowledge of all his affairs than any-one here. I've been going through his desk and files here at the office."

"Everything?"

"Yes, everything."

"Personal journals, memoranda, private notes he made to himself, expense records, the whole ball of wax?"

"Everything."

"Have you turned up anything interesting?"

"I don't know what you mean."

"Was Ephraim looking into the operations of the law firm? Was he concerned about the cash flow? The balance sheet? Did he find some evidence of hanky panky in these hushed halls? Have *you* found any evidence of hanky panky?"

She fidgeted, stared at me, then said, "I don't think that's any of your business. If he was looking at the operations it was normal, routine."

I stared back at her. She was agitated all right but that could have been reaction to me or to Saint Martin's death. I was sure they had been close, possibly closer than just attorney and chief assistant. Ms. Day could probably shed light on a lot of this mystery, but I figured she'd be the toughest one to crack. If I pushed her too hard, she'd be baying to her personal attorney. I hoped the paper shredder in Eppy's office was a good one. It was probably running hot and heavy these days.

"So nothing you've discovered is out of the ordinary or peculiar." I made another scribble in my little book. "Have you found any references to these names? Gina Moskowitz, Santangelo, Luscious Lucinda, Polly, Nathan Noble, Cleveland, Ohio." I pronounced each name carefully, watching Ms. Day. She shook her head with each name, but I was sure she was lying about some of them. I figured

I'd scored a hit with Santangelo and possibly Nathan Noble, the one I called Cheap-suit. Noble was that ex-P.I. from Detroit. I made notes in my little book, filled two meaningless pages.

"Thank you, Ms. Day. You've been most helpful." I let her get to the door before I said, "By the way, were you sleeping with Eppy?" It stopped her cold. Then she jerked the door open and flung one brief angry look over her shoulder at me as she stalked out.

I hit the buzzer and P. Hall appeared in the doorway. He must have come down that long hallway at the speed of light. Or he might have been waiting just outside. I wondered if the room was bugged.

So it went through the morning. I interviewed partners, secretaries, associates, and even George Saint Martin, in from Oregon for his father's funeral. He looked a lot like his father. Nobody was what you'd call forthcoming. Nevertheless, a good detective learns from evasions and non-answers as well as from the bald truth. And I'm very good.

I took a break around noon and buzzed P. Hall again. When he appeared I asked about lunch. "I want to review my notes. Can I get something sent in?"

"Of course, sir. A light pasta salad perhaps? We use a caterer in the building. Very highly thought of."

"I'll pass on that. I'd like a large hamburger and some French fries. Call Benny's. They're over in Butler Square and they deliver. Oh, and a cold Heineken, too." I smiled. P. Hall grimaced and went out. Fifteen minutes later there was a rap at the door and in he came with a sack. The grease from the hamburger inside was already staining the sack and P. Hall held it out from his body as if he were carrying a dangerous snake. Or a piece of fried meat.

"How much?" I fished for my money clip as I stood to take the sack.

"It's been taken care of." He set the sack on the table in front of me. He was peering down at the little notebook, trying to read my scrawls upside down.

"I hope you tipped the delivery boy," I said, tearing open the bag. The redolence of fried beef and potatoes filled the room. I slid the sack along the table closer to my chair. It left a shiny smear of grease on the table top. P. Hall looked over and noted the defilement. I sat down and popped a crisp French fry into my mouth. Then I smiled up at P. Hall and snapped the cap off the Heineken, adding another foreign odor to the room.

"I'll buzz you when I'm ready for my next appointment. Okay?" P. Hall's mouth twisted again and he went out without a word. I sat back in my chair and put one red Ked on the top of the table. I wondered if they had a camera monitoring the room along with the audio bug.

I hoped so.

Chapter 40

I SHOVED THE greasy sack and empty beer bottle aside, swiped ineffectually at the grease stains with one of Benny's cheap nonabsorbent napkins. Then I signaled my lackey, P. Hall. When he appeared, I smiled and asked for my main man, my real target, Preston Bryce.

"I'll see whether he's available, sir."

"Oh, he's available. He's been sitting in his office for at least half an hour, probably shuffling papers about and wondering what's going on." P. Hall looked the tiniest bit startled and then only for an instant. Five minutes later, he reappeared in the door and ushered in Mr. Preston Bryce.

I stood and nodded. "Mr. Bryce. Thank you for seeing me this afternoon." He surveyed the almost empty room and then walked slowly to a chair and slowly sat down. His demeanor, his whole persona, was different from the first time I'd seen him a week or so earlier. Then, he'd seemed shattered, hanging on to life by rote, just barely going through the motions. Today he had a lawyerly appearance. Today he had presence, an aura. In part it was the clothes; then he'd been casually dressed in an old sweater and wrinkled wash pants, whereas today he was all suited up to look exactly like what he was, a sharp corporate attorney who would deal you to death at the merger table, a man who did his homework, who had all the facts at his fingertips, a man to be feared if you were on opposite sides; a man you might fear if you were on the same side. This was a man who would give nothing away unless he wanted to do so. He'd probably be an excellent poker player. I made a note in my little book to ask my friend Pete Hautman about that. Poker, I mean.

"Thank you for seeing me," I said again. He walked down the length of the room. He took his time. Finally he picked the same position Ms. Day had chosen, only on the opposite side of the table, his back to the windows. He was the only one all day who forced me to look at the light. I had to squint slightly, and his face wasn't as clear as it might have been.

"We try to be accommodating. However, Mrs. Saint Martin was not very forthcoming. She merely said that she had engaged you to look into some of her late husband's activities, and that we might be able to assist in the inquiry by making available certain members of the firm to answer your questions. Frankly, I—we—questioned that, but she was quite insistent."

"I gathered that Mrs. Saint Martin has a measure of influence in this firm."

"We have done as she asked. It would have, perhaps, been more fruitful for you had we known more exactly what it is you are investigating." He hadn't looked at me so far. It wasn't that he was avoiding me. He was sending a message, telling me I was so insignificant as to be nearly invisible.

"Your employees have been most . . . forthcoming," I responded. "Everyone has been quite helpful." That was largely bullshit, taken one by one, and Bryce must have known it. I was certain he'd been kept informed of the questions I was asking and had an idea about my direction. But, as any experienced interviewer will tell you, unless you make plain the answers you are looking for, the answers you get often reveal more than what's on the surface. Especially when they're put together with the evasions and hesitations from several people.

I'd asked everyone so far about money, about cash flow inside the firm. Were questions being raised? Had the subject of odd or unusual fund transfers come up at the weekly partners' meetings? Any out-of-the-ordinary auditing going on? So I asked Preston Bryce similar questions just because he was expecting them. In earlier interviews, I'd detected—that's what I do, remember?—tiny hesitations, minor evasions, lots of denials. I was sure there was something going on having to do with the movement of cash in the firm, movement that was probably off the books. It could be Ephraim discovered outright embezzlement, or loot being funneled to a lobbyist or politician, or, it could have been something much less sinister, and probably was. I didn't much care, except it gave me a tiny hook, something to jiggle and probe at, the way you poke at a cavity or a slightly loose tooth with your tongue.

"Mr. Bryce, tell me about the money."

"I beg your pardon? What money?"

"It's clear that considerable sums of cash are not well handled in this firm. I want to know about that."

No expression. "Nonsense. The last independent audit raised no significant questions."

"Oh, I'm aware of that." I hadn't been, but it didn't surprise me. I tore off a corner of Benny's paper napkin and rubbed ineffectually at the grease stain by my elbow. "Are you denying that this firm never handles sums of cash, cash it must take possession of for days or sometimes weeks? Cash which, for various reasons, is not deposited in bank accounts? H'mmm?"

Bryce looked at me. "I don't believe the subject is within the scope of your charge. But as I said, the most recent audit—"

"Look, we're both grown-ups here, Bryce. We both know that under the right circumstances, auditors can be flimflammed or even colluded with." I raised my voice ever so slightly. "Mr. Bryce, who is Alice Moskowitz? How did you meet Polly La Famme?"

I rose from my chair and leaned toward Bryce. I slapped my hand on the table top for emphasis. My hand hit the cold smear of grease on the table and slipped, but I carried valiantly on. "Start with Alice Moskowitz, Mr. Bryce."

He was not cowed. He sat back and minutely adjusted the crease in his trousers. "I don't know an Alice Moskowitz."

"Yeah? Maybe you know her as Gorgeous Gina."

"Oh. Is that her last name? Moskowitz?"

"Never mind that. She was blackmailing you, wasn't she?"

"She had a videotape. She threatened to play it for my wife."

"How much did she take you for?"

"They sold me the tape for five thousand dollars."

"They? Who's they?"

"I didn't deal with Gina directly, she sent some oily, fat man to see me. Walker, I think his name was. He never mentioned her name, but it was obvious they were in it together. Later, I discovered they had only sold me a copy of the tape."

Pretty naive for a big-time corporate attorney, I thought. But you never know about people when they were out of their element. "So Walker approached you again."

"Yes." Bryce nodded and clasped his hands on the edge of the table. The tips of his fingers turned white. "This time Walker swore it was the original and I'd never hear from him again."

"And you believed him. Did you meet him here?"

"Certainly not." Bryce sounded indignant at the idea. "Ms. La Famme dealt with him the second time."

I considered that. It was possible neither Gina nor Walker knew how big a fish they had on the line. Preston Bryce didn't make headlines the way trial lawyers did. On the other hand, that might have been their pattern. Take a few bucks from a lot of people and try never to rile anyone enough so they'd go to the cops or take more direct action. Still, Walker was dead, wasn't he? And while five big ones wasn't exactly pocket change for the other guys at Harcourt, Saint Martin, Saint Martin, et cetera, it was probably pocket change to a man with Bryce's income.

"All right, now let's talk about whips and chains. The last time I saw you, you had a pink band across your forehead. I think I know why." Now I got a reaction. Not much of one but his gaze became more intense. "Somewhere along the line, you went looking for something different. You thought you needed some new thrills, right? The domination scene entered your life, right?"

"That's the most ridiculous thing I've heard in a very long time." Bryce took a slow measured breath and looked up so he could gaze at the book-filled wall across the table.

"Bryce, I know one of the foundations of your success and of people like you is research. You try to have the answers before the questions get asked, am I right?"

No response. Bryce sat there and swiveled his head until his gaze raked across my face. He was basically expressionless.

"Let me give you the benefit of some of *my* research. For years you've been doing mergers, acquisitions, working in tense, pressurized circumstances. Even in friendly mergers there is always tension, an adversarial relationship at some level. You've led many teams from this firm into such situations. And you've been successful, with millions, even billions of dollars riding on your work. For the clients and for the firm. Right?

"I think you got high on the feeling of control, the absolute high of winning, of discovering secret accounts or concealed debts, and slapping the opposition with your knowledge at crucial and subtle moments in the negotiations. But after a while that wasn't enough. You began to look for other highs. Something that would restore your edge."

Bryce sighed, favored me with a pitying look. "Please do go on. This is fascinating."

"I also think you discovered something in your wife that surprised you."

Bryce sat up. His look was no longer pitying. "Mr. Sean, I married a particular woman, a woman secure in her own vision of the world. We were suited to each other. She died under the most tragic circumstances. I'd advise you to be very careful."

I'd been snarling at him, now I softened my voice. "Bryce, I was at the morgue. I saw the whip marks on her body." Bryce sat still and looked at the polished table top.

I changed the subject. "Tell me about Polly La Famme." Bryce wet his lips. I hadn't asked for any water, so I couldn't offer him a cooling drink unless I flashed P. Hall. I didn't flash. Making Bryce comfortable wasn't on my list. "Polly La Famme," I said again.

"Magda and I met her in New York a few years ago, at an ABA meeting."

"American Bar Association," I said.

"Correct. She was working for the convention. As I recall it, we had occasion to see her more than once during the meeting and her demeanor, her ability to deal well with complications, favorably impressed me. My wife and I had been talking about hiring someone who could manage the household and our growing social obligations."

"So you hired Polly La Famme? A woman you hardly knew?"

"Not at all. Polly—Ms. La Famme—had expressed to my wife an interest in traveling to the Midwest. We suggested she might look us up if she ever came to this area. When we returned to Minneapolis (he meant Deephaven), Magda did a background check on Ms. La Famme, and as a result, we offered her a position on a trial basis. About three months later, she arrived and has been with us ever since. Until her death last week."

I blew out my breath. "So, did Polly La Famme locate Lucinda the Luscious?"

"Who? I don't know anyone by that name."

"Sure you do. She didn't tell me, but I know you know her and I know you use her services. You probably started out in New York. There are several domination services there. Discreet, expensive. Polly La Famme probably found them for you. But you couldn't be running to New York all the time, could you? So you had to find somebody local. And Polly took care of that, didn't she?" I flopped back in my chair and stared at Preston Bryce across the polished yards of table top. "And if I could find Mistress Luscious Lucinda, the cops can too. And we know what that revelation would do to your career, don't we?"

Chapter 41

THERE'D BEEN NO threat in my voice, but Bryce got the message, that was clear. Even if I didn't say anything, the continuing investigation by the Minneapolis cops into the murder of Polly La Famme could turn up the connection between Gina and Lucinda and Bryce.

"Do you know anything about Walker's murder, Mr. Bryce? Anything at all?"

He nodded. Too easy, I thought. He's giving up something to divert me from heavier stuff. Well, I never look a gift horse in the mouth, to coin a phrase. "Tell me," I said.

"I have reason to believe Gina had a boyfriend. In South Dakota. I think he killed Walker."

I made a note, a legitimate one this time. "How do you know?"

"I engaged a private detective. He developed some circumstantial evidence that the man was here at the time of Walker's death and has the expertise to arrange the murder."

"What have you done with the information?"

"Nothing to date."

"All right." I didn't much care how Bryce knew, or thought he knew, that a boyfriend had killed Walker. It wasn't my case, but if I carried Bryce's information to my friend, Detective Ricardo Simon, it might deflect police interest in Bryce, so I said, "It's possible I could pass that information to the police in effective but anonymous fashion." I raised one eyebrow. Bryce looked back at me, expressionless.

"Let's go back to Mistress Lucinda, the luscious Lucinda."

Bryce leaned back. I sensed relaxation in the set of his body. Had I given up some tiny advantage without being aware of it? "I have already told you, I don't know anyone by that name. Whether or not I have ever used the service of such a woman, or of the kind of woman you suggest she may be, if I have, is a private matter. I categorically deny any such accusations. Such comments are sheer speculation. Furthermore, Mr. Sean, if you or your associate try to make such accusations public, I can assure you, you'll be put out of existence. You know I have the power." Now he was look-ing at me. I had the sense of looking at a shark questing about for food, and I was its prey.

"In fact, Mr. Sean, if you persist in these patently false accusations with the police or even continue to pur-sue your own investigation, the result will be the same." Bryce's expression hadn't altered in the least. The muscles in my thighs twitched. They do that sometimes when I miscalculate.

There was nothing much Bryce could do to me. Oh sure, he could ruin my business, at least in the short term, but I could rebuild, or move out of town. Right now, mov-ing wouldn't have been much of a problem, given my rift with Catherine. But now I knew he had me by the short and curlys. All it had taken was those three words, 'or your as-sociate,' and what was just as bad, he knew I knew. The ad-vantage had shifted to the other side of the table. I couldn't try to force him to do anything without exposing Catherine and her enterprises to absolute ruin right along with me. His connections, or those of the law firm, would make it almost easy. Hospital patient massage contract up for re-newal? No problem, a word or two on the ear of a key board member and that would be that. Suddenly, building inspec-tors would call at the school. The subtle and not-so-subtle ways to ruin Catherine were many. Bryce let me hang there for a moment, then said, "Now, Mr. Sean. Is there anything else you wish to ask me?"

I thought fast. I'd reached the end of my prepared questions for this man, and I needed time to assess Catherine's exposure and figure out how to protect her from possible fall out. I'd been cultivating a somewhat inept aura, but I didn't want to dissemble so completely that I'd raise suspicions in the man across the table. I decided on a different tack.

"Actually there is, Mr. Bryce. For some time now you've been having me investigated."

"I have?"

"Don't be coy. There's been a detective nosing around me and asking questions of the people in nearby offices. He's reporting to you. Why? What's he looking for?"

"I have no idea who or what you are talking about." Bryce frowned at me. He looked genuinely puzzled.

"That's an odd thing to say because I saw you with the man only a few days ago. The two of you were talking intently, so I assume he was reporting to you or getting his instructions. You were seen together at the Holiday Inn, in Bloomington."

His expression cleared as if he'd just made the connection. "I see." He leaned forward. "You are mistaken in this as in so many things. I was just doing a favor for—" Bryce stopped abruptly. "I think, Mr. Sean, this interview is at an end. Report whatever you will to Mrs. Saint Martin. I shall do the same. Good afternoon." And with that he stood up and left.

I thought about Preston Bryce's threat. It wasn't idle. The police department could receive anonymous tips that her employees were using the massage business as a front for drug selling or prostitution. I knew there were almost endless ways a powerful, well-connected man could destroy someone's business. And I couldn't expose Catherine to that. I sat there for a few minutes more, staring at the window and the sun-washed buildings below. Then I remembered that others might be watching and listening. "Well, Mr. Preston Bryce, we shall have to see what there is to be seen," I muttered. I scribbled for a couple of minutes in my little book, careful to keep from exposing the pages to a possible watchful glass eye. Then I stood up and put the book into my inside jacket pocket. I grabbed Benny's empty sack of grease and balled it up. Using my famous nod-and-go move, I faked out the opposition guard, made a perfect hook shot into the corner wastebasket, and danced out the door. Jerry West would have been proud. I wondered what Catherine was doing.

Chapter 42

THE RUMBLE OF THUNDER distracted my morose thoughts. I glanced at the sky. Huge, ominous, thunderheads were piling up. The sun still shone on my little patch of backyard green, but that would change in just a few minutes. I tossed down another swallow of scotch. It was my second drink, even though it was still early evening.

After I'd left the hallowed halls of Harcourt, Saint Martin, et cetera, skipping past the expressionless P. Hall, I called my favorite florist from the IDS lobby. Yes, I have one. Another ex-client. He'd have a second dozen red roses delivered later in the afternoon. I went to my office and entered my mental notes about my interviews into the computer. The notes weren't extensive. My interview with Preston Bryce was the most provocative, but not for what I learned. He gave me some new information, like the fact that he'd not been the principal at the meeting with the detective at the Holiday Inn restaurant, but not entirely what I'd expected. For several days, I'd focused on Bryce as the likely killer of Polly and possibly his own wife, probably to cover some kind of fraud as well as the domination stuff. But he'd seemed honestly devastated over his wife's death during our first interview. Today he'd been a different man. He'd parried every thrust. Bryce had only talked about things that already were known to the police or were not, in his view, consequential. Then he'd produced the bald threat against my associate. This was not a man to take lightly, and I knew he hadn't made the threat against Catherine casually. But if Preston Bryce hadn't killed those women, who had? I grunted. Things were always clearer to Sam Spade.

I called Catherine at home and at her office. Left messages both places. Impassioned pleas, actually. Then for an hour I stared at my walls. She didn't call back. So I went home. What in hell was I going to do if she wouldn't talk with me? And worse, if she went out of my life altogether?

The sun departed behind massing storm clouds. There was no wind and the temperature seemed to rise. Impossible. I was having difficulty breathing the thick atmosphere. The scotch helped, but only a little. I had to find a way to solve this case quickly, if only to protect Catherine. Maybe Mrs. Saint Martin could help. The telephone rang.

"Mr. Sean? You are difficult to locate, at times. Will you spare me a moment?"

"Certainly, Mrs. Saint Martin."

"I am distressed. I have had a report of your interviews today at the firm and I must tell you, you seem to be moving far afield."

"Excuse me? I wasn't aware there were going to be limitations on my investigation. Besides, I think the deaths of Magda and Polly are related."

"I'm afraid I don't agree, and unless you can show me some compelling evidence to the contrary, I'm going to have to ask you to focus on the Santangelos' missing daughter and on Magda's murder and nothing else. Goodbye, Mr. Sean." I was able to deduce from the click and hum that she'd broken the connection.

A bright flash of lightning revealed a car parked at the curb beside my driveway. Whose? I realized that the light had grown dim. Booming thunder rattled the windows and I smelled the ozone released around me. The air seemed to crackle and pressure changes smacked against my ears. Upstairs I cracked the bedroom windows and changed into a light cotton shirt and shorts. Even those movements brought perspiration. When I went back outside on the deck after refreshing my drink, the sky had grown to a dark slate color and lightning was snapping overhead with increasing frequency. Doom was definitely approaching. Even the neighbor's dog was silent. The clouds churned faster and it began to rain.

Huge, fat, stinging drops slammed down on the deck and raised puffs of dust in the yard where the grass had departed. I kicked off my topsiders—shoes I wear only at home—and walked to the edge of the deck. The roiling clouds pressed closer, bright lightning flashed again and again, became an almost continuous flare against the clouds and illuminated the now gently waving tree branches. The heavy raindrops smacked into the oak leaves overhead like a drummer's arrhythmic cadence. Behind me, I could hear the heavy hiss of rain walking slowly down the street. When I looked to my left, the houses beyond my next-door neighbor had disappeared behind heavy sheets of water. It was a real gully washer.

Now the banging and crashing overhead was constant. When the heavy rain reached me, I was instantly drenched, felt almost beaten to the deck. There was little wind, and the rain fell as if from a fire hose in the sky, a torrent of warm water. My glass filled to overflowing, the scotch washed away into the yard.

"Sean!" Through the crashing storm sounds I thought I heard my name. I turned around and Catherine came through the sliding door. Her hair was plastered to her skull and water streamed down her face. We held out our arms and walked into a mutually forgiving embrace that lasted until the storm cell departed, as quickly as it had arrived. The world around us was washed clean, quiet, cooler, and peaceful.

"I listened to your last two messages twice. You can certainly be eloquent when you want to be, and the roses are gorgeous."

"I'm glad you've come. But I think I should warn you, I would have started camping outside your building in an hour or so."

She smiled and her fingers smoothed my damp cheeks. "I know, my dear. But not for long, because I would have dragged you upstairs. I apologize. I said awful things."

"You were provoked. I'm sorry. I'm not used to being told what I should do and I reacted badly. Overreacted."

We were sitting side by side in warm puddles of water on the chaise, arms entwined, under dripping oak leaves. Night had come with the passing of the storm, and there were no lights anywhere in the neighborhood. "Let's go upstairs," Catherine whispered into my mouth when we broke another long kiss.

* * * * *

I LOOKED AT my watch. "It's almost midnight. The lights are still out."

"Did we lock up?" Catherine's voice came out of the dark on the other side of my queen-sized bed.

"I don't remember, but I'll check and then I want to talk with you about Saint Martin." I padded naked down the short hall to discover the front door was indeed unlocked and ajar. Catherine came down the hall a moment later and handed me a short terry robe, companion to the one she had slipped on.

"Power's out. Since we can't make coffee, how 'bout a little brandy?" She'd wisely brought the small flashlight I keep beside the bed and I took it to shine on the bottle while I poured two snifters. We settled on the couch. "Now, what's the story with the Saint Martins?"

"First, I took your advice and told Mrs. Saint Martin to be careful." I quickly went over the information I'd picked up from my interviews at Harcourt, Saint Martin, et cetera, then I told her about the threat from Bryce.

"Did he mention me by name, Sean?"

"No, but he didn't have to. We all know I don't have associates. You're the only one I've ever even referred to as an associate."

"And that was only the one time, at Saint Martin's, right?"

"Right. I've been thinking about that. It's possible Bryce was just using a phrase, but I don't believe it. Which raises the interesting question, what's his source? How did he figure out that you and your business would be a soft spot?"

"Did you get the impression he had done a background check on me?"

"Exactly. I'm sure that Preston Bryce knows Gorgeous Gina, that dancer from South Dakota. He also knows Lucinda the dominatrix, probably by way of Polly La Famme."

"The second murdered woman."

"Yeah, the one I didn't protect. Anyway, I think he probably introduced his wife Magda to S & M. It's possible she was killed to keep her quiet. If it got out that he was patronizing a dominatrix it could damage his value in the law firm. Might cost the firm a bundle."

"How does the Cleveland business fit?"

"I think the Saint Martins learned about the Santangelos and about Magda's vanished twin sister after Polly La Famme arrived to become the factotum at the Bryces. Polly must have met the twin in New York. I think she saw Magda at that ABA meeting and told the twin. Then she maneuvered her way into the Bryce household and later brought the twin sister into the picture." I sipped my brandy.

"Meanwhile, Bryce is exploring his darker side with prostitution and domination."

"Exactly. But remember, the woman in the morgue, positively identified as Magda Bryce, had been whipped."

My companion ran a hand through her tousled hair and stretched. "So you think that both Magda and Bryce were into the domination scene?" she asked.

"I'm not certain of that. I'm more certain that the woman who came to see me as Magda was actually her twin sister. I also feel pretty sure it wasn't the first time that the sisters had run the substitution bit." I told Catherine about the unusual events I'd turned up in my interviews at WAMSO, the Women's Association of the Minnesota Symphony Orchestra, and North Memorial Hospital.

"It's as if there were two different Magdas. But why, Sean?"

"I think Magda played along with her twin and Polly for a while. I don't know why. But I'm pretty certain the twin filled some of Magda's duties in the community while Magda did other things."

"Maybe she had a lover, or was recovering from being whipped?"

"Possibly, but when I interviewed Lucinda, she told me it was rare for whipping to leave lasting marks, and certainly not scars. So I wonder if that whipping wasn't perhaps some kind of payback just before she was killed."

"All right." She took a sip of brandy and stared thoughtfully across the dark living room. "Why were you assaulted here and then shot at when we were at the Saint Paul Grill?"

"I think those attacks happened because someone else found out about the twin deception Polly and Magda were running and was afraid I'd learn something that would kick dirt on their precious world."

"Preston Bryce."

"Possibly, but the fit isn't comfortable."

"Do you suppose whoever killed Magda hoped she'd never be found or identified?"

I shook my head. "The body wasn't hidden well enough for that. Besides, forensic science is pretty good these days. I heard a presentation by a Bureau of Criminal Apprehension forensic artist once. She said—" Catherine leaned toward me and put a finger on my lips. "Not tonight, okay?"

"Okay, let's talk about Bryce's threat to take you down if I persist. I've kicked that around a lot. The only thing I can figure is to turn over what I know to the cops and make sure Bryce knows I'm out of the picture for good."

"You'd do that?

"For you? In a New York minute. I know it isn't much, but it would probably work. He didn't say it in those words, but Bryce must figure that if my investigation stops, he'll get away with it. Whatever *'it'* is. But he must know the cops aren't going to let go." I shook my head. "I'm still not seeing a clear picture here. There's an important element missing."

"And what about Polly La Famme?"

I blew out my breath in a gusty sigh. "Yeah, I think about her, too. I hate to give it up because I'm somewhat responsible for her death."

"Then don't give it up. It's sweet of you to offer, Sean, but you don't have to do it to protect me. Even if the cops do figure it out eventually, I think you'll get to the answer faster."

"Which may be important. I think the longer Harcourt, Saint Martin, Saint Martin, Bryce, et cetera, maintains things as if normal, business will go on as usual. Maybe they have a couple of big deals that are just about to close. Maybe they need time to move some money out of reach of somebody.

Bryce's threat may be a delaying tactic. But it doesn't matter now. I'm not going to let Bryce ruin what you've worked so hard to build."

"No chance of that. Suppose a client accuses a masseur of impropriety? Suppose one of my students screws up? The business could be gone in a day. I have protection."

"Insurance?"

"You bet. And not just policies. All my important assets are separately protected. Even if Mr. Preston Bryce came after me personally, he'd have to get past my insurance company, then my lawyers, and then my accountants. My guys are very good at their jobs and they aren't local.

"My funds would be hard to find and harder to extract. I could walk away from every tangible asset in the city and never miss it, financially. Oh, it's all legit and I pay my taxes, but I believe in being careful. You don't have to worry about me one little whit."

"Out-of-town hired guns," I smiled.

"I haven't been entirely forthcoming with you about some of this."

"Oh?" I shifted around so I could look her more directly in the face.

"Remember I said I'd built up a small portfolio of investments?"

"Sure."

"That's true as far as it goes. I've been successful, but my dad left me a pretty good inheritance to start with, and the out-of-town guys came with it."

"No kidding. I guess I withdraw my offer." I'd lit a candle and in the dim glow I could see Catherine's smile. I smiled back and touched her nose with my finger.

She raised her arms to me and said, "C'mere and let me show you just how much I appreciate your offer to exit the field of combat on my behalf."

Chapter 43

IT WAS ALREADY noon by the time I made it to my office the next day. I had more to think about after Catherine took her lingering departure. I'd earlier assumed that Preston Bryce might have been discovered with his hand in the cookie jar, embezzling funds out of some of those merger packages. But I wasn't hip to the ins and outs of all that moola to know if that was even possible. Still, if Polly had discovered Bryce the embezzler, she'd be dangerous to Preston, even if she wasn't blackmailing him. So he'd want to get rid of her. But if she didn't know because Preston wasn't stealing funds, someone else shot her. Who? I was missing something.

The telephone on my desk rang and I leaned for it. "Yeah?"

The owner of the voice in my ear must have been reading my thoughts. "I have some more pieces of your puzzle." Alain Russol sounded a wee bit smug.

"So tell me." I was in no mood for games this particular afternoon.

"The missing Santangelo twin is named Heather. The Santangelo relatives took her to the east coast. There she became part of a larger family named La Famme."

"No shit!" Connections were falling into place.

"Right. When she entered the working world, Heather Santangelo La Famme became an employee of a large convention packager who happened to get the contract for the ABA convention the critical year in question. She and another woman named Polly were in charge of that particular contract."

"Sisters?"

"Foster sisters, to be precise. Those are now the known facts. Rumor and innuendo suggest that both women led pretty wild lives in the Big Apple, though they came with good recommendations from their employer."

"Good work, Alain. You are worth every penny of the hefty fee you're going to charge."

"Yeah, well, you better not show your smilin' Irish face around here for at least a year, or my Betty will bean you with a frying pan. She's still pissed about our disrupted vacation."

"I'm sending her flowers. Thank you again, my friend."

I broke the connection and called Catherine. After I related my conversation with Russol, she said, "Sean, I've been thinking about your interviews with Preston Bryce and the others. Didn't it strike you that Bryce seemed to be a much different man than he was the first time you talked with him?"

"I'll say. At the office he was everything I'd been led to believe a big-time, successful merger lawyer would be, but I see what you're getting at. I put his putty-like appearance at our first meeting down to his distress over his wife's death. But it might have been something else entirely. That band of pink flesh on his forehead. Maybe he'd just finished a session in his private dungeon. What if he was having an affair with Magda's sister, Heather? Maybe Bryce and all of those women were into the domination scene. Either way, there are some signs of instability, wouldn't you say?"

"Still a lot of speculation."

"I know, I need more facts."

"I have a favor to ask. I want to meet Mr. Bryce. See him, Sean. Talk to him. Not about your case, but about his threat to me."

"Now there's an interesting idea. How 'bout I set up an appointment and we'll both lean on him. With a little pressure, who knows what might ooze out of his pores."

"Ughh. I'm not fond of the image, but that's the general idea. But away from his office."

"I'll call him. Try to set things up to go out to Deephaven."

"Isn't it Minnetonka?"

"Wherever. I'll call you right back."

I discovered that Preston Bryce was not in the office so I called his home. The female person who answered switched me to Bryce after a moment of intense persuasion on my part. "I think we have a few more things to sort out, Mr. Bryce, before I make a formal report."

"A formal report? I thought this ridiculous business was settled and you were going to conveniently disappear from my life."

"Not exactly."

"Subtleties seem to go right by you, Mr. Sean. I can and will crush you if you persist."

"I can't just drop it. That would raise more questions than there are now. My client would never let it go."

"I assume you won't tell me who your client is, of course, although it's fairly obvious, given the pressure we took from Mrs. Saint Martin to let you interview the staff. So I suppose I can't object this time either. However, I seriously doubt we have anything of substance to discuss."

"Suppose I show up about two this afternoon and we'll find out?"

"Very well."

"Thank you, Mr. Bryce, and by the way, give my best to Ms. La Famme." I gently hung up, not waiting to hear his response. I was, by God, in a tree-shaking mood, especially now my lady Catherine had assured me she was nearly invulnerable. It gave me life. It jazzed me up. I wiggled my toes in my red Keds and thought a minute. I wondered if he'd have his lawyer there. I didn't care. I was ready to eat a lawyer or two for lunch. Instead I called the Saint Martin home. Mrs. Saint Martin answered.

"Good morning, Mrs. Saint Martin. I have some new reports for you. I thought I could run out there midafternoon, say after three?"

"Excellent. That time would be most satisfactory. I look forward to seeing you again. If you wish to bring your associate, that would be fine."

Chapter 44

WE CONFRONTED Preston Bryce alone in his cool study, or library, or whatever it was. I figured it was a measure of his sense of security, or maybe his arrogance, that he was alone. No attorney.

Although the house was air conditioned, the temperature got pretty warm pretty quickly. "Look, Bryce. I'm tired of this. I never asked to be involved in your life in the first place. Your hired punk came to my house and beat on me. Then my friend and I get shot at, and your other hired hands are mooshing around, bothering my friends."

"Nonsense, Sean. That's preposterous. You can't prove any of that." Bryce's voice was quieter than mine, but he didn't look at all relaxed. His use of my last name wasn't a bit friendly. I assumed he wasn't going to dignify the exchange by calling me mister. We sure weren't on a first name basis, so ipso facto, he must have been using my last name.

We'd been snapping at each other for several minutes. Me the terrier, Bryce the stolid, unflappable St. Bernard. I'd been poking and prodding, trying to get through his defenses. He seemed to have forgotten yesterday's threat as quickly as we forget yesterday's ad slogan. I figured this was his attempt to draw me out, learn from my questions, just as I had done while quizzing his staff. Through all of it, Catherine sat in a side chair, hands clasped on her purse, feet flat, knees together and back straight. Only her eyes moved, shuttling back and forth between us.

"I don't have to prove it, I know it. Remember, I saw you meeting with that tall drink of water at the Holiday Inn last week." He waved that off with a small gesture. "Your hoofprints are all over this mess. I'm not sure how Polly La Famme fits here, but I've got you with a prostitute and a dominatrix. I've got enough—"

"That's quite sufficient," Bryce interrupted. "Your taste-less remark on the telephone earlier was completely out of line, as you are now. Have you no shame? Ms. La Famme is dead. After losing my wife, this is all quite rude. And I have already warned you." Bryce shook his head, and in what I was sure was a practiced move, slowly rose from his chair, and turned toward the window.

I waited until his back was almost turned. "Oh, I wasn't talking about Polly La Famme," I said in my best steel-quiet tone. "I was referring to Heather, Magda's sister."

That got a reaction. It didn't last long and he covered well, but I'm experienced and I saw it. I suspected that two or three years ago there would have been no reaction at all, but the man was beleaguered and possibly falling apart. He swung around toward me, his mouth open to respond. He'd gone paler than normal.

"Mr. Bryce." I'd never heard Catherine use that tone of voice and I looked in her direction. She was standing now, feet together, hands holding her purse at waist level. Her shoulders were back. *Regal* was the word that came to mind. Her voice snapped out at him. "Mr. Bryce. I understand you have made threats against me."

"What?" Bryce turned his head to meet this new attack. His shoulders started to sag.

"Threats, Mr. Bryce. Against my business and against my person."

"I—don't—"

"Really? Isn't it true you told Mr. Sean that if he pur-sued this investigation you would move against him and his associate? That's a pretty clear threat, and since I'm Mr.

Sean's only associate, I take the threat personally."

"I—"

"Mr. Bryce, I suggest before you take any action you'll surely regret, that you contact my attorneys." Catherine stepped forward and slapped a white business card onto Bryce's desk.

"Can we get back to Heather La Famme?" I asked in a mild voice. Bryce's gaze swung from the card Catherine had put down to my face. I could see bewilderment in his eyes that I suspected had seldom if ever before been there. "I know Heather is your dead wife's sister. I suspect she's more to you than just your sister-in-law. I believe and I expect to prove that you, Heather, and Magda were running a deception in town for at least the last year. I also think—"

"Mr. Bryce!" The door slammed open and a clone of P. Hall advanced swiftly into the room. Whoever he was, he knew his stuff. One glance and he placed his not inconsiderable body between me and Preston Bryce, breaking the wire of connection that ran between us. He pressed Bryce into his over-padded chair and said without turning around, "This interview is over. Now. You must leave."

"I'll show you out. This way, please," said a quiet voice.

I turned my head to see a woman standing in the doorway. Another retainer. This one was chunky and sturdy, and I got an instant impression she could handle herself in a scuffle. Never mind that she was dressed like a household servant in this time of the servantless wealthy. Odd, I thought. P. Hall-the-second had got Bryce settled in his chair and was leaning over him, still blocking our view. I looked at Catherine and she raised one hand, palm up. We both realized we'd get no more from this interview. The woman in the doorway turned and gestured at us to follow her.

"Is Heather La Famme here this afternoon?" asked Catherine as we proceeded to the front door.

"I'm sorry, there's no one here by that name." She reached the front door and with hardly a pause pulled it open, admitting a wall of hot, sticky, summer air.

"How long have you been employed here?" I asked, stepping onto the sun-blasted stone steps. The bright sun hurt my eyes and I reached for my sunglasses.

"We don't talk about the family's private business," she said, and closed the door behind Catherine's departing heels.

"Well, zipp-i-dee-do," I said.

"Do you suppose that bodyguard was listening?" wondered Catherine as we eased into my car's oven-hot front seat. "His entrance was awfully fortuitous."

"Fortuitous?"

"It means—"

"Yeah, yeah, I know what it means. Yes, my darling, I think they were monitoring us the whole time and when Bryce began to show signs of caving under the pressure, they intervened. Which leads me to wonder how long he's needed that kind of propping up."

"I'm no psychologist, Sean, but I bet he's been deteriorating for a couple of years. They might even control him with drugs and protection from long periods of stress. Those were some pretty strong accusations you were throwing around in there. You've been holding out on me."

I cranked up the air conditioner, which seemed to be working after two trips to the repair shop. "No I haven't. Those were ploys, attempts to rattle the man. I guess I believe what I said, but I don't have any proof. At least not enough to go to the cops."

"Polly comes to town and inserts herself into the Preston Bryce household, right?"

I nodded. We were rolling south now, headed along winding tree-shaded avenues toward Deephaven and the

Saint Martin estate. The air conditioner blew cool air on our faces.

"About the same time people in the law firm began to see warning signs of cracks in the steel exterior of their lead M & A attorney, Polly invites her foster sister to join in the fun and games."

"I still can't figure out whether Bryce knew that his wife was into whips and chains, or if that was a one-time occurrence."

"Sean, pull over a minute will you?"

I frowned and glanced at my companion. Memories of our dustup a few days ago in her apartment prompted me to quickly find a parking spot out of the sun. I shut down the engine and turned to her.

She searched my face with her green eyes for a minute, a serious look about her.

"I don't want you to take this the wrong way. I know you use wisecracks and humor to deflect some of the awfulness you sometimes deal with."

"True. Gallows humor. Like cops you sometimes see laughing together at a crime scene. It allows us to continue."

"Yes, but there's a deeply disturbing element to this and I want you to know how much it bothers me."

"The whip marks on Magda's body."

Catherine nodded. "Exactly. If she had an aberrant need … if she willingly submitted, actively participated, that's one thing. But there's every possibility that she wasn't willing. That she was being abused. That she was coerced. That's a power trip so many women, even in these supposedly enlightened times, are subjected to. It isn't just poor or uneducated women. It happens at all levels of society, and I just want to be sure you take that into account."

I looked at Catherine and nodded. "I guess I hadn't considered it in that light. It's hard for me to believe a well-educated woman like Magda Bryce couldn't just walk away. But I'll never walk in those shoes. So if you tell me it's so, I'll take your word for it. Without reservation."

For a silent moment, we said nothing. Then her mouth curved upward and she said, "I knew you would. Now tell me what you think. Was Preston Bryce lying about Magda and Polly and the rest?"

"Sure. At this point, denial is about all he has, since his attempt to intimidate us out of the picture isn't working."

"All right. Here we have this powerful, prominent attorney paying for services of a dominatrix, while his wife, her twin sister, and the twin's foster sister are all playing at other games, sort of a *ménage a quatre*. As you pointed out last night, maybe the whip marks on Magda's body were done as a kind of punishment just before she was killed. More and more I think that's the way it was."

"Okay, I'll buy that. Then, the Saint Martins became involved, because I got invited to scope out the family Santangelo in Cleveland."

"Do you think they knew about the link between Polly and Heather at that point?"

"Dunno, my sweet, let's ask Mrs. SM," I said as we rolled smoothly into the Saint Martin driveway.

Chapter 45

A ROUND, pleasant-appearing, grandmother-type woman, who told us she was the housekeeper, greeted us. This one, I thought, didn't look like a bodyguard. In spite of the broad, sun-bright windows that almost filled one whole side of the house, and which took advantage of the view, the interior was comfortably cool. Saint Martin must have installed a brutally large air conditioner. Grandmother-cum-housekeeper led us to yet another book-lined study. My rubber soles squeaked on the tile floor and I fielded an amused glance from Catherine. This study was on the south side of the house. The drapes had been pulled to reduce the glare and heat, so lamps were lit, giving a friendly, welcoming air.

Mrs. Saint Martin looked up from a settee where she was examining some official-appearing documents. They were legal-sized anyway. I noticed she laid them upside down on the table beside her when she rose to greet us. "Good afternoon, Mr. Sean, Ms. Mckerney."

"Good afternoon, Mrs. Saint Martin," Catherine said.

"Thanks for seeing us now," I said.

"Please, sit down. Would you care for a cool drink?"

We both chose iced tea. The grandmotherly housekeeper nodded and went away.

Mrs. Saint Martin smiled at us with a faintly inquiring expression and then said into the peaceful silence, "You have some reports for me?"

"Yes, here is the final report from the man I hired in Cleveland." I held up the brown mailing envelope I'd carried in from the car. "He confirms what I suspect you knew all along. Polly La Famme and Heather La Famme are foster sisters and Heather is, in fact, the lost twin sister of Preston Bryce's wife, Magda Santangelo."

"Is that so? You have proof, I suppose."

"Yes. Notarized copies of all the relevant documents, birth certificates, employment records from New York, school records and so on, are coming."

"I see. Copies of the documents?"

"It's usual practice for the investigator to retain copies, and I assume my man in Cleveland will do so. I won't. Our formal association will end when I hand over the documents. I still have a few questions about this case, however."

"Really? I would have assumed you had already resolved any lingering questions when you talked to Preston earlier this afternoon."

"Ah," I said. "Now, why am I not surprised that you know we went to see him before coming here?"

"I imagine you must have told me when you called for this appointment. Isn't that what happened?"

"No, ma'am, it isn't. I'm not now nor have I ever been in the habit of discussing my cases with outsiders. I don't even make reports to my clients about my activities during the run of a case."

"Are you positive of that? Surely you have discussed this case, as you call it, with your associate here? Perhaps she made an injudicious comment to someone?"

Catherine started to say something but Mrs. Saint Martin held up a hand and smiled, not warmly. "Please don't misunderstand me. I'm not accusing you of anything. I just want to be sure you are on secure ground when you make these statements." She turned her head and looked at Catherine. "And what about you, my dear? Have you unresolved questions about this case?"

My associate looked calmly at Mrs. Saint Martin and said quietly, "Not at this time, Mrs. Saint Martin." Mrs. Saint Martin transferred her glance and her smile back to me.

I smiled also. Not warmly. "Yesterday, when I was interviewing the staff and attorneys at your late husband's law firm—"

"Thanks to my assistance, I believe."

"Yes, ma'am. You are a woman of powerful influence. I was surprised, frankly, that the firm agreed to your request. Unless of course, diversion was the idea."

"I beg your pardon?"

"It's a fairly common tactic. Persuade your adversary you want to cooperate in every possible way to lull said adversary into believing that what he gets is everything there is. In this situation, you figured you'd let everyone in the IDS Tower talk to me without any hesitation or any apparent reservations. You assumed, correctly, that almost no one in the law firm knew anything of substance. But Preston made a little slip."

"Mr. Sean, you appear to be reaching for the most tenuous of connections."

"Am I? When Magda came to you for help, she was tired of the games, she was ready to get out of the marriage, and certainly ready to get away from her sister's corrosive influence. I think she'd decided hiring a private detective to collect some concrete evidence was necessary. You remembered me, didn't you? I think you remembered me from years ago when I appeared at a certain pool party out here, and I suspect you made a few additional inquiries." I waved at the wall behind her. "Or perhaps you persuaded your husband to find out about me. But you made a mistake. You gave Magda my name before you learned enough about why she wanted it.

"I think Magda also talked to your late husband. I thought it was odd at the time that Ephraim didn't recall my name being on the short list he provided Magda. It's not the sort of thing a top attorney would forget, is it? He didn't forget. My name wasn't on his list. But it was on yours."

"Really, Mr. Sean, I have no idea what list you are talking about." Mrs. Saint Martin frowned and fingered the pearl necklace at her throat.

"I think Magda came to you for help when she discovered the game she and Polly and Heather were playing in the community had been extended to Preston's bed. I think you offered her support, including my name because you thought I could be handled. But then you discovered it wasn't just the marriage Magda wanted out of. She was ready to blow the whistle about more than just Preston's adultery. Either Magda told you about certain other things, nasty things that could have done serious damage to Preston's value as the leading Mergers and Acquisitions guy, or you already knew about that. If Preston Bryce was revealed as a kinky sort, his career would be compromised, and that would have meant a lot less money rolling into your bank account. Your reputation in the community would be seriously damaged.

"You thought fast and came up with a plan. You diverted Magda from meeting me and sent Heather to my office instead. Heather had been substituting for Magda all over town without a hitch, why not in an interview with me? You had no way of knowing how much I had already been told so you figured the interview better take place, only Heather could defuse the whole thing."

I glanced at Catherine and continued into the semi-polite silence. "Once Heather reported to you that I was apparently clueless about the reason Magda had made the appointment, you knew your only problem was keeping Magda quiet."

"This is all totally preposterous."

"Is it? I think you've been controlling this thing from the beginning. I should have tumbled sooner, when you told me that the investigation into the Santangelo thing was actually *your* contract and Ephraim was acting as your agent. I think you've been propping up Preston so he could finish whatever business is on the table. You couldn't stand to lose all that money if Preston was revealed as a flake. And when Magda threatened to blow the whistle on the whole sordid business, something had to be done and quickly.

"Then there's Polly La Famme. It was one thing for her to have a cushy job with the Bryces and play a few games by substituting Heather at WAMSO and the hospital." I paused for breath. Mrs. Saint Martin stared at me through narrowed eyes. "Why'd they do that, by the way? Was it because Magda couldn't meet those obligations at times? Or was it just more kicks, like let's put something over on the Midwesterners? Then the deception game got serious. It moved on to putting Heather in Preston's bed. Is that why Magda was killed? Because she finally objected to the whole twisted mess? Was that your idea, to give Preston a little boost from some illicit sex? Something Magda wouldn't agree to?"

"Magda. Magda was contemptible! She threatened—" Mrs. Saint Martin stopped in mid-sentence. She struggled to regain her calm. But her eyes blazed at me. Somewhere in the house I heard a faint cry and the sound of a door slamming. Mrs. Saint Martin turned into a marble statue. "I think, Mr. Sean, this meeting is over." Her voice was flat and devoid of emotion.

"Oh, is it? Well let me give you one more little piece of evidence. Remember that slip I said Preston made? When I was interviewing him, he suggested that if I persisted in my accusations he'd ruin me and my associate. Mrs. Saint Martin,

I don't have an associate and only once did I ever introduce someone as my associate. It was that time Catherine and I came here to see your husband, the time he wanted to hire me to go to Cleveland. The only reason Preston Bryce would have used that title for Ms. Mckerney is if you or Ephraim told him about Catherine."

I stood up and paced a few steps back and forth. "Ephraim wouldn't do that unless Preston was a party to the deception. Ephraim never talked about his dealings, except with the people involved. You remembered the title I gave her; it was your contract." I sat down again which turned out to be a mistake. "I'll bet you're the one who suggested Preston lean on Catherine if I got out of hand."

The door to the study blew open with a bang and loud angry voices cascaded over us. I looked over my shoulder and there stood Preston Bryce. Fury mottled his normally bland face with angry red splotches. Apart from that and his slightly mussed hair, he was much as he'd been when we left him.

Except for the large black semi-automatic pistol in his hand.

The boom of the gunshot slammed into my ears. It went high so the bullet must have ruined some book on the shelves behind Mrs. Saint Martin. I didn't bother to look. Bryce stood there spraddle-legged and swung the gun wildly back and forth. The hole at the muzzle end looked enormous as it went by. I cringed. I wasn't heeled and nothing that I could use as a weapon came to my skittering glance.

"Goddammit," he roared. "You've been screwing around with my life for too long. I told you and told you, you b—"

Bryce swung the weapon in our direction again and I sensed an eruption of movement beside me. A body launched itself off the chair and slammed me across the chest. Catherine and I went over the back of the sofa onto the floor. Almost simultaneously there were two more shots, one that sounded like a toy gun. Then there was a crash and the thump of a body falling.

When I slid out from under Catherine and rose to my knees, Preston Bryce lay sprawled in the doorway, the big automatic still clutched in his hand. The smell of burned gunpowder stung my nose. I looked at Mrs. Saint Martin, who hadn't moved from her chair. She was holding the proverbial smoking gun. In this case it was a small, pearl-handled twenty-five-caliber Beretta. Where she'd got it from I had no idea, but her aim was true. Bryce had a hole in his throat, a bullet in his brain, and was dead on the floor.

Chapter 46

THE POLICE AND CRIME scene technicians were still doing their work in the study, but Preston Bryce's body had been removed by the medical examiner. Detective Henry Holt came into the living room or drawing room, I wasn't sure which, and looked down at us. A paramedic had given Catherine one of those refreeze chemical packs to hold on her bruised shoulder, the souvenir of her effort to get both of us out of harm's way.

We'd given statements covering the facts as we knew them. Mrs. Saint Martin had been taken somewhere; I didn't know where and I didn't much care where. If I never encountered that lady again it would be soon enough.

"Well, you two feel like talking?" Holt asked.

"About what?" I grumbled. "I hurt, Catherine hurts and is still very shook up. We've given our statements and—"

"Yeah, yeah, but this lady doesn't look all that shook up and maybe you'd like to fill in some of the gaps. Course, if you want, we can go downtown."

"Excuse me, detective, but since this is a little out of your jurisdiction, maybe you can tell me why you're here?"

"Call it professional courtesy, Sean. The chief here in Deephaven is a friend of the County Sheriff who gets along good with my chief, and since I've been handling the Bryce and La Famme killings in Minneapolis, they asked me along this afternoon on the assumption this thing was connected. Now, you wanna explain all this or what?"

"Or *what* what?" Catherine muttered *sotto voce* in my ear.

"All right. Here's what I think," I said. "I think Magda Bryce was killed because when she learned about her husband's affair with her long-lost twin, Heather, she threatened to go public with the adultery, his growing fixation on the domination stuff, and probably other information she had of Preston Bryce's deepening breakdown. I think Heather and Polly were enlisted by one or both of the Saint Martins as part of an elaborate plan to prop up Bryce for as long as possible until they could get more lucrative mergers completed. The motive behind all three murders was plain old greed."

"Are you saying Ephraim Harcourt Saint Martin was behind this whole thing?"

"Yes. Or Mrs. Saint Martin. Who else had the clout?"

"So you were wrong about Bryce embezzling funds?"

"Yes. I think Ephraim and the rest of the people at Harcourt, Saint Martin, Saint Martin, et cetera, began to see signs of deterioration in their main money man several years ago."

Holt said, "Preston Bryce."

"You'll probably find carefully concealed medical interventions going back months if not years, somewhere in the records. Eventually, Bryce began to patronize the seedier side of life here at home. Visiting New York and overseas domination services would be much easier to conceal. But when he started going to our local strip clubs, visiting women like Luscious Lucinda and Gorgeous Gina—" I broke off. "Incidentally, what's happening with the Walker killing?"

"We got the whore's South Dakota boyfriend. He's confessed."

I nodded and resumed. "Both Mrs. SM and Ephraim were the puppet masters. Heather and Polly were brought here as part of an elaborate scheme to prop up Preston and keep him out of the newspapers."

"So, you think Magda Bryce was killed because she threatened to blow the whole thing open," Holt said.

"Yeah. I think Magda talked separately to the Saint Martins about hiring a detective to help her build a case for divorce. But she said more to Mrs. SM and must have threatened to go public with all of it. Divorce over adultery is one thing, but the Saint Martins couldn't stand a complete exposure of Preston Bryce. They were afraid that if Preston's proclivities were made public, it was inevitable that the Saint Martins' prior knowledge and acquiescence would also become public.

"Heather, masquerading as Magda, came to see me, mainly to find out how much I knew. It could have ended there. I might have testified that Magda was alive when she'd already been killed."

"But since you didn't have any damaging information at the time of the phony interview, why'd they kill Magda?" Holt wondered.

"I think the Saint Martins discovered Magda was fed up and was about to blow the whistle. It all happened quickly. Heather was conning me, and out here Magda was telling Mrs. Saint Martin that she was going public with the whole thing. Mrs. Saint Martin realized that the interview with me by Heather could be used to cover everybody in on the game who needed an alibi. The twins and Polly had been playing the substitution game, mostly for their own amusement, whenever Magda wanted to get out of her civic obligations. I expect Heather Santangelo can tell you more about that."

"When we find her. Apparently she left town yesterday on one of those feeder airlines that stop at several cities. Her ticket was paid to New York. Problem is, she never arrived there. She left the plane at an intermediate stop."

"Probably Cleveland."

"So then what?"

"I think Saint Martin decided to get me out of the picture when he learned Mrs. SM had sent Heather, masquerading as Magda, to my office. He brought the people in from Detroit to frighten me off. If Catherine hadn't been with me the night someone shot at us at the St. Paul Grill, I might have walked away from the whole thing. After all, at that point I didn't have a client, but that shooting pissed me off.

"Then Eppy and Mrs. SM decided to buy me off by trying to send me to Cleveland. I think they also wanted to find out about more Heather, but it was mainly an effort to get me out of Minneapolis for a while. Another delaying tactic."

Holt scratched his ear. "Seems like an expensive and elaborate plot, just to keep some hotshot attorney in action a while longer."

"We aren't talking about chicken feed here. You'll find that Preston Bryce was worth tens of millions to the firm and its partners in annual billings," I said.

"If, as you say, the Saint Martins and their partners were propping up Bryce, why'd he come here to kill you?"

"Oh, he didn't come here to kill me."

"What?" Holt's retort was sharp and Catherine snapped her head around to me.

I looked at her. "Remember, Catherine, just as you slammed me off the sofa, what Bryce was shouting?"

"Of course. He accused you of messing around in his life for too long, then he started to call you a bastard. I thought he was about to shoot you. That's why I—"

"Think about it. I'd only been involved in his life for a week at the most and then not heavily until the last couple of days. When you lunged at me, I was looking at him. His mouth was forming the word *bitch*. He was talking to Mrs. Saint Martin."

"Oh, my God."

I nodded. "He might have killed all three of us in the end, except your lunge at me distracted him just enough and Mrs. Saint Martin was quick on the draw. I think she took the opportunity to silence the only one left who could say for sure why Magda and Polly were killed. She knew the money machine represented by Preston Bryce was broken, anyway."

"What about Polly La Famme?" Holt said.

I looked down at the floor at Holt's sensible shoes. Catherine squeezed my fingers. She knew how I felt.

"Polly. She's the one real regret I have in this. I suspect she realized the game was out of control, or maybe she saw a chance to get a payoff. Maybe she figured out who killed Magda. I don't know. But she was really frightened the night she called me, the night she was murdered. *Damn*. I could put up with being targeted as a lousy patsy and all the rest of it, but I should have paid more attention to the note she passed me on the street. I shouldn't have shrugged it off, especially after that gaunt fellow whacked me and stole it. I should have talked to her right away. If I had, Polly La Famme might still be alive. By the way, didn't you tell me she was killed with a small caliber bullet?"

Holt nodded.

"You ought to check that pearl handled job of Mrs. Saint Martin's, Holt. I won't be surprised to discover that's the pistol that killed Magda, Polly and Bryce. As I said earlier, it all comes down to good old-fashioned greed. The Saint Martins didn't want to see the money faucet shut off, and after Eppy died, Mrs. SM took complete control. I'll bet Mrs. Saint Martin knew more at any step along the way than her husband did. For all we know, his cancer may have affected his judgment."

Holt nodded.

"Detective Holt," said Catherine. "The sheriff's people have released us. Can we go now?"

I looked up to see him nod again. Catherine took my hand and without further words we went, the white rubber tread of my red Keds squeaking on the expensive tile floor of the Saint Martin's entry way.

Two weeks later, Catherine was sitting behind me on my chaise. She was expertly massaging my head. On the jazz station we were turned to, the news announcer reported that Mrs. Ephraim Saint Martin, wealthy widow of the prominent, recently deceased attorney, had just been arrested and charged with the murders of Magda Bryce and Polly La Famme.

I told you I was pretty good at my job.

About the Author

In a previous lifetime Carl Brookins acquired a broad liberal arts degree in a flexible program from the University of Minnesota, for which he is ever grateful. He's old enough to have had several interesting careers, including writing, performing and producing television, community theater, and counseling and teaching adult college students.

He writes the Whitney/Tanner sailing mystery series, and an academic series of mysteries featuring Jack Marston. He's a member of Sisters In Crime, The Private Eye Writers of America and The Minnesota Crime Wave. His website address is www.carlbrookins.com.